PALM BEACH PREDATOR

A CHARLIE CRAWFORD MYSTERY (BOOK 6)

TOM TURNER

TRIBECA PRESS

ISBN: 9781720113171

Published by Tribeca Press.

www.tomturnerbooks.com

Palm Beach Predator/Tom Turner – 1st ed.

JOIN TOM'S AUTHOR NEWSLETTER

Get the latest news on Tom's upcoming novels when you sign up for his free author newsletter at **tomturnerbooks.com/news**.

ONE

In her mind, Claudia Detwiler had already spent the commission money. She'd book a Danube River cruise on Viking, the one that started in Budapest and ended up in Prague. Someone had told her that you pronounced it *Buda-pesht*, so she planned to enunciate it properly and impress her fellow travelers with her worldliness right off the bat. And even though she lived with Jake Dawson, she'd be traveling alone. After all, everyone was always telling her that she could do much better than Jake. And you never know when a handsome German industrialist or Danish count might be bunking in the stateroom next door.

She also needed to chic up her wardrobe a bit. She'd gotten about all the mileage she could out of her hard-shouldered Versace suit and her Herve Leger Band Aid dress, which fit fine back in her rail-thin days, but not anymore. Then she planned to take some tennis lessons from the cute pro at the Racquet Club for the dual purposes of losing a few pounds and meeting people who might eventually be looking to buy or sell a house in Palm Beach.

Speaking of which, Bill and Jessica Donaldson had already seen the house which Claudia was driving to three times. They were going there again because they wanted their children to see it. Kids and houses were a dicey mix, because you never knew what might come out of their spoiled little mouths. "But, Mom, I can't stand that pukey carpet in my bedroom" or "How are we supposed to play Ultimate on that puny, little lawn?"

So, short Bill—height, hair length and attention span—was riding shotgun in Claudia's Range Rover, while round and fidgety Jessica sat in back with loudmouth Willie and princess Emma. One big, happy quintet, heading for the house on North Lake Way.

Claudia had planned ahead by dispatching her window washer, Diego, that morning to make sure there were no saltwater stains on the windows, thus ensuring that Bill and Jessica would once again swoon over the ocean view. It had cost her a hundred dollars but was well worth it...so she hoped, anyway.

Bill leaned toward Claudia. "If we had a quick closing—like, say, two or three weeks—do you think we could get it for less?" he asked, which was the first sign that he might be considering floating a lowball offer.

"I know they turned down twelve five," Claudia said, meaning twelve million five hundred thousand. She'd heard that, anyway but wasn't absolutely sure if it was true or not. Bill chewed on that for four or five blocks until Jessica piped in.

"I know it comes with the furniture," she said, "but we're not in love with much of that stuff. In fact, we'd probably have to pay Goodwill to come take most of it away."

Yep. A lowball offer was definitely headed her way. It almost seemed as if the pair had rehearsed this tandem act of disparaging the exquisite edifice around the breakfast table that morning.

Shit, maybe Diego wasn't such a good investment after all.

"I don't know what they valued the furniture at," Claudia said, trying to hold things together. "Maybe not too much."

In the rearview mirror, Claudia watched Jessica nod but not say anything. Another glance back caught Jessica concentrating hard. Like she was cooking up yet another gambit to knock the price down.

Claudia drove into the driveway, trying to come up with a way to restore the Donaldsons' former enthusiasm. "I just love how the driveway meanders in," she said, "then you see it—ta-da!—the big reveal of this extraordinary house."

Bill and Jessica didn't respond despite Claudia's zealous hype job. The big house did have nice curb appeal, though it would have been a lot better if it had another fifty feet of frontage. The neighboring houses felt a little too close on both sides.

It was then that Claudia realized that the listing agent, Mimi Taylor, wasn't there. Her car anyway. Mimi was normally so prompt for her showings.

Claudia parked and everyone got out. She pointed at the Canary Island date palm. "That's a real specimen," she said. "I've never seen one that big."

"It's nice," Bill said coolly.

He seemed to have been much more excited about it the first time they came. That is, before he slipped into stealth negotiating mode.

They walked up the six steps to the landing. Willie was bringing up the rear, picking his nose with impunity. Emma yawned as she played a game on her iPhone. Well, at least she was preoccupied and might not bitch about the carpet.

Bill smiled at Jessica as Claudia fiddled with the lockbox to get the key. "We're just going to go ahead on in. Mimi, the listing agent, is probably right behind us."

Bill and Jessica nodded.

She took out the key, pushed it in the keyhole, then turned it, opening the door. The five of them walked into the foyer, and Claudia spread her arms wide. "Welcome to Casa... Donaldson!" she proclaimed as they walked into the living room. It truly was a fantastic ocean view, though she noticed that Diego had missed a spot on the upper-right-hand corner of a window.

"See what I mean about the furniture?" Jessica said to her husband, though the comment was clearly meant for Claudia's benefit.

"I wouldn't be so sure Goodwill will even take it," Bill said.

Claudia was beginning to hate this family of negative thinkers, nosepickers, and smartphone savants. She decided to zero in on the check-writer, Bill, as Jessica and the kids peeled off in the direction of the master bedroom.

"In analyzing the comps," Claudia said, "the price is really good on a per-square-foot basis."

Bill nodded as his eyes wandered along the crown molding.

"As you can see, they spared no expense on the details." Claudia watched Bill's eye drift over to where Diego had missed the spot.

"I've never had a place on the ocean," Bill said. "Do you need to clean the windows all the time?"

"Oh, gosh, no," Claudia lied. "Just every once in a while."

"How often is that?" Bill asked. "Once every couple of days? Every week?"

Claudia started to answer but was interrupted by the piercing scream of Jessica. Then Emma joined in. Then Willie, the little nosepicker, hollering way louder than his mother and sister put together.

TWO

The woman's naked body lay face up in a Jacuzzi bathtub in the spacious master bathroom, her head just below the granite tub surround. On the surround, the words *Reclining Nude* had been scrawled in Crest toothpaste. An empty tube lay discarded on the floor in front of the tub.

Something in Palm Beach homicide detective Charlie Crawford's past academic life told him that *Reclining Nude* was the name of a famous painting. Back at Dartmouth, he had taken a gut course in art, which turned out to be one of his favorite classes ever. Every now and then he'd go to the Norton Museum in West Palm or hit a gallery or two on Worth Avenue, even though he couldn't afford to buy anything.

Crawford and his partner, Mort Ott, had ID'd the body, having located the deceased woman's purse on a counter in the kitchen. Her name was Mimi Taylor, and the business card in her wallet said she worked at Sotheby's Real Estate at 340 Royal Poinciana Way in Palm Beach. Crawford and Ott had been joined at the scene by the medical examiner and two women from the Palm Beach Police Department's Crime Scene Evidence Unit.

Bob Hawes, the medical examiner, had reached the official verdict that Taylor had been strangled to death—this, about an hour after Crawford and Ott had, unofficially, come to the same conclusion.

Crawford Googled "Reclining Nude" and found a painting by that name by Amedeo Modigliani that had sold for $170 million three years before at a Christie's auction. It depicted a naked woman, not in a bathtub but on what appeared to be a burgundy-colored sofa.

Going back to his search results, Crawford found another painting called *Reclining Nude*—this one by Picasso. The Picasso was considerably more abstract. He'd take the Modigliani over the Picasso any day but didn't have $170 million lying around.

Crawford motioned Ott to follow him out of the bathroom so they could have a private conversation. Ott followed him out into the large master bedroom.

"So, for starters, no clear evidence of rape," Crawford began.

Ott nodded. "But obviously she didn't walk in here with no clothes."

"So the killer either had her strip while she was still alive or took her clothes off after he killed her," Crawford said. "I'm guessing he was either someone she was showing the house to or else was already here."

"Well, if it was someone she showed the house to, he wouldn't have been stupid enough to have called her on his own phone. Or given her his real name."

"Exactly. So he'd have used a burner and a fake name."

Ott nodded. "Or could have met her here," he said. "Called her on the burner and told her he saw her name and number on the sign and wanted to see it right away."

"Yeah," Crawford said. "Could be. Or could have been a burglar she caught in the act. Except if it was, he would have taken her cash and credit cards." He had a second thought. "Plus that whole thing with the toothpaste and staging her body...gotta be premeditated."

"So you're ruling out burglary?" Ott asked.

"I'm not ruling out anything yet. Let's just call it unlikely."

"I agree."

"So, two other things," Crawford said, glancing around the room. "The vic's car isn't here, and neither are her clothes."

"Maybe the perp took her car. Clothes, too."

"Which means he didn't drive here."

"Or...maybe there were two of them?"

Crawford cocked his head. "Yeah, but I'm not getting that vibe."

One of the CSEU techs walked into the master bedroom. Her name was Dominica McCarthy, and she and Crawford had a history.

"What's your take?" Ott asked her.

"Damned if I know, Mort," Dominica said. "I'm just the hair, prints, and DNA girl."

Ott chuckled. "You're a lot more than that," he said. "Whatcha got so far?"

"I got lots of everything," Dominica said. "Which tells me one of two things. Either the house has been shown a lot lately, or else the cleaning people haven't come around in a while. Or maybe both."

"A lot is better than a little, right?" said Crawford with a smile. "What are you focusing on?"

"The hair and DNA in the tub and that toothpaste tube."

"Think you might lift a print off the tube?" Crawford asked.

"Maybe," Dominica said. "A partial anyway. What do you guys got?"

Ott smiled. "Being the art connoisseur I am, I know that both Picasso and Mogigliano did paintings called *Reclining Nude*."

Dominica chuckled. "I believe it's Modigliani."

"Close enough," Ott said.

"By the way, did any of you recover a cell phone in the bathroom? Or anywhere around there?" Crawford asked.

Dominica shook her head. "Sorry."

"That would be very helpful," Ott said.

"I hear you," Dominica said, walking toward the door. "All right boys, wrap it up by the weekend, will you?"

"Do our best," Crawford said as Ott nodded.

BACK IN HIS OFFICE AT THE POLICE STATION ON COUNTY ROAD, Crawford called the Sotheby's office, identified himself, and asked to speak to the real estate firm's manager, whose name he had just learned from the receptionist was Arthur Lang.

"Yes, hello, Detective, this is Arthur Lang."

Crawford could tell by his tone Lang knew what had happened to Mimi Taylor.

"Hi, Mr. Lang, I'm calling about the death of your agent, Ms. Taylor."

"So horrible," Lang said. "I—well, I still can't even comprehend it."

"I know and I'm very sorry," Crawford said. "I'd like to ask you some questions if it's okay."

"Of course," Lang said. "Ask me anything."

"Thank you," Crawford said. "First, I need to know who her next of kin are, if you know."

"Yes, I looked that up shortly after I heard what happened. Her mother's name is Mrs. Andrew Taylor, and she lives up in Vero Beach."

"So Ms. Taylor was never married?" Either that or she had been married and kept her maiden name, Crawford figured. Or had been divorced and had taken it back.

"As far as I know, she never was," Lang said.

"And do you have her mother's phone number?"

Lang said yes and gave him the number. "I also suggest that you speak to another agent here named Carrie Nyquist. Mimi and Carrie were best friends."

"Is she in the office now?"

"I think so. I saw her a little while ago," Lang said. "I can transfer you, if you'd like."

"Before you do," Crawford said, "her license shows her address is 2500 South Ocean Boulevard. Do you know if that's current?"

"Yes," Lang said. "One of those condo buildings at the south end. Just south of the Par Three golf course."

"You don't happen to have a key to her condo, do you?"

"No, but Carrie might."

"Okay, thanks. If you could transfer me over to Ms. Nyquist now... Oh, and Mr. Lang, I'd like to come to your office tomorrow morning and speak to all your agents if that's possible."

"Sure, I understand," Lang said. "How's ten o'clock?"

"That's good."

"I'll send out an email and tell my agents it's a mandatory meeting."

"Thank you again," Crawford said. "Now, if you could transfer me, please?"

"You're welcome. Here goes."

Crawford waited a few seconds.

"This is Carrie," said the voice.

"Hello, Ms. Nyquist, my name is Detective Crawford, Palm Beach Police. Just like to say, I am very sorry about the loss of your friend Ms. Taylor. Would you mind if I asked you some questions?"

The woman sighed deeply. "Oh, God, I'm still in shock. She was the best..." And with that she began to cry.

"I'll make this brief. Was Ms. Taylor ever married?"

"No, but she had been living with a man until recently. For almost three years. Lowell Grey is his name."

"And had she been seeing anybody else since then?"

"Yes, but she wouldn't tell me who."

"Why not? Do you know?"

"I could guess."

"Because the other man was married?"

Nyquist didn't respond.

"Ms. Nyquist?"

"I think he might have been."

Crawford tapped his desk with his fingers. "Did Ms. Taylor ever mention anyone she was...scared of, possibly? Anyone who ever threatened her? Or who may have been physically abusive to her?"

Carrie Nyquist sniffled. "No. She never mentioned anyone. I mean, Mimi was a woman who worked very hard but had a pretty simple life. She wasn't a party girl or a social butterfly like a lot of the women in this business."

"Mr. Lang told me about her mother up in Vero Beach. Do you know whether she had any other immediate family?"

"No. She was an only child."

"One more thing. Do you happen to have a key to her apartment?"

"Yes, actually I do," she said. "Mimi used to have a dog. Sometimes she'd go out of town for a day or two and I'd go feed and walk it."

"I understand," Crawford said. "Could I stop by and get that key from you? I'm going to need to go inspect her apartment."

"Sure," Nyquist said. "I'll be in and out the rest of the day. I'll leave it with the receptionist, who's here until six."

"Sounds good. Thank you very much. Oh, also, Mr. Lang's going to ask all agents to come in tomorrow morning to meet with me and my partner, so I hope to see you then. I'll probably have some more questions at that point. Thanks again."

"You're welcome," Nyquist said. "See you tomorrow morning."

Crawford clicked off and thought about what he'd say to Mimi Taylor's mother. It was pretty much the same script every time, just different names. He and Ott alternated making the calls. It was a job neither one wanted.

Claudia Detwiler was in a foul mood. The *Reclining Nude* murder had probably killed her sale of the house on North Lake Way, and now Jessica Donaldson wasn't returning her calls.

The drive back to her office after they found the body of Mimi Taylor had been a quiet one. Except for that little pain in the ass Willie, who'd whimpered all the way home, as if he'd just crashed his Luke Skywalker Landspeeder into a bridge abutment.

The Palm Beach EMS team had gotten there ten minutes after Claudia put in the 911 call, and an EMT had paid particular attention to Jessica Donaldson, who seemed to be in shock. He'd offered to take her to Good Samaritan Hospital, just over the north bridge in West Palm, but she said she was okay. Her daughter and husband were doing fine and her son...well, Willie was Willie.

Now Detectives Crawford and Ott had come to her office to interview her. The three of them sat together in the real estate agency's conference room.

"During the entire time you were at the house on North Lake Way, Ms. Detwiler," Ott was asking, "did you ever see anyone else there?"

"No," Claudia said. "No one."

"And did you notice her cell phone there, by any chance?" Ott asked.

Claudia shook her head. "No, sorry."

Unlike his short, stout, balding partner, Charlie Crawford looked nothing like a cop. He looked more like a male model who'd just popped out of a *GQ* ad (minus the snappy threads). He had burned out on high-profile homicides in New York City three years before and migrated south. Ott preceded him by a year, having left high crimes and misdemeanors in Cleveland in the rearview, along with other things he wouldn't miss: like dirty snow and the flaming Cuyahoga River. He hooked up with Crawford almost three years back, and they had a mostly copacetic relationship. As Dominica McCarthy had observed, they had a quite functional marriage of opposites.

"So, you and your clients walked into the house and were going through it when Mrs. Donaldson and her son and daughter walked into the master bathroom?" Crawford asked.

"That's pretty much it," Claudia said. "I was with the husband when the wife and two kids went into the master and master bath. I ran in when I heard the screaming."

"Did you ever go up to the second floor?" Ott asked.

Crawford knew what Ott was thinking. Maybe the killer had gone up there to hide if he heard Detwiler and the Donaldsons come into the house.

"No, we never got that far," Claudia said. "The police came, then the paramedics. We left a little while after that."

"We understand that Mimi Taylor was the listing agent for the house. Is that correct?" asked Crawford.

Claudia nodded.

"Did you make an appointment with her before going to the house?"

"Yes, I did," Claudia said. "She was going to show the house to my customers. I thought it was odd she wasn't there, because she's normally so prompt."

"So you've worked with her before?"

"Oh, yes, quite a bit," Claudia said.

"Was anyone else around?" Crawford asked. "Like a landscaper maybe, or a pool man or a caretaker?"

"Nobody that I saw," Claudia said. "Oh, wait a minute, I forgot. I sent over my window cleaner in the morning. Maybe he saw something."

Ott noted that in his well-worn notebook then looked up. "What's his name? And number, if you have it."

Claudia scrolled down on her iPhone. "His name is Diego. I don't remember his last name...wait a minute, here it is, Diego Andujar." She read Ott his phone number.

"And, Ms. Detwiler, just so we're absolutely clear," Crawford said, "you were with the husband, Mr. Donaldson, when you heard Mrs. Donaldson screaming. Correct?"

"Yes."

"And where were you?"

"In the living room. He was admiring the view of the ocean and the beach."

Crawford nodded. "Did you happen to notice anybody walking away from the house toward the beach when you were looking out?"

"No, sorry, I didn't."

"You mentioned having worked with Ms. Taylor fairly frequently. Did you know her pretty well?"

"Not that well," Claudia said. "I just knew her as a good agent. I sold another listing of hers last year."

"What do you know about her?" Ott asked.

"What do you mean? I just told you."

Crawford hadn't had a chance to catch Ott up on his conversations with Arthur Lang and Carrie Nyquist.

"I just wondered what you know about her relationships with men or her personal life in general." Ott said.

Claudia exhaled and glanced out the window. "I remember hearing that she had a long-standing relationship with a man, but I think they may have broken up."

"Do you know any more about it?" Ott asked.

Claudia shrugged. "Sorry."

Crawford nodded and glanced over at Ott. "I can't think of any more questions, for now."

"Me neither," Ott said, standing up. "Could we get your card in case we need to get back in touch with you?"

"Sure." She reached into her purse and pulled out two cards. She gave one to each of them.

Crawford and Ott stood, facing the agent from across the conference table.

"Oh, one last thing," Crawford said. "Could you give us the cell phone number of Mr. or Mrs. Donaldson, please? Just in case we need to talk to them."

Claudia gave them the numbers. "Be my guest. I'm afraid my conversations with that family are *finis*."

On the way back to the station house, Crawford put in a call to Diego Andujar. It went to voice mail, so he left a message. "Mr. Andujar, my name is Detective Crawford, Palm Beach Police Department. Please call me as soon as possible." He left his number.

"Why does that name sound familiar?" Ott asked.

"I don't know," Crawford said. "Third baseman for the Yankees maybe? Except it's Miguel."

Ott shook his head. "The guy I'm thinking of boosted cars."

"Really?" Crawford said. "Wonder if he boosted Mimi Taylor's."

"Let's get the guy," Ott said. "Meanwhile I'll check him out on FDLE." Ott was referring to a website that contained a database of individual criminal records.

"While you're at it, see about getting a search warrant for Mimi Taylor's place," Crawford said. "If you're right about Andujar having a record, he wouldn't be a guy I'd give access to a twelve-million-dollar house."

Ott smiled. "*If* I'm right."

"You were one time back in 2016."

THREE

TURNED OUT, OTT *WAS* RIGHT. ONE DIEGO ANDUJAR OF WEST Palm Beach had been convicted of car-theft several years back.

"How the hell did you recognize that name?" asked Crawford. "It's not like you're in burglary."

"'Cause the car he boosted was my neighbor's. An old Mercedes shitbox," Ott said. "She came over to my house bawling her brains out, telling me how much she loved the car. I told her I'd make sure to get a good guy on it. And sure enough, Benny Carbone, ace West Palm PD burglary dude, caught Andujar in the act."

"How long ago was this?"

"When I first got down here. About four years ago."

"So I'm guessing Andujar did a couple of years and got out?"

"Yeah. Probably."

"I'll put in another call to him," Crawford said. "And if I don't hear anything in a couple hours, we'll go track him down."

Ott nodded.

"In the meantime, I was thinking we go around to a bunch of real estate offices in Palm Beach. Get 'em in a room and ask 'em what they know. You know, sketchy people they may have dealt with. Or maybe someone knows something about Mimi Taylor that might be helpful. I already got one set up for Sotheby's at ten tomorrow. Next, I'm gonna talk to Rose, see what she knows."

Rose Clarke was the top real estate agent in Palm Beach and also a friend of Crawford's. A close friend. A friend with benefits, to be precise.

"I was just going to suggest that," Ott said. "Seeing how she knows everyone."

"And everything," Crawford added as he dialed her cell.

"Hello, Charlie," Rose answered, not sounding like her usual bubbly self. "I was wondering when I was going to hear from you."

"Hey, Rose," Crawford said. "How you doing?"

"Not too well," Rose said. "Poor Mimi."

"I know. Pretty horrible what happened," Crawford said. "Did you know her very well?"

"Not too well," Rose said. "But I liked her. She was always easy to work with."

"Do you know how long she was with Sotheby's?"

"I don't know for sure. I'd guess about ten years."

"Have you heard anything at all?"

"You mean, like how it could have happened?"

"Yeah, or who might have done it?" Crawford asked. "We both know how the rumor mill gets cranking in this town."

"Oh, do we ever," Rose said. "No, I haven't heard anything at all, but it's early still."

"I heard she had just broken up with a guy after a long relationship."

"Yeah, Lowell Grey. She was too good for that bum."

"What can you tell me about him?"

Rose paused, cleared her throat. "Well, I'd describe him as one of the many guys in Palm Beach with too much money and too much time to screw around. She was better off without him."

"And I guess she finally figured that out," Crawford said. "You know if she had another male friend after him? And, if so, who?"

"Of course."

"Who?"

"It'll cost you."

"Giovanni's at seven thirty tonight?" Crawford was thinking... a quick dinner then back to the station.

"Deal."

Giovanni's was a no-frills but exceptionally good Italian restaurant on Clematis Street in West Palm Beach.

"That also gives you plenty of time to keep your ear to the ground and come up with a long list of suspects. Oh, also, can I ask you a big favor?"

He heard a faint chuckle.

"Yes," she said.

"Me and Mort are gonna go around to real estate offices and talk to agents. Can you tell me the names of the ones we should talk to? I know a few of them. I'm going to Sotheby's, obviously."

"Right," she said. "Well, I'd start with the big ones. Corcoran, Douglas Elliman, Fite, and Brown Harris."

Crawford wrote the firm names in his notebook. "That's great. Thanks, Rose."

"No problem. Tell me if you need more."

"At first, I thought about getting all you agents together in one big room somewhere."

"Forget it," Rose said. "You'd need to rent out the convention center. Someone told me there's one agent for every fifty people in Palm Beach."

"But only one of 'em sells houses like you do."

"Mmm," she said. "Flattery will get you everywhere."

By five o'clock, Crawford had not heard back from Diego Andujar, so he and Ott decided to track him down. After that, they'd go to Mimi Taylor's condo at the south end of Palm Beach.

Crawford had gone and picked up the key that Carrie Nyquist left for him at the agency, and Ott had gotten a search warrant from Judge Shanahan.

To get started, Crawford called back Claudia Detwiler and asked if she had Diego Andujar's address. She did. She told him he lived in a little garage apartment in West Palm and said he did occasional odd jobs for her at the houses she listed.

He thanked her, went and got Ott, and they drove from the station on South County Road to the address in West Palm.

The house in front and to the side of the garage apartment was a broken-down grey stucco one-story that had numerous cracks and a broken drain pipe. A brand-new Chevy Cruze was in its driveway.

"You know why people care more about what they drive than the dump they live in?" Ott asked.

"Why's that?"

"'Cause that's where people see them the most, in their car," Ott said. "Think about it...who ever sees them in their house except relatives and friends?"

Crawford glanced over and shook his head. "Hang around you much longer and I'll know the meaning of life."

Ott nodded.

The driveway to the left of the house led to the narrow, two-story garage apartment. At the end of the driveway in front of the garage sat a dented white Geo.

"If he still boosts cars, he would have copped something nicer than that piece of shit," Ott said as they both got out of the Crown Vic.

They walked up to the apartment and Crawford knocked on the door. They heard a TV on inside, but after a full minute nobody had come to the door.

Crawford pounded on it again. Harder this time. Still nothing, except now they no longer heard the sound of the TV.

Crawford turned his back to the door and kicked it three times with the heel of his foot. "Open up. Police."

Finally, a short woman in her thirties wearing a striped top opened the door. She looked scared.

"Mrs. Andujar?" Ott asked.

She nodded.

"Palm Beach Police. Where's Diego?"

"I do not know," she said with a heavy Spanish accent.

Crawford put his hands on the frame of the door and leaned forward. "Listen, if we go inside and find Diego hiding under a bed or crawling out a window, we're gonna take him in for resisting arrest. Do you understand?"

She was silent.

"Do you understand?" Ott repeated loudly.

She nodded but didn't move.

"So, go get him," Ott said. "And don't you go crawling out a window. I'd hate to have to tackle you."

"And you'd hate it even more," added Crawford.

The woman turned and went back in. Crawford blocked the door from closing with his foot.

A few moments later, a slender man in a black Puma track suit appeared. His eyes darted back and forth between the detectives, avoiding their gazes.

"Why were you hiding?" Crawford asked.

"I wasn't hiding," Andujar said.

"Well, what do you call it when your wife says you're not home but you are?" Ott asked.

Andujar didn't have an answer to that.

"Claudia Detwiler told us you went to 1441 North Lake Way and washed the windows there this morning. Is that correct?" Crawford asked.

"Yes, I did," Andujar said.

"When were you there and for how long?" Ott asked.

"I got there at nine and left about two and a half hours later," he said, shifting from one foot to the other.

"And who did you see there during that time?" Crawford asked.

"No one. Ms. Detwiler told me the owners are up north somewhere."

"What about Mimi Taylor?" Ott asked.

"I don't know who that is," Diego said.

"You sure?" Ott said. "Nice-looking, blonde woman in her thirties? Real estate agent?"

"I'm sorry, but there was no one else there when I was there," Diego said.

"Okay, I'm gonna ask you again," said Ott. "Why were you hiding just now? And don't tell us you weren't, 'cause your wife—who doesn't lie so well—said you weren't here."

Diego sighed and looked down at his shoes. "I didn't want to get in trouble with the police."

"Again, you mean?" Ott said. "Yeah, we know about your grand theft auto."

"He has been an honest man since that," Diego's wife said. "A very hardworking, honest man."

"Thank you for that vote of confidence, Mrs. Andujar," Ott said. "And when did your husband get back home this morning?"

"Around noon, or a little before that," she said.

"So, you cleaned those windows and came straight home?" Crawford asked.

"Yes, I did," Diego said.

Ott looked over at Crawford.

"Next time, call us back when we call you," Crawford said.

"I-I was going to," Diego said lamely.

"When?" Ott said, shaking his head. "Next month?"

"All right, Diego," Crawford said. Then to his wife, "Give me your cell number, too. We might need to contact you again."

Ott took down Mrs. Andujar's number, and they walked back out to their car.

"What did you think?" Ott asked as he started up the Crown Vic.

"I think Diego's got a nice, loyal wife," Crawford said.

"So, Diego walked out of Moore Haven Correctional and down

the straight and narrow," Ott said. "You're not usually so trusting, Charlie."

"It's not that I'm trusting, it's just a big reach that Diego staged the body like that and had a clue what *Reclining Nude* meant."

THEY GOT TO MIMI TAYLOR'S CONDO BUILDING AT 5:45. THERE was a man in a uniform just inside who gave them a welcoming smile. "Gentlemen, can I help you?"

Crawford held up a key on a chain. "Going to Ms. Taylor's apartment. We're detectives, Palm Beach Police Department."

The man's smile disappeared. "I heard about what happened," he said. "Terrible thing."

Crawford nodded. "What's your name, sir?"

"Winston."

"Mind if we ask you a few questions?" Crawford asked. "I'm Detective Crawford and this is my partner, Detective Ott."

"Sure, fellas, ask away."

"How long you been workin' here?" Crawford asked.

"Fourteen years."

"Okay, so you've probably been here longer than Ms. Taylor?"

"Yeah, I think she bought her place about four or five years ago."

A man and a woman walked in. Crawford nodded to them.

"Welcome back," Winston said to them.

They waved, smiled, and proceeded to the elevator.

Crawford waited until he had Winston's attention again. "We're interested in who visited Ms. Taylor here."

"Well, her mother every so often. And her friend...Carrie, I think her first name is. A couple of other women who worked with her, I think."

"We're more interested in men friends," Ott said.

"Oh, gotcha. Well, a man by the name of Lowell used to stop by once in a while but not in the last six months or so."

"He was her boyfriend, then?" Ott asked.

"I think so, yes."

"And did he spend the night?" Crawford asked.

Winston nodded tentatively, like maybe he was uncomfortable with people knowing he noticed things like that.

"So, he *was* her boyfriend?" Ott said. "But not anymore?"

"That would be my guess," Winston said. "Not like I really know for sure, though."

"We understand," Crawford said. "But since Lowell Grey, no men friends?"

Winston thought for a second. "No. Not on my shift."

"Were there ever any incidents...in the apartment?" Ott asked.

"Incidents?"

"You know, loud parties. Something the neighbors may have complained about? Anything at all out of the ordinary?"

"Oh, God no," Winston said. "Ms. Taylor was a perfect lady. Couldn't ask to meet anyone nicer."

Ott took out a card and handed it to Winston. "Okay, well, thanks for your time. You think of anything that might be helpful to us, give me a call."

"I will. I sure will," Winston said with a smile.

Crawford nodded and followed Ott to the elevator, which had a faint smell of suntan oil and perfume.

Mimi Taylor's condo was a one-bedroom on the eighteenth floor. Expensively decorated, though a little on the minimalist side. It had a spectacular view of the ocean.

"How 'bout I do the bedroom and bath, and you do the living room and kitchen," Crawford said.

"You got it," Ott said, taking out a pair of vinyl gloves from his jacket pocket.

Crawford went into the bedroom. It was very white. From the wall color to the puffy comforter to a tufted chaise longue that looked more decorative than functional. Off to the side facing the ocean, a glass-topped desk had all of its contents neatly arranged. In the center was a MacBook Air computer with its cover up. Crawford walked over to it and put his vinyl gloves on. He looked down at the screen and saw that it was on. He thought he was the only one who never turned his computer off. It only had fifteen percent life left, so he plugged the charger in.

He clicked the email icon and scanned down the received emails. He saw a lot of women's names, then three emails in a row from someone named Stark Stabler.

The name was a blast from the past. Stark Stabler was a professional tennis player whom Crawford had watched compete one summer at the U.S. Open, back when he was a kid. He remembered Stabler as a second-tier player but still really good. It had to be the same person. How many Stark Stablers could there be?

He read the chain of emails, going from last to first.

The latest from Stabler read: *I agree. Tomorrow morning 10:00 at L.N.*

Based on the date, that would have been the morning Mimi Taylor had been murdered.

Crawford scrolled back, eager to follow the thread of emails.

He went to the Sent list and saw that Mimi Taylor had started the email conversation. Her first email was written about a half hour before Stabler's last:

Hi S,

We need to talk about you-know-what.

M

To which Stabler responded:

I've already said all I'm going to say on the subject.

Only a minute went by before Taylor responded.

If that's your final answer, you're forcing me to do what I really don't want to do.

Two minutes later, Stark Stabler shot back.

Don't threaten me Mimi.

Five minutes went by before Taylor responded.

Let's be grown-ups and work it out at L.N.

There it was again. L.N. It could have stood for a million different things.

Crawford scrolled down, looking for more emails between Taylor and Stark Stabler that could help elucidate the murkiness of their most recent one.

"Whatcha got?"

Crawford was startled. He hadn't heard Ott come in.

"Jesus, you scared me."

"Big, strong guy like you jumpy?" Ott said.

Crawford turned to Ott. "Ever hear of a guy named Stark Stabler?"

"No, who's he?"

"A tennis player from like twenty-five years ago."

"I didn't grow up knowing guys who played country-club sports," Ott said.

"He's a guy we need to talk to right away."

"First name Stark, huh? My sports heroes all had rugged American names like Bronko and Raw Dog" — Ott shook his head derisively and rolled his hand from side to side— "Stark's a little..."

Crawford ignored the comment and pointed down at the emails.

Ott read through them quickly. "What the hell's L. N. mean?"

"That's what I've been wondering. Seems like it's a place," Crawford said. "One of the many questions I have for this guy."

"Ten o'clock was about the time she got killed," Ott said.

"I know."

Ott raised his arm and took a pull on a bottle of Heineken.

Crawford hadn't seen it before and gave Ott an astonished look.

"What the hell you doin'?" Crawford asked.

"What's it look like? Having a beer."

"I can see that," Crawford said, shaking his head. "Why don't you go see if she's got a steak in the freezer. You can grill it up out on the balcony."

"Hey, man. What's the big deal? It's seven o'clock, been a long day, it's cocktail hour, and I got thirsty."

Crawford just shook his head. "You find anything, besides her beer supply?"

"I don't really know," Ott said. "There are a couple of DVDs in there we might want to take a peek at. Kinda look like homemade jobs."

"Okay. Anything else?"

"Six sets of keys," Ott said. "I'm guessing probably for her real estate listings."

Crawford nodded. "Well, I'm going to take this computer. See what else I find in her emails or wherever else."

Ott nodded and took another sip of the Heineken, finishing it off.

Crawford rolled his eyes.

"What?" Ott said with a defiant shrug. "Not like she's gonna drink it."

FOUR

Crawford and Ott left Mimi Taylor's condo building at 7:20 and drove the ten minutes back to the station to get Crawford's car.

Crawford was on his way to pick up Rose Clarke for dinner, when he got a call on his cell.

"Hey, Charlie, it's Red Noland." Noland was a homicide detective with the West Palm Beach Police Department. "So, I heard about your murder and wanted to talk to you about it. I might have some info for you."

"Yeah, sure, Red, where you now?"

"At my station."

"I'll be there in ten minutes," Crawford said.

This took precedence over dinner, even though Rose would, no doubt, be able to provide useful info as well. Crawford didn't like the idea of cancelling at the last minute and hoped she'd understand. She had once accused him of having his priorities messed up. How solving a murder was more important to him than anything in his personal life. He'd denied it but not very convincingly.

Red Noland was known to be the best homicide detective on the

West Palm Beach force. Crawford had worked with him personally and found his reputation to be well deserved. If Red wanted to talk, it would be worth listening to.

Crawford called Rose and she answered. "Hi, Charlie."

"Hey, Rose, I apologize, but something came up on my case. Can we do a rain check?"

Dramatic sigh. "Yes, Charlie, as long as you're not cutting me loose for another woman."

"That would never happen, Rose," Crawford said. *Unless, of course, it's Dominica McCarthy*, he refrained from saying. "I just got a call from a West Palm detective about the Taylor homicide. He's got something to tell me and it might take a while. Maybe tomorrow or the next day?"

"I understand. Tomorrow's good but not Thursday."

"Let's do it tomorrow. I'm sorry," he said.

"It's okay, I understand. Bye, Charlie."

Crawford pulled up to 600 Banyan Boulevard in West Palm, the headquarters of the West Palm Beach Police Department, and parked on the side street.

He walked inside and asked for Red Noland. Noland, less than average height, stoop-shouldered and, no surprise, flaming red hair, came out and got him and they went back to his office.

"So, I heard bits and pieces about your murder up on North Lake Way," Noland said.

"Yeah, just when I was beginning to think Palm Beach was the safest place in the universe again," Crawford said, sliding into the hard wooden chair opposite Noland's desk.

"Compared to West Palm it sure as hell is. Twenty-seven homicides here last year," Noland said. "You could always come over and help us out."

West Palm Beach had roughly ten times the population of Palm Beach and, therefore, ten times as many homicide cops. But it still wasn't enough.

"I'd miss my partner too much," Crawford said.

"Bring him along," Noland said with a grin.

"Thanks," Crawford said, "but we're pretty happy where we are. So, whatcha got?"

Noland leaned back in his chair and put his hand on his chin. "I got two homicides that may have some similarities to yours."

Crawford leaned toward him. "Really? Tell me about 'em."

"Okay, the first one took place on a boat at Palm Beach Yacht Club on the Intracoastal six weeks ago. A woman who had just gotten separated from her husband was strangled in her cabin. A friend found her naked about eight to ten hours after the ME figured it happened."

"Anything weird like mine? I mean, any message left behind or anything?"

"That thing with the toothpaste? Nah, just naked in bed, but, like yours, there was no rape."

"How old was she?"

"Forty-one. She worked at a bank. Pretty high up," Noland said. "Apparently she had been staying on the boat for about a week. The husband was staying in their house."

"Okay, and the second one?"

"Just last week," Noland said. "A woman, mid-thirties. She had been working late at the library on Okeechobee. The library had officially closed, and another woman who worked with her had locked up and gone home. We're guessing someone rang the buzzer and the vic opened up—probably figuring it was a coworker. Anyway, she was found naked in one of the back rooms—but again, not raped."

"But strangled?"

"Yup, just like the one on the boat and yours."

Crawford nodded but didn't say anything, thinking, *Realtor. Banker. Librarian...*

"It struck me as kind of strange," Noland said.

"What did?"

"Taking a woman's clothes off, then not...assaulting her."

Crawford nodded. "Yeah, I know what you mean," he said. "So, you thinking serial killer maybe?"

Noland shrugged. "I don't know what the official definition is, or how many it's gotta be, but, yeah, maybe."

Crawford nodded.

"But yours has that extra wrinkle," Noland said.

"You mean the message left behind?" Crawford said.

"Yeah. Not being much of an art guy, I looked it up. Pablo Picasso and somebody Modigliani had paintings named that, right?"

Crawford nodded.

"Got any clue what it's supposed to mean?"

"Nope. Maybe nothing," Crawford said. "I had a case up in New York where the killer left chicken bones around a corpse. Papers called him the Chicken Bone Killer, and me and my partner kept trying to come up with the significance of chicken bones. We finally brought him in, and he just said he was hungry, had a box of KFC with him."

Noland looked at his watch. It was already past eight. "You got me hungry, Charlie. You eaten yet?"

"Nah, let's go get a bite."

THEY WERE AT ROCCO'S TACOS ON CLEMATIS STREET, A HIGH-quality, low-rent joint that Red Noland summed up thusly, "Margaritas and tacos...is there anything better?"

Crawford nodded and took a pull on his margarita. He planned to switch over to water after one. Maybe two.

Noland was telling him that he and his partner had been on the two West Palm murders 24/7 and so far had come up dry. "We've interviewed every mutt within a hundred miles. Thought we were getting somewhere with this one sketchy-looking dude we caught on camera near the library, but he was with a woman who alibied him."

"Your two vics," Crawford asked. "They got anything in common?"

"Not really. Just that they were attractive women who seem to have been at the wrong place at the wrong time."

"But they didn't have any connections? Mutual friends? Worked together? Anything at all like that?"

"Not that we've found out," Noland said.

"So you think it was random?" Crawford asked. "No pattern and they weren't specifically targeted?"

"That's what I'm thinking today, but ask me tomorrow and it may be different." Noland licked the salt from the rim of his glass. "The woman on the boat apparently was going through a real knock-down-drag-out divorce with her husband, a rich doctor."

"So I assume you got in his face pretty good?"

"Yeah, my first thought was he might have hired a hitter. Took the wife out so she couldn't take him to the cleaners. But he didn't crack at all when we put him in a room," Noland said. "The other woman was a divorcée who moved down from Cincinnati about a year ago. She wasn't in a relationship, just seemed to live a quiet life."

"Yeah, that seemed to be the case with my vic. Except she had a couple of relationships we're looking into. Including one with a married guy."

"That's not real unusual over there, is it?" Noland asked, referring to Palm Beach.

"I don't keep track." Crawford took another pull on his margarita and set it down. "There's this other thing..." And Crawford proceeded to tell Noland about the back-and-forth emails between Mimi Taylor and Stark Stabler. And about the mysterious L.N.

"But you got no clue what it stands for?" Noland asked.

"No, just that it seems like it's a place."

Noland thought for a second. "Lake..."

Crawford shrugged. "Yeah, I thought that, too... hey, how 'bout a look at your suspect list."

Noland reached into his pocket. "One step ahead of you." He

pulled out two pages and held them up. "Thirty-seven of the baddest bowwows in Palm Beach County, right here."

Noland handed the list to Crawford.

Crawford looked down the list of names and the crimes they were convicted of and smiled. "Burglars, arsonists, rapists, murderers...my kind of guys. Can't wait to meet 'em."

FIVE

Crawford looked up Stark Stabler's number and called him from his office at eight a.m. He got Stabler's voice mail and asked him to call back ASAP. Then he started calling real estate offices. By the time he and Ott left for their ten o'clock at Sotheby's, he had three other meetings scheduled for later in the day. When Crawford called Sotheby's to confirm that Ott and he would arrive at ten, office manager Arthur Lang told him that Sotheby's had eighty agents, but many of them were part-time and he expected around three-quarters of that number to be in attendance.

Crawford and Ott walked into the office at 10:05. Arthur Lang, a nattily dressed, short man with sunny blonde hair, a color he hadn't been born with, was waiting for them in the reception area. He led them back to a large open space divided into cubicles. Faces looked up expectantly as the three came into the room.

Lang led Crawford and Ott to a corner of the room and turned toward the Sotheby's agents.

"Okay, guys," Lang said. "As I told you, we have two detectives from the Palm Beach Police Department with us today, and I urge you to give them as much help as possible so they can solve Mimi's tragic death as quick as they can. So with that I'm just going to turn it over to them" —Lang opened his hand toward Crawford and Ott— "this is Detective Crawford and Detective Ott."

Crawford nodded to the assembled agents. "Thank you, Mr. Lang. My name is Charlie Crawford." He looked out at the agents, the majority of whom were women, and realized he hadn't seen as much bling and expensive-looking clothes since Dominica forced him to watch ten minutes of *The Real Housewives of Beverly Hills* one night. Granted, these women were way less flashy, but they weren't wearing your average work clothes either. Not by a long shot.

"First of all, I would just like to say how sorry my partner and I are about the loss of your coworker Miss Taylor. We know she was a good friend to many of you and we are, of course, eager to solve this right away. And second, we'd just like to open it up to you folks. Maybe you know something, or saw something, or can volunteer something that might be helpful to us. And anything at all would be appreciated."

A woman in a green silk top and bold cleavage raised her hand.

"Yes," Crawford said, pointing at her. "You don't need to raise your hand, you can just go ahead and speak."

She nodded. "So, my question is, was anything stolen from the house?"

"Not that we're aware of," Crawford said. "Why, what were your thinking?"

"Well, 'cause there's this pair of guys who have come to open houses and stolen stuff." A few heads started nodding around the room. "What happens is one distracts you, you know, with a bunch of questions, while the other is filling his pockets—"

"Or his man-purse," another woman added.

"Yeah, the tip-off is when they walk in and the tall one's wearing a trench coat on a sunny day in the eighties," said another.

Half the room was nodding now.

"I heard about this," Ott said. "I'm Detective Ott, by the way. I think our burglary team looked into this. I believe several of our men have gone undercover at a number of open houses but haven't been able to locate the two you're referring to."

"A friend of mine who's an agent down in Manalapan told me the same two were spotted down there," a man said, turning to the woman who had first brought it up. "A tall guy with longish hair and kind of a fat guy, right?"

"Yeah, they go after stuff like iPads, tablets and Echoes," Bold Cleavage said. "Even stole a small painting at this one place where I gave an open house. I lost the damn listing 'cause of that."

"Oh, yes, I remember that," Arthur Lang said, shaking his head at the memory.

"But you have no reason to believe that those two men have acted in a...violent manner, do you?" Crawford asked. "Or could have been murderers?"

"They never did anything physical, as far as you know?" Ott asked.

"Well, no," Bold Cleavage said. "But then we had the squatters."

Half the agents in the room groaned.

"The what?" Crawford asked.

Bold Cleavage turned to a man in a pink-and-white bow tie next to her. "Well, you tell 'em, it was your listing."

Bow Tie was shaking his head. "So, I had this listing. Way, way overpriced. I never showed it and kept thinking the owner was going to drop the price. Half a year went by and, first, this family of squirrels moved in. So I got the Orkin guy to come over and get them out, and then I gave an open house, and—" he took a long, deep breath "—well, apparently, from what I pieced together after, what happened was this guy hid in a closet and came out after the open house was over and I had locked up. Next thing I know, about two weeks later, I go to the house to show it—like I said, I hardly ever showed it—and my key didn't fit. So I hear this Grateful Dead music inside and look through the window and see a bunch of people passing a bong—"

Ott leaned over to Crawford and whispered. "I remember hearing about this. Just before you came down."

"—so I call you guys" —Bow Tie flicked his head at Crawford and Ott— "and the police come and ask the guy who answers the door what he's doing there. The guy says he's just visiting, that his friend, who's at the Winn-Dixie at the moment, is renting the place. I go, 'No, no one's renting the place. There's no lease and it's on the market.' So the cops leave after a while and the guy comes back with a bunch of groceries. I was *so* pissed. It turned out he had the balls—'scuse me, the temerity—to have the locks changed and kicked me out of the house. Can you believe it? So I called the cops *again*. They come back, and he claims he has a lease but it's at his office. One look at this guy and you know...no way a druggie like that's got an office anywhere, 'cept maybe at a crack house."

Crawford thought about cutting the guy off but knew that was not exactly in keeping with the spirit of the free-flowing meeting.

"So the poor owner, who's up in Chicago by the way, has to hire an attorney to prepare an eviction notice, then they serve the deadbeat in *the owner's* house. Then, after he still doesn't move out, they have to start a lawsuit to evict. I mean, are you kidding me? Three weeks later, the squatters are still in the house—"

Crawford saw a few people's eyes glaze over, including Ott's. It was time to move on.

"Sir, sorry, I don't know your name—"

"Miller. Brad Miller."

"Mr. Miller, you have no reason to suspect that that man, or any of his friends, is a murderer, do you?"

"No, I have no reason to think that, even though he threatened me. I guess maybe I'm just pissed off I spent so much time on all this nonsense and the damn house has still never sold."

"I understand," Crawford said, looking around the room. "Regarding Ms. Taylor, did she ever mention to any of you that she might be afraid of someone, or maybe there was someone she had reason to believe might harm her?"

The agents looked around at each other and heads began to shake.

"I'm just so afraid now," said a female agent with blue-framed glasses; other agents started nodding their agreement. "I mean, there's a homicidal maniac out there somewhere."

"Yes, will you please just catch the guy?" Bold Cleavage said. "We can't be worried that every time we walk into a house some guy's going to jump out of a closet and kill us."

"We hear you loud and clear," Crawford said, "which is why we're here."

"We've brought along a lot of business cards," Ott said, reaching into his jacket pocket. "And we want to urge you to call us if you have any additional thoughts, or if there was something that you didn't want to bring up in front of the group."

"Thank you all very much," Crawford said. "We appreciate your time and assure you we'll be doing everything possible to apprehend this perpetrator."

Crawford and Ott thanked Arthur Lang and headed toward the door.

"Excuse me, Detective?" came a woman's voice.

Crawford swung around to see a woman who looked somewhere between forty-five and sixty depending on the light, the angle you saw her from, and whether you'd had a few cocktails in you.

"Yes, ma'am?" Crawford was no expert on face-lifts, but if you'd been around Palm Beach long enough you knew one when you saw one.

"You're Rose's friend, right?" She was trying to smile but was having a tough time with all the botox that had, no doubt, been pumped into her face.

Off to the side, Ott chuckled his annoying chuckle, and Crawford wanted to haul off and smack him.

"Rose Clarke?" Crawford asked innocently.

The woman nodded. "There's only one Rose," she said, batting her inch-long eyelashes.

"Yes," Crawford said. "*We're* friends of Rose."

Might as well drag Ott into it.

"She told me nice things about you," the woman said. "And how cute you were."

"Oh, well, great," Crawford said. "Did you have anything to tell us about Mimi Taylor or our investigation?"

"No," she said. "I just wanted to get a look at you close-up."

Crawford couldn't get out the door fast enough.

SIX

"Good place to pick up chicks," Ott said as they slid into the Crown Vic. "Your mother's age, that is."

Crawford wasn't going to dignify that with even a grunt.

"Though there were definitely some young, hot ones there too," Ott added.

"Is that what you were doing, checking out the women?"

"No, Charlie, I was trying to get some info that would help solve our murder," Ott said, "but we didn't. We just heard people talk about weirdo house crashers and bellyache about how their jobs sucked. All you gotta do is listen to me if you want to hear that shit."

"Thought you liked your job."

Ott nodded. "Yeah, I do. Except when Rutledge gets involved," he said, referring to their boss, chief of the Palm Beach Police Department.

"I still think going around to the real estate offices is a good idea," Crawford said.

"I do too."

"Well, good. As usual, we're on the same page."

Crawford and Ott had just left the Corcoran real estate office on Royal Poinciana Way after having previously gone to Brown Harris, Douglas Elliman, and the Fite Group.

"I never thought about how vulnerable they are," Ott said. "Sitting alone in a house during an open house. Anybody can just walk in."

"Yeah, I know, that last story was pretty scary," Crawford said.

He was referring to what an agent had told them about two well-dressed men who had walked in at the tail end of an open house she was giving. They appeared to be a father and son, she said—big smiles and lots of apparent interest in the house. She was about to give them the tour, when one of them casually pulled out a snub-nosed pistol from his jacket, while the younger one went and locked the front door.

"Okay, honey, we're going to make this quick and easy," he said. "Where's your purse?"

She pointed to her purse across the room on a sofa.

The younger of the two went over and got it. He emptied the cash from her wallet and found her checkbook.

"How much you have in your account?" the older one asked.

"Oh, a couple hundred dollars," the agent said. "Maybe a thousand."

"Don't lie to me," the older one said, pressing the pistol barrel to her head. "How much is in it?"

She told Crawford and Ott she was not about to die over money.

"About fifteen thousand," she said.

The younger one handed her a pen. "Start writing," he said.

"Fourteen thousand nine hundred and seventy-five dollars," the older one ordered with a smile. "You're gonna need the rest for dinner tonight. Maybe a drink or two."

The older one went to the bank with the check, while the

younger one stayed with the agent to make sure she couldn't call the bank and cancel the check.

A half an hour later, they were gone and so was all but twenty-five dollars in her account.

As far as concrete leads on the Mimi Taylor murder, Crawford and Ott had nothing after having gone to the four offices. But they didn't consider it a waste of time because now almost two hundred agents had their business cards and could attach faces to their names. If something suspicious were to happen or one of the agents remembered something that might be helpful, Crawford felt confident they would call.

After Corcoran, they went back to the station. Crawford put in a third call to Stark Stabler, and then he and Ott split up the thirty-seven profiles provided by Red Noland, the West Palm Beach homicide cop.

Crawford went through eight of his and already had two that were of particular interest. One was a murder suspect who seemed to have gotten off on a technicality. The victim was a woman whom the suspect had apparently had a dispute with over work he had done at her house. A witness, who was a friend of the suspect, told Red Noland's partner that the suspect had admitted to him having strangled the woman.

Crawford had a number for the man, whose name was Art Nunan, and he called him.

"This is big A, you know what to do," said Nunan's voice mail.

"Detective Crawford, Palm Beach Police, call me right away." He left his number.

The second person of interest was a convicted murderer named Buddy Lester, who had been released after doing twenty-five years at Raiford prison.

The day after Lester got out, he spent five hours in a bar, picked up a woman, and strangled her in her apartment but failed to kill her. Lester was arrested, but the woman recanted and said it was a case of mistaken identity. Red Noland told Crawford that he suspected a friend of Lester's had gotten to her and either threatened to kill her or paid her off.

Crawford called Lester, but his phone just rang and rang.

As he picked up the next file, he glanced at his watch.

It was 7:45. He was supposed to pick up Rose at 7:30 for a 7:45 reservation at Giovanni's.

He dialed Rose's number. She picked up after the second ring.

"Hello, tardy Charlie."

"I'm sorry," he said. "I'll be there in five."

"Don't break the speed limit," Rose said. "You'll have to arrest yourself."

THEY GOT TO GIOVANNI'S AT 8:05 AND FORTUNATELY Crawford's table hadn't been given away. He was a regular, after all. Not to mention a good tipper.

Rose, five feet ten inches tall with a near-flawless distribution of body parts, was wearing a clingy beige dress that showed a lot of leg and thigh and toned, tanned arms. She sat as Crawford held her chair.

"Thank you. Those perfect Ivy League manners of yours."

"Trust me, about the only thing I learned in college was how to drink prodigious amounts of grain alcohol," Crawford said. "So, I went to Sotheby's, Brown Harris, Corcoran, Douglas Elliman, and Fite Group today and heard a lot of war stories."

"Like what?"

"About squatters, thieves, and worse."

"But no help on Mimi's murder?"

"Not really, but it's still early." Then, remembering, "I met a friend of yours at Sotheby's who's about five three, a little on the chunky side, and probably spent about ten grand on what I believe they call 'facial-reconstruction surgery.'"

"Ten?" Rose said with a laugh. "Triple that. So, you had the pleasure of meeting flirty Katie. She actually couldn't be nicer."

"Yeah, she seemed it," Crawford said. "Anyway, I have a couple more real estate companies tomorrow."

"Well, I guarantee you that I can top whatever war stories you heard today," she said.

"Okay, let's hear."

Rose smiled. "Did I ever tell you about the couple who lived in a trailer park up in Riviera Beach who were looking at fifty-million-dollar houses?"

"No, I'd definitely remember that one."

"So, normally I'm very careful about vetting buyers before I take them out." Rose shrugged. "'Cause time is money."

"How do you vet 'em?"

"Well, for instance, if a guy tells me he works on Wall Street, I know enough people there so I can check him out. Find out whether he's a lowly stockbroker on commission or a managing director making five mill a year. Google's also made things a whole lot easier. So anyway, I get a call from an agent in our Boston office, whom I don't know, telling me she's making a referral."

"That's where she tells you about a buyer, and if you sell 'em a house, she gets a piece of the commission, right?"

"Very good, Charlie, you've been paying attention," Rose said. "Her name is Gail somebody and she tells me her referral is this very understated couple but that the husband started a high-tech company on Route 128 in Boston which he just sold to Sun Microsystems for gazillions. Well, I'd heard of Sun Microsystems, of course, so I said great, thanked her, and told her she'd get twenty percent of the commission if something came of it." Rose shook her head and smiled. "Two days later I get a call and this guy says he's the one whom Gail in Boston sent my way. I go, 'Oh, yes, Mr. Bialecki, I was hoping I'd hear from you.' Which I was 'cause Gail said he wanted something on the ocean or Intracoastal for between twenty-five and fifty million."

Crawford did the math; even after paying Gail in the Boston office a referral fee, Rose could still make upwards of a million dollars.

"So what happened?"

"First of all, this couple showed up at my office in a Dodge Dart. And not even a nice Dodge Dart. A real beater. He's wearing ten-dollar blue jeans with these cheap suspenders, and she looks like the wife in that Grant Wood painting *American Gothic*."

"You mean with the husband and his pitchfork."

"That's the one," Rose said. "So, I remember what Gail said and figured that sporting outfits from the Depression era is what she means by 'understated.' So, I haul 'em around to every house between twenty-five and fifty mill, and I'm paying close attention to hear the brilliant tech-guy Hal say something genius but never do. Oh, I forgot one big thing, the wife, Darla, never talks. I figure, okay, she's a mute...probably not the first mute to ever buy a house, right?"

Crawford shrugged. He didn't know any mutes.

"So, after three days and a couple tanks of gas in the old Range Rover, Hal finally makes his move. He says, 'We really like that one on North Ocean Way, the one just north of the S curve, and we'd like to try it out for a week.'"

"I go, 'You'd like to *what*?'"

"'Try it out,' he said again. Said they wanted to see which they like better, being on the ocean or on the Intracoastal. And I'm thinking, *Well, that may be how you do things up in Beantown but not here, my friend*."

Crawford chuckled. "Hey, I'd like to do that too."

"Everyone would...except the owners," Rose said. "So, Hal got really insistent. He says, 'I don't know why that's so unreasonable. After all you test-drive a car, why not test-drive a house?' To which I said the obvious, 'You don't test-drive a car for a week, just a half hour or so.' So then he came up with something priceless, and finally I'm thinking, 'Aha, so this *is* the genius who started the high-tech company.'"

"What'd he say?"

"He said, 'If I'm paying, say, fifty grand for a car, then a half hour test-drive is enough.' Then he closes his eyes like he's thinking really hard, doing the math, maybe. 'But if I'm paying five hundred times that for a house, then I deserve a lot longer test-drive.' 'Like a week?' I asked. 'Uh-huh, like a week,' he said."

"I gotta hand it to him," Crawford said, "he *is* beginning to sound like a guy who started a tech company and sold it for billions."

Rose smiled and put her hand on Crawford's hand. "Except, he never did."

"What do you mean?"

"So I decided to follow Hal and Darla, in their orange Dodge Dart, figuring they're down from Boston probably staying at The Breakers or the Four Seasons."

"And?"

"And instead they end up driving into the Breezy Shores mobile park up in Riviera Beach. Only thing is it's not even on a shore but right next to a landfill. I let them park and go into their little aluminum chateau. Meantime, I'm getting really pissed for wasting three whole days. I storm up to the front door after they've gone inside and beat on the door. Darla opens it with a shocked look. 'What the hell are you doing here?' she says."

"Wait, I thought she was a mute?"

Rose snickered and shook her head. "Only reason she didn't ever talk is because *she* was Gail, the fictitious referral agent from our office up in Boston."

Crawford laughed. "Ho-ly shit," he said, "you gotta be kidding."

"No, the two were poor as church mice and just wanted to get a taste of the high life."

"That's incredible," Crawford said. "Definitely tops any other war story I heard today."

"I got more."

"But before you tell me," Crawford said, "you were going to fill me in on Mimi Taylor's most recent boyfriend."

"Let's order first," Rose said. "Telling you about the exploits of Hal and Darla worked up an appetite."

Crawford signaled for the waiter. He came over and they ordered.

"I can see you're champing at the bit," Rose said.

"It's that obvious, huh?"

Rose smiled and nodded. "Okay, so does the name Stark Stabler mean anything to you?"

"Sure does. The tennis player. I've been calling him all day long."

"How'd you find out about him?"

"Emails from Mimi Taylor's computer," Crawford said. "So, tell me what you were going to say."

"Well, he's probably in his mid-fifties now and married to one of the Kittredge sisters—"

"As in—"

"Yup. As in those three-wheeled green-and-yellow tractors. As in, rich as hell but, poor thing, got whacked pretty hard with the ugly stick."

Crawford smiled. "Haven't heard that expression in a while."

"So Stabler was Mimi's boyfriend. I'm guessing it had been going on for six months or so. And what I heard was Mimi was pressing him to divorce Sally Kittredge and marry her. And supposedly he said he would but never actually planned to."

Crawford put his glass down. "I'm going to make a wild guess here. Stark was reluctant to give up the Kittredge lifestyle."

She nodded. "That would be my guess."

"So let me go down the road a little further," Crawford said.

She gestured for him to proceed. "Be my guest."

"Scenario goes something like this: Mimi says to Stark, 'If you don't agree to marry me, I'm going to go to Sally and tell her about us.'"

"I never thought of that, but yeah, it definitely makes sense," Rose said. "So you're thinking that Stark, who's not about to kill the golden goose, might have killed Mimi instead."

"It's a little extreme but possible," Crawford said. "I have another question for you."

"Fire away."

"Stark and Mimi went back and forth with a bunch of emails which kept referring to the initials L.N. Got any clue what that might stand for?"

Rose took a sip of her wine and thought for a second. "L.N., no, I'm drawing a blank."

"That's so unlike you."

"But if I come up with something, I'll let you know."

Crawford nodded as their dinners arrived.

"As usual, keep this under your hat," Crawford said.

"Don't worry."

They ate for a while, then Rose put down her fork and smiled her mischievous smile. "So, speaking of war stories, I have to tell you what happened last week."

"I'm all ears," Crawford said, as he took a bite of his veal scaloppini.

"I went to one of my listings on Barton because I wanted to freshen the place up with a bouquet of flowers. I had a big showing there that afternoon," Rose said. "When I drove in I saw the pool guy's truck but didn't see him at the pool. So, I walked in and saw the cleaning lady's cleaning supplies in the kitchen but didn't see her."

"Stop," Crawford said. "I already know where this is going."

"Just two clues and you've got it solved?" Rose said. "Well, I'm going to tell you the rest anyway. So I put the bouquet down on a table in the living room and hear a noise upstairs."

"Wait a minute, I'm going to guess," Crawford said. "Springs from a bed?"

Rose laughed and shook her head. "I didn't know what it was, so I went up the stairs and it got louder."

"Moaning?"

Rose shook her head again. "I still didn't know. But, curious girl that I am, I just had to find out."

"Of course."

"So I go into the master bedroom, where it seems to be coming from. It was a sound I'd heard before but couldn't quite identify."

"And?"

"The noise gets louder, but they're not there, so I go a little further, and I see in a mirror in the master bath the cleaning lady leaning over the sink—buck naked—and the pool guy is right behind her thrusting away...and then it dawns on me. They're both a little on the chubby side, and you know that distinctive sound of flab on flab—"

"Okay, okay." Crawford held up his hand like a traffic cop halting traffic, laughing despite himself. "Speaking of initials, you ever heard of...TMI?"

SEVEN

Crawford got a call from Dominica McCarthy, crime scene tech and *special* friend, the next morning. The gist of it was she had lifted twenty-two different fingerprints from the master bathroom of the house on North Lake Way. Dominica added that she was unable to get a good print from the toothpaste tube.

An hour later, Crawford was looking across his desk at Art Nunan, or Big A, as he'd referred to himself on his outgoing voice mail message. But the fact of the matter was, he wasn't big, he wasn't tall, he wasn't even fat. He was just...average.

Ott was there, too, and looking at Nunan askance. "So, Big A, where were you the day before yesterday from noon until two thirty?"

"At the pound," Nunan said.

Ott's brow furrowed. "The one on South Dixie?"

"What?" Nunan said quizzically. "I'm talking about the dog track. What are you talking about?"

"Thought you meant animal rescue. Come on, man, gotta be more specific."

"What were you doing at the dog track?" Crawford asked.

"Playing poker," Nunan said. Then proudly, "I'm a professional gambler."

"I thought they just had nickel-dime games there," Ott said.

Nunan frowned. "They got the Tenth Annual Butch Jones Poker Classic goin' on now."

"What the hell's that?"

"Twenty grand in cash prizes if you win," Nunan said. "Can't believe you never heard of it. Named after one of your fallen compadres."

Ott nodded. "You got people who can confirm you were there?"

"Yeah, the boys that hang out there."

"Tell us about a woman named Louise Hyam," Crawford said to Nunan. She was the woman who had been strangled to death after Nunan had apparently done work for her and had a financial dispute.

Nunan looked out the window then back at Crawford. "I had nothin' to do with that."

"That's not what your friend Duane had to say."

"Duane's not a friend. He's a scumbag."

"What happened at Louise Hyam's house?" Crawford asked.

Nunan sighed and shook his head. "I went there to shampoo her carpets. Three rooms. Because I couldn't get a dog shit stain out in this one bedroom, she was only gonna pay me for two rooms. I told her it was a permanent stain. So, she got all bent out of shape and told me to leave. She was gonna stiff me on the whole job."

"Yeah, and that was it?" Ott asked.

"She called the cops, said I threatened her."

"Did you?"

"Fuck no. I was gonna take her to small claims."

"And later that day she was found strangled to death."

Nunan held up his hands. "Don't look at me."

"That's exactly what we're doing," Ott said. "Give us the names of your poker buddies who saw you there day before yesterday. Guys who work there, too, if you know them. While you're at it, you parked there, right?"

Nunan nodded.

"Show us your parking stub."

"I never keep shit like that."

Crawford shook his head and asked a question he felt he needed to ask every suspect on the case. "You have any interest in art...Art?"

Nunan frowned. "What the hell kind of a question is that?"

"Hey, don't get insulted," Crawford said. "Do you?"

"You mean, like paintings and shit?"

"Yeah, paintings and shit."

Nunan scratched his chest. "No."

Crawford shrugged. "Okay."

Nunan was still eyeing him suspiciously.

"We're done," Crawford said. "You can go, but do yourself a favor and come up with a convincing list of witnesses who can alibi you so you're not our number one suspect anymore."

Art Nunan was only their number one suspect because they didn't have anyone else, though Stark Stabler was certainly a person of interest. It seemed that Nunan probably was not their man, assuming he was, in fact, at the West Palm Beach dog track at the time Mimi Taylor was murdered.

Crawford and Ott were on their way to an address that Red Noland had provided. It was in Lake Park, which was north of Palm Beach, and the home of convicted murderer Buddy Lester. Crawford had not been able to reach Lester by phone, so they had decided just to show up on his doorstep.

They walked up the four steps to the door of the tidy white-brick ranch. The doormat said, "Hi, I'm Mat." Ott pressed the doorbell.

A few moments later, a woman in a platinum blonde wig and a hooded housecoat opened the door.

"Morning," Crawford said. "Detectives Crawford and Ott to speak to Buddy."

The woman shaded her eyes. "He do something?"

"That's the question," Ott said. He had his hand around his pistol butt inside his pocket, just in case.

The woman turned back inside. "*Buddy!*"

A few moments later, a balding man in a strappy T-shirt and grey cargo shorts appeared.

"Who are you?"

"Detective Crawford and Detective Ott," Crawford said. "We're looking into a homicide in Palm Beach."

Lester smiled. "I've never been there in my entire life."

"Ten miles away and you've never been there?" Ott asked.

"Never. Why would I want to go see a bunch of big houses and fancy cars? Just make me feel inadequate."

Crawford kind of knew what he meant. "Where were you the day before yesterday between twelve noon and two o'clock?"

Lester looked at the woman. "Was that when we went to Costco?"

She nodded. "We went to the Dollar Store first," she said. "Then spent over an hour at Costco. I had to wait in line for two prescriptions."

"We like the meats there," Lester said. "Got cheap gas too. Cheaper than any other place around."

"So you have receipts for all this?" Ott asked.

"I save all my receipts for a month," the woman said. "So, yeah, I do."

"That's a good idea," Ott said.

"Thank you."

"Can you get them, please?" Crawford asked.

"But I told you I've never been to Palm Beach," Lester said.

Crawford smiled at Lester. "You'd be surprised, but not everyone tells us the truth."

The woman walked back into the house.

"They got good wines too," Lester added.

"So I hear," Crawford said then cocked his head, figuring if

Buddy Lester was interested in wine, maybe he was interested in art. "You got any interest in art, Buddy?"

He got the same perplexed look Arthur Nunan had shot him.

"Not really, why?"

"Oh, I don't know," Crawford said, "you just look kind of cultured."

"I do?" Buddy said with a shrug.

The woman came back with two receipts. Lester chuckled. "The detective here thought I might be into art," he said to her.

She chuckled louder. "Oh, yeah, opera too."

Lester smiled at her.

"So, I guess not," Crawford said, as the woman handed him the receipts.

He looked at the times on the Costco receipts. The one for the main store said 12:57, and the one for the gas station there said 1:25. The one for the Dollar Store said 12:13.

They were in the clear.

"Thank you," Crawford said. "See how easy that was?"

Lester smiled back at him. "Yeah, but it kinda hurts, you not believin' me in the first place."

EIGHT

Ott shook his head as he got into the car. "Well, that was a big fuckin' waste of time."

"Hey, news flash. Half this job is," Crawford said. "So, we gotta bear down on Stabler and that guy Lowell Grey."

"Yeah, and find out what the hell L.N. stands for."

Crawford nodded. "I'm not waiting around for Stabler anymore —let's go to his house," Crawford said. "South Ocean, number 411."

As he had found in his two and a half years in Palm Beach, most people were about as eager to get back to a detective as they were to call back a collections agent.

Ott's cell phone rang. "Hello."

"Detective Crawford?"

"No, this is Ott. You want Crawford?"

"Yes, please."

Ott handed Crawford his cell phone and whispered, "Some babe."

"Hello?"

"Hi, Detective Crawford," the voice said. "My name is Holly

Pine. I'm a real estate agent at the Fite Group and wondered if I could talk to you."

"Sure, absolutely," Crawford said. "About Mimi Taylor's murder?"

A hesitation. "Well, yes."

"Sure, shall I come by your office?" Crawford asked.

"Well, see, I hardly ever go there," Holly said. "I pretty much just operate out of my home office. So—"

"I'd be happy to come there. I just need your address."

"I'm on Coral Lane...231 Coral Lane."

"Could I come right over. Say, in fifteen minutes?"

"Uh, sure, make it a half hour, though, would you?"

"Sure, see you then, Ms. Pine."

Crawford clicked off and handed Ott his phone.

"Jesus, Charlie. You're so damn eager."

"In case you hadn't noticed, Mort, we don't have much goin' on."

"Yeah, I know," Ott said. "But we still got a lot of names on Red Noland's list to go through."

"I know."

"So what do you wanna do?" Ott asked. "Drop me at the station and go see this real estate chick?"

Crawford looked at his watch. It was 12:15. "She's ten minutes away. Might as well get a quick lunch. I'll flip you for where we go."

For something quick, it was always between Krystal's, Ott's choice, or Burger King, Crawford's choice.

"You flip," Crawford said.

"You can't multitask?"

"Flipping a coin, catching it, then turning it over, and putting it on my wrist is pretty tough when I'm driving."

Ott took a quarter out of his pocket and flipped it up in the air. "Call it."

"Heads."

Ott caught it and put it on his wrist.

"Tails," Ott said.

"Shit," Crawford said. "You know, I went to Krystal's website once, and their burgers looked like shit even there."

"Is that what you do with your spare time? Visit fast-food websites?"

"I wanted to see if they admit to making their burgers out of roadkill."

Ott laughed. "Krystal's fries beat the King's fries, any day of the week."

"They're so greasy they slip out of my fingers."

"Use a fork," Ott said. "Hey, by the way, I checked that Bacon King you always have."

"Yeah, what about it?"

"Eleven hundred thirty calories," Ott said. "And you have two of 'em."

Crawford reached over and gave Ott a pat on his ample gut. "You busting me for my eating habits...Slim?"

CRAWFORD ROLLED INTO THE DRIVEWAY AT 231 CORAL LANE AT 12:45, well nourished, even though he wouldn't admit it.

"What do you suppose she's going to tell us?" Ott asked as he opened the car door and got out.

"Who knows? Hopefully something that gets our asses in gear," Crawford said, scoping out the well-tended, two-story stucco house.

They walked up the steps and Crawford pressed the buzzer. Holly Pine's doormat said simply *Welcome.*

A woman who was no stranger to the makeup brush and who appeared to be in her late thirties opened the door. Her eyes lit up when she saw Crawford then dropped to the floor in apparent disappointment at seeing Ott off to his right.

"Oh," she said, "I didn't realize both of you..."

Crawford immediately noticed a few things were off about Holly Pine. For one, the buttons on her shirt were not lined up right. The top button was unbuttoned, but the second one down was in the third buttonhole. So, Crawford's first impression of her was that she was slightly lopsided. His second observation was that the lipstick on her upper lip had strayed off course a little.

"Hello, Ms. Pine, I'm Detective Crawford, and this is my partner, Detective Ott," Crawford said. "Thank you for calling and, if you would, tell us why you called."

"Come on in," Pine said, "and I'll explain."

They followed her in, through the large foyer, into the living room.

She sat down in a beige wingback chair, and Crawford and Ott sat on a couch opposite her.

Crawford thought he knew why she asked them to come to her house in a half hour instead of straight there. Clearly, she had wanted to spend time in front of the mirror doing her face. He noticed a not-so-subtle shade of rouge on her cheeks, her eyebrows were flawlessly penciled and her hair...not a strand out of place.

"First, can I get either of you something to drink?"

"Thank you, Ms. Pine," Crawford said, glancing at Ott, who shook his head, "but we're fine."

"Are you originally from around here?" she asked, looking at Crawford. "You know how they say all Floridians are from somewhere else."

"Originally from New York," Crawford said, getting impatient. "My partner's from Cleveland."

"Oh, really, where in New York? That's where I'm from too."

"New York City. Ms. Pine, if you could tell us—"

"I'm from Oyster Bay. Know where that is?"

"Sure. On Long Island," Crawford said. "Ms. Pine, if you could tell us what you called us about, please?"

Holly Pine leaned forward and dropped her voice, like she suspected there might be a spy behind her curtains. "Mimi had a boyfriend who was married."

On the off chance she might be referring to someone other than

Stark Stabler, Crawford whispered back, "And what do you know about this man?"

"I heard he used to be a professional athlete. A golfer, I think, and that his wife is very rich."

"Thank you," Crawford said starting to get to his feet. "Was there anything else you heard?"

Yet another waste of time, Crawford thought. Plus, he'd had to scarf down a Krystal burger while they waited for Holly Pine to powder her nose.

"No, that's it," Pine said. "Sure I can't get you something to drink?"

Crawford got to his feet, Ott right behind him.

"No, thank you very much, Ms. Pine," Crawford said, "but we have another appointment we have to get to."

That was news to Ott.

"CHRIST," CRAWFORD SAID BEHIND THE WHEEL OF THE CROWN Vic, "we could have had a nice relaxed lunch at Green's." The combination luncheonette-general store-pharmacy on North County Road where they ate lunch when they weren't in a hurry.

"If you asked ol' Holly whether I was tall, short, fat or skinny," Ott said, "she wouldn't have a clue."

"What are you talking about?"

"She got all dolled up for you, Charlie. What do you think I'm talking about?"

Crawford just shook his head and looked at this watch. "We're meeting with Mrs. Taylor in forty-five minutes, and then we're going to Stabler's house and break the goddamn door down, if we have to."

"In the meantime, I'm going to get to the bottom of the L.N. thing."

Crawford had first spoken with Corinne Taylor two days before, on the day of her daughter's murder. It was one of the more difficult notification calls he had ever made, not that they were ever easy. She had kept sobbing uncontrollably, which was understandable. Crawford suggested he and Ott come up and visit her in Vero Beach, but she volunteered to come to Palm Beach. She said that was where her daughter would probably like to be buried, since she had lived there so long.

They went back to the station and scrolled down the remaining names on Red Noland's suspect list.

A while later, Crawford got a call on his cell. He looked at his watch. It was 2:35.

"Hello."

"A Mrs. Taylor to see you, Charlie," Roberta, the receptionist, said.

"Thanks, be right there." He swung by Ott's cubicle on the way up front.

"She here?" Ott asked.

"Yeah, I'll bring her back to my office," Crawford said, walking out to the reception area in front. "Meet you there."

Corinne Taylor, standing at the receptionist's area, had ramrod straight posture, round, frameless glasses, and a sad, faraway look that she probably had before the death of her daughter, Mimi, but which appeared more intense now. She looked to be in her mid- to late sixties.

Crawford approached her. "Hello, Mrs. Taylor," he said. "I'm Detective Crawford. Again, I'm so sorry about your loss."

"Thank you, Detective. I appreciate it," Corinne said.

"If you would follow me back to my office, please?"

"Of course."

They walked back to his office, and Crawford introduced her to Ott, who also expressed his condolences.

"Mrs. Taylor, if we could ask you some questions about Mimi, please?" Crawford asked.

"Yes, of course, go right ahead."

"How long had your daughter lived in Palm Beach?"

"Just about twenty years," Corinne said. "She moved here right after graduating from college."

"Where did she go to college?" Ott asked.

"Rollins. Up in Winter Park."

"Oh, sure," Crawford said. "Good school. And she was there the full four years?"

"Yes, though she did her junior year abroad."

"Where, exactly?"

"Italy. She could speak enough Italian to get by."

Crawford tapped a pen on his desk as Ott took notes in his well-worn leather-bound pad.

"Mrs. Taylor, we're most interested in your daughter's relationships with men. We feel that might advance the case," Crawford said. "If you would start with what you know about her most recent relationship and go backwards, please?"

Corinne sighed and looked down. "I think it's safe to say Mimi was not the best picker of boyfriends."

Crawford raised a hand. "Could you expand on that a little, please?"

"She'd talk to me about them a little," Corinne said. "Kind of bemoan her lack of luck with men. I always listened carefully and tried to give her the best advice I could, but what could I really do? I mean, I couldn't pick them for her."

"Of course."

She exhaled slowly and frowned slightly. "So, all I know about the last man was that he was married."

"She never told you his name?"

"No, because the conversation never went anywhere. I mean, I told her right off the bat that a relationship with a married man was just...well, just plain folly."

"And before him?"

"A man named Lowell Grey. At least he was single." Corinne sighed again. "In the old days, he would have been called a playboy. Maybe they still call 'em that. Anyway, he was a man who never worked, had a lot of fancy cars, played polo...getting the picture?"

Crawford nodded. "How long did they go out for?"

"Um, maybe two or three years," Corinne said. "The problem was, Lowell seemed to have girlfriends the way he had polo ponies. Lots of both."

"I understand," Crawford said. "And before Grey?"

"It gets a little blurry," Corinne said. "There was a man I liked who seemed very stable. He ran a stock fund up in New York. Mimi brought him to meet me in Vero, and I thought, 'Finally, this is the man.' Bu-ut, it turned out his fund was just one big Ponzi scheme. I'm pretty sure he's still in jail now. The government wanted to make an example of him, Mimi told me."

"Sorry to hear that," Ott said, and Crawford nodded.

"Then there was a real estate agent she worked with, but that lasted about a minute and a half," Corinne said then smiled. "I think the love of her life was a man she met in Italy."

"While she was there for her junior year abroad?"

"Yes, he was older. An architect. He ended up moving here—well, not here but Miami. His firm did a lot of office and condo buildings there. Very sleek and ultramodern. Mimi showed me pictures of them in magazines like *Architectural Digest*. I really liked them."

"So, what happened?" Crawford asked. "To that relationship?"

Corinne's face slowly morphed into a frown. "That's a very good question. Mimi never really told me."

"So this took place in her early twenties?" Ott asked.

"Yes, early to mid," Corinne said with a sigh. "He may have been the one that got away."

Crawford and Ott both nodded.

"Then when she was in her late twenties, I think it was...along came the psycho."

Ott's head jerked up from his note-taking. "The psycho?"

Corinne nodded. "That was my nickname, which, needless to say, I didn't share with my daughter. He's a man by the name of

Hardy Johnson, who was the most hyper man I've ever met. Literally could not stand still. Which was I guess why he raced speedboats and motorcycles. There was a part of Mimi that seemed drawn to wild, reckless men like him. Men who liked to live in the fast lane," she said, using finger quotes then shrugged. "Me? I don't get it. They're always so unstable."

"So how long did that last for?" Crawford asked.

"A year maybe," Corinne said. "He lives down near Mar-a-Lago. Supposedly he's toned down a little, Mimi said."

"Who else was there, Mrs. Taylor?" Crawford asked.

"Oh my God, isn't that enough?"

"Do you happen to know...did any of these men ever threaten your daughter? Ever say anything that made her fear for her life? Anything like that at all?"

Corinne thought for a second. "Not that I know of," she said. "But I'm not sure she would have ever told me something like that. You know, wouldn't want me to worry."

"In the days before your daughter's death, did you see her or speak to her?" Ott asked.

"No," Corinne said, "but she planned to come up for Mother's Day."

That was a month off.

"So, no communication with her in the last week?" Crawford asked.

Corinne shook her head.

"What about...do you know if any of these men were art enthusiasts, by any chance?" Crawford asked.

Corinne frowned. "That's an odd question. Why do you ask?"

"Oh, just something we found in the bathroom where Mimi's body was discovered."

Corinne Taylor's eyes got suddenly misty, and she started to sob for the first time.

"I'm sorry, Mrs. Taylor," Crawford said, realizing he had gotten a little clumsy at the mention of her daughter's body.

Corinne held up a hand. "It's okay," she said. "No, I don't remember any of them being art enthusiasts."

"Okay, well, thank you."

Corinne looked at Crawford then Ott. "What do you think happened?" she asked. "You've had two days to look into it."

Crawford exhaled. "To be perfectly honest with you, Mrs. Taylor, as much as we'd like to, we don't have a theory or a prime suspect at this time."

Ott nodded. "But we will."

Corinne's eyes suddenly turned steely behind her glasses, and she seemed to stare straight into Ott's soul.

"You have to...*you must.*"

NINE

THIS TIME, OTT WAS BEHIND THE WHEEL. HE NORMALLY DID the driving because both he and Crawford knew he was the better driver. And every once in a while, they'd needed to drive extremely fast—like when a killer was trying to escape from them. On those occasions, both preferred that Ott be in the driver's seat. Ott had once let Crawford off the hook about his mediocre driving by pointing out that the driving he had done had mostly been up in New York City, so how could he possibly be expected to pursue a perp without ramming into a garbage truck or a yellow cab?

It was now a few minutes past three, and Crawford and Ott were headed to Stark Stabler's house on El Brillo Way.

"I felt bad hearing about Mimi Taylor," Ott said. "Seems like she went out with every shit-bum loser between here and Jacksonville."

"I know, and this guy Stabler seems like the last in a long line of 'em."

Ott shrugged. "Who knows? Maybe you'll end up liking him. One of your boyhood sports heroes and all."

"Not exactly. Like you, most of my boyhood sports heroes were football players. With a few hoopsters thrown in."

"Like who?"

"The hoopsters?"

"Yeah."

"Well, there was a long list of big-time Knicks like Willis Reed, Patrick Ewing, Bill Bradley, Earl Monroe, Dave DeBusschere, Walt Frazier, Bernard King...Who were yours?"

Ott didn't hesitate. "LeBron."

"Yeah, and who else?"

"That's it. Unless you want to count Foots Walker."

"Who the hell is—"

Ott nodded. "Exactly. Just LeBron," he said as he rolled into the driveway of the big Mediterranean house on El Brillo.

Ott whistled as he eyeballed the castle-like house. "Tennis has been very good to Stark."

Crawford shook his head. "Don't kid yourself. His wife's been very good to Stark."

They both got out of the Crown Vic and walked to the front door.

"Who's the wife again?" Ott asked.

"You know those green-and-yellow farm vehicles?"

"Sure do," Ott said. "Company started out in some backwater in Iowa. What I love is how a few generations later, the great-grandsons or great-granddaughters of these hardworking Midwest burghers find their way down to Palm Beach and end up never doing jack shit."

"I know what you mean," Crawford said, as Ott pressed the doorbell.

An Asian woman in a light-blue uniform came to the door. "Yes, may I help you?"

Crawford thought about saying, "Yes, we want to talk to the man of the house about a murder" but made do with, "Detectives Crawford and Ott to see Mr. Stabler, please."

"Ah, I'll go see if he's available."

"If he's here," Ott said with a smile, "he's available."

The woman gave him a nasty look, harrumphed off, and Crawford and Ott cooled their heels for a few minutes, which did little to improve their moods.

Finally, a figure appeared in the doorway. Crawford recognized him as a stouter, shorter, balder version of the man he had seen at the U.S. Open. He had a pencil-thin mustache that Crawford wanted to tell him worked okay on old matinee idols but not on him.

"I'm sorry I didn't call you back," Stabler said. "I've just been terribly busy."

"I'm Detective Crawford and this is my partner, Detective Ott," Crawford said. "Is your wife here, Mr. Stabler?"

"What difference does that make?"

"A big one," Ott said. "Is she?"

"Yes," Stabler said.

"Then, for your sake, I suggest we conduct this interview out in our car," Crawford said.

"O-kay," Stabler said. "This won't take long, will it?"

"It'll take as long as it takes," Crawford said.

"That's not really an answer," Stabler said.

"I'm aware of that," Crawford said. "Follow us, please."

They turned and walked down the steps as Stabler followed them to the Crown Vic.

"What is this about?"

"I'm sure you've guessed already," Crawford said.

Ott opened the front passenger door for Stabler.

Stabler grimaced at the sight of the Vic's crusty, well-worn exterior then got in.

Ott sat in the seat behind him, then slid over so he could see Stabler's face. Crawford opened the driver's side door and slid in.

"So, Mr. Stabler," Crawford said, "we're investigating the murder of Mimi Taylor. And, please, don't say '*Who*?'"

Stabler sighed and lowered his voice. "I knew Mimi."

"Yes, very well, in fact," Ott said.

Stabler didn't answer.

"You were having an affair with her," Crawford said.

"Where'd you get that from?" Stabler protested.

"Front-page headline in the *Glossy*," Ott said, referring to the local Palm Beach paper. "Come on, doesn't matter where we got it, just that it's a fact."

Stabler shook his head and cast his eyes down like he was being picked on.

"Let me ask you this, Mr. Stabler, would you prefer we have this conversation in your living room?" Crawford asked.

"Within earshot of the missus," Ott added.

"O-kay, o-kay," Stabler said. "I was getting ready to end the whole thing with Mimi."

"Why was that?" Crawford asked.

"She was a very needy woman."

Crawford had already developed a strong aversion to the man. "Seems you needed a thing or two yourself."

Stabler shot him the double stink-eye.

"We know you were in a relationship with Ms. Taylor for a number of months until the time of her death." Crawford said, turning to Ott, "Hand me that computer, will you, Mort?"

Ott handed him Mimi Taylor's computer, next to him on the back seat. Crawford opened it and pressed the email icon. He scrolled down to the email conversation between Mimi and Stabler three days ago.

"In this first email, Ms. Taylor said she wanted to talk to you about 'you know what' three days ago. What is 'you know what,' Mr. Stabler?"

Stabler sighed. "I was in the process of breaking up with her."

"So that's 'you know what'?" Ott asked.

Stabler nodded.

"I'm not buying it," Crawford said, "'cause a few minutes later you say, 'I've already said all I'm going to say on the subject.' Then a minute later Ms. Taylor says, 'If that's your final statement, you're forcing me to do what I really don't want to do.' What is she referring to, Mr. Stabler?"

Stabler looked like a trapped animal. "I-I don't know."

"Sure you do," Crawford said. "She's threatening to tell your wife about your affair."

"Isn't that right, Mr. Stabler?" Ott chimed in.

Stabler said nothing.

"Next you email her, 'Don't threaten me Mimi,' and she responds, 'Let's be grown-ups and work it out at the L.N.' What is the L.N., Mr. Stabler?"

There were beads of sweat on Stabler's forehead now. He shrugged.

"You don't know what she means, the L.N.?"

Stabler shook his head nervously.

"Well, then you're the only one in this car who doesn't," Crawford said. "You see, my partner just went through Ms. Taylor's computer very thoroughly, and found a few references to the L.N."

Ott took over. "The first one was back about five months ago, close to the beginning of your relationship. You emailed Ms. Taylor, 'Meet me at the *love nest* at eight o'clock. I'll have bubbly chilling on ice.'"

"So the L.N. is the love nest, and bubbly is champagne," Crawford said. "And we want to know exactly where the love nest is."

Stabler sighed again then mumbled something inaudible.

"I didn't hear you," Ott said.

"Three-two-seven Granada."

"In West Palm?"

Stabler nodded.

"Okay," Crawford said. "Glad to see your memory came back. Back to the original email chain, your last one reads, 'I agree. Tomorrow morning at 10.'"

"Which would have been a few hours before Ms. Taylor was murdered," Ott said.

Stabler threw up his hands in protest. "Hold on, I had nothing to do with that. We met at that time, then she left and I left."

Crawford glanced at Ott to gauge his reaction. Ott looked dubious. "Okay, so what took place at that meeting, then? And don't bullshit us anymore."

Stabler sighed again. The man was a world-class sigher. "We broke up, once and for all. You're right, she had threatened to tell my wife, but I talked her out of it. More like I implored her to" —he dropped his voice— "and offered to pay her some money."

Crawford glanced at Ott again.

Ott smiled. "So, you 'implored' her with exactly how much money?"

"A hundred thousand," Stabler said. "I figure the whole thing worked out to about a thousand bucks per roll in the hay."

Crawford watched Ott roll his eyes in disgust.

"So, the morning of Ms. Taylor's death, when did you leave the *love nest*?"

"About twenty minutes after we got there."

"So, ten twenty?" Ott asked.

Stabler nodded.

Crawford caught Ott's eye and motioned with his head. "We're gonna step outside for a few moments," Crawford said, and he and Ott opened their car doors.

They walked away from the car. "What's your gut?" Crawford asked Ott.

"Could be our guy or could have happened like he said."

Crawford nodded. "Yeah, I got no strong hunch yet."

"So, let's turn up the heat," Ott said.

"I agree. Turn it up, play it like we're sure he did it."

Ott nodded and turned toward the car.

"Hang on," Crawford said. "Stay here a few minutes. See if we can't get him a little more stressed out."

Ott smiled.

For the next few minutes they talked about sports and a Netflix series Ott had been binging on then went back to the car, their expressions hangman grim.

"Mr. Stabler," Crawford said, sliding back to the driver's seat, "did you strangle Ms. Taylor at 327 Granada then take her to the house on North Lake Way?"

"What?" Stabler said, dabbing at the sweat on his forehead with a handkerchief. "I told you I left there at ten twenty. Same time she did. She couldn't have been more alive."

"She was going to tell your wife, wasn't she?" Ott asked.

"No. Christ, I *told* you."

"Yeah, just like you told us you didn't know what the love nest was," Ott said. "When, in fact, it was you who came up with the name in the first place."

"When you took Ms. Taylor's body over to the house on North Lake Way, was someone else there?" Crawford asked.

Stabler started to speak, but Ott cut him off. "Did you see a car in the driveway, a man cleaning the windows, then did you drive around for a while, then come back?"

Stabler shook his head violently. "I went to the Poinciana and played golf at twelve thirty."

"And you've got people who can say they saw you there?" Crawford asked.

Stabler nodded.

"So that still leaves a two-hour gap," Ott said, "between approximately ten thirty and twelve thirty."

"Before I played, I hit some balls on the range," Stabler said. "Putted for a while too."

"For two hours?" Crawford asked skeptically. "When you played, were you in a foursome?"

"No, I played alone."

"When did you finish up?"

"About four. I went around pretty fast."

Crawford scratched the side of his face. "It would have been possible to play the first hole or two, get seen by a bunch of people, then go get in your car, drive up to North Lake Way, and kill Mimi Taylor. Then come back and finish up the last couple holes."

"Yeah, it doesn't take that long to strangle someone," Ott said.

Stabler rubbed his face with both hands for a long moment then threw his head back. "For Chrissakes, that didn't happen. I played eighteen holes, went to the bar, had a drink, then went home."

"That's your story," Ott said, glancing at Crawford.

"Why don't you give us a list of people who saw you? On the range, on the course, in the bar, wherever," Crawford said. "We'll see whether it checks out."

Stabler nodded. "Fine," he said. "Are we done here?"

"No," Crawford said. "So, if you gave Ms. Taylor a hundred-thousand-dollar check at 327 Granada, that would have helped your case. We'd have found it in her purse, and it would prove you paid her off so she wouldn't say anything to your wife. But, the problem is we didn't."

"I was going to give it to her," Stabler said. "I don't carry my checkbook around with me."

"That's too bad," Ott said. "Sure woulda helped your cause."

Crawford pulled out his wallet, took out a card, and handed it to Stabler.

"Send me that list of people at the Poinciana to the email there."

Stabler took the card and nodded.

"One final question," Crawford said, figuring—what the hell—might as well try to leave things on a good note.

Stabler looked wary.

"Still got that nice topspin backhand?"

TEN

It turned out Stark Stabler didn't play tennis anymore. Like so many professional athletes after retirement, he ended up being a golfer.

"So?" Crawford said to Ott on the ride back to the station. "What's your take?"

"Best guy so far," Ott said. "He could have made that whole thing up about the hundred-grand payoff. Killed her at the love nest, took her body up to the house on North Lake Way, then left it there."

"But why? Why bother taking the body up to the house?"

Ott shook his head. "That's a good question," he said. "I still like your scenario. The two of 'em left the love nest, then Stabler started to think twice about the whole thing. She mentioned she was going up to the house, so he started to play the Poinciana just to be seen, then cut it short, went up to North Lake Way, killed her, then went back out on the course at the Poinciana to alibi himself again."

Crawford nodded. "Definitely could have happened." Then he thought for a few moments. "We also gotta talk to Lowell Grey."

"Sure do."

Crawford's cell phone rang. "Hello."

"Charlie, it's Red Noland. Got a few minutes?"

"Yeah, sure, what's up?"

"I mean, can you come to my station. I got a live one here."

"Me and my partner will be there in ten." He clicked off, then turned to Ott. "West Palm police station on Banyan. Red Noland says he's got a live one there."

"What's that s'posed to mean?"

Crawford thought for a second. "Umm...not dead?"

They walked into the West Palm Beach station on Banyan, and the receptionist directed them back to Red Noland, who was waiting in a room with no windows and no amenities. The door was locked, and Noland was seated at a table with a man who had a pock-marked face, splayed teeth, and, as they soon found out, an attitude.

Crawford rapped on the door. Noland saw his face through the glass and let them in.

"Hey, Red," Crawford said. "This is my partner, Mort Ott."

"I heard of you, Mort," Noland said.

"That can't be good," Ott said.

"A regular at Mookie's, right?"

"Had a few beers there, yeah."

The three turned to the unsmiling man.

"Got a fella here with a bad memory," Noland said. "Johnny Cotton meet Detective Crawford and Detective Ott."

"Hello, Johnny," Crawford said.

"Johnny," Ott said.

Cotton didn't say a word.

"So, here's what I got on Johnny," Noland said. "Five years back, he took a little trip up to Redfern Correctional for manslaughter, which got pled down from murder one. What happened was—" Noland glanced at Cotton "—you want to tell 'em, Johnny?"

Cotton didn't say a word.

"What happened was," Noland went on, "Johnny had himself an eighteen-year-old girl in his apartment and, according to the testimony, he and the girl got amorous and Johnny ended up strangling her to death. But Johnny's attorney was able to convince the judge that it was in the act of having sex."

"Wait," Ott said. "Don't tell me. The old erotic asphyxiation gambit?"

"Bingo. You heard that before, huh?"

Ott nodded. "Oh, yeah."

"So, lo and behold, we catch Johnny on a camera at the Palm Beach Marina two weeks ago—"

"Which turns out to be the same night that woman was strangled on her boat, I'm guessing?" Crawford said.

Noland nodded. "You got it. But then we got something even better. I tracked down Johnny here working for a landscaper. Guess where?"

"Palm Beach, maybe?" Crawford said.

"Not only Palm Beach, but last Tuesday he was at a house three doors down from that one on North Lake Way where your reclining nude was found. And" —Noland held up a hand— "it gets better."

Cotton took a sip of a Coke.

"What happens is," Noland continued, "the rest of the crew go to buy something for lunch, but Johnny's brought a sandwich with him and stays right where they've been working."

"Three doors away from our murder house?"

Noland nodded. "Yup. And the other boys come back twenty minutes later and ol' Johnny's right where they left him."

"So, the question is, did he take a little walk to the house three doors away?" Ott said.

"That *is* the question. Well, did ya, Johnny?" Noland asked as all three eyed Cotton.

"No, I didn't," Cotton said in a gravelly voice, just north of a growl. "And since when is it illegal to walk around in a marina looking at boats."

"Since never," Noland said. "But it's all about your timing."

"At both places," Crawford added.

Noland nodded.

"How long you been out of Redfern, Johnny?" Ott asked.

"A month or so."

"And what exactly were you doing that night at the marina?" Ott was slipping into his easygoing, let's-have-a-beer-and-shoot-the-shit persona.

"Just walking around," Cotton said. "I was at CityPlace before. Just looking at stuff."

"Were ya now?" Ott said, nodding. "You buy anything there?"

"Nah, on a landscaper's salary you can't afford much in that place."

Ott nodded. "Did you talk to anybody at either CityPlace or the marina?"

"Asked a few questions in one of the stores."

"Was it a woman you spoke to?"

Cotton nodded.

"And what about at the marina. You talk to anybody there?"

"What you tryin' to get at?"

"Were you looking to meet women by any chance, Johnny?" Ott asked. Then, with a smile, "'Cause I sure would be if I just got out of the joint."

Cotton frowned. "Told you. I was just walkin' around lookin' at the boats."

"Did you happen to see any women on any of the boats?" Ott asked.

"Goddamn dog with a bone, man," Cotton said. "I wasn't paying any attention to the people on the boats. Just the boats."

"So you never saw a good-looking woman on a boat called—" Ott turned to Noland, "What was it, Red?"

"The *Seabreeze*."

"Yeah, on a boat called the *Seabreeze*?"

"Nope."

Ott nodded.

Crawford cocked his head to one side, then the other. "Let me ask you about something else," he said. "You look like a man of culture. You like art at all?"

Cotton smiled for the first time. "Oh, yeah, man, when I'm not picking weeds and mowing grass, you'll be sure to find me in a museum."

Crawford chuckled. "Sense of humor, huh?"

"No," Cotton said. "*You* got the sense of humor. Art? Are you fuckin' kidding me?"

Crawford glanced over at Ott, who had a smirk on his face.

"Johnny," Ott said, "you said a couple of times how you like to walk around."

"Yeah, so?"

"When you were working at that house on North Lake in Palm Beach day before yesterday, did you take a little walk on your lunch break?"

Cotton shook his head. "Nope. Ate my sandwich and nodded off for a half hour. I was tired, picking all those weeds and shit."

"So, if we went around and showed your picture to the neighbors, none of them would have seen you, right?"

Cotton thought for a second. "Well, they might have seen me working at the house."

"But not walking along the road or going into the driveway of that house where the woman was killed?"

"Or coming out?" Ott asked.

"Hell, no."

"Okay," Crawford said, taking his iPhone out of his jacket. "So, you won't have a problem if I take your picture and go show it to the neighbors, will you?"

Cotton's eyes narrowed. Like, he indeed might have a problem with that. "Yeah, I would actually. 'Cause this guy up in Redfern was in for twenty years before they found out it was mistaken identity. Don't take my picture, man."

Crawford had an idea. "We found a mailman who saw a guy come out of the house in question. Got a decent look at him, too. So this would be your chance to get off the hook, since you're saying it wasn't you."

"Still don't want you taking my picture."

"You realize," Ott said, "you're getting us all a little suspicious."

"Hey, man, I don't give a fuck what you are."

Ott shrugged and looked at Crawford.

Crawford stood up. "Okay, Johnny, nice talking to you," he said. "Guess we're just going to have to use your mug shot from five years ago to show that mailman."

"It would be nice if there really was a mailman," Ott said as they drove over the north bridge to the station.

Crawford nodded. "Yeah, no kiddin'. So, what's your take on Cotton?"

Ott thought a few moments. "I don't know, man. The guy was right there. But if it was him he would have grabbed Mimi Taylor's purse. And the art thing...I'm not sure he'd even know how to spell 'reclining.'"

"Unless he was playing us."

Ott shrugged.

Crawford's cell phone rang. "Hello."

"Hey, Charlie, it's Glenna." The receptionist at the station.

"Hey, Glen, why are you whispering?"

"'Cause I got a wack-a-doodle here who wants to see you."

"Oh, yeah? What's his or her name?"

"Holly Pine."

The real estate babe who went heavy with the makeup brush.

"She say what she wants?"

"Just that she wants to talk to you."

Crawford sighed. "All right, we're on our way back."

"She just wants to talk to you. Not Mort."

"Aw, he'll be hurt," Crawford said, clicking off.

"You talking about me?" Ott asked.

"Holly Pine, that agent at Fite, is at the station. She wants a private audience with me."

Ott frowned. "I *am* a little hurt."

Ten minutes later Crawford and Ott walked into the station. Ott kept walking back to the serenity of his cubicle, while Crawford went over to Holly Pine, who was reading a year-old magazine.

"Hi, Ms. Pine," he said and she looked up and beamed.

"Oh, hi, Charlie," she said. "I hope you don't mind if I call you Charlie. Detective is such a mouthful."

Crawford noticed two things. One was Glenna smirking behind the reception desk and the second was that somehow Holly Pine had gotten a deep, dark tan since he saw her last. Then he realized it stopped halfway down her neck. It was clearly something that came in a tube, not from the sun.

"Charlie's fine," he said.

"You can call me Holly."

Another silent smirk from Glenna, who was pretending not to listen.

Crawford sat down across from Holly and waited for her to volunteer something. But she just kept smiling her goofy smile.

Finally, he asked, "So, did you think of something else...I mean, about the murder of Mimi Taylor?"

"Well, as a matter of fact..." She lowered her voice.

Crawford leaned closer. "As a matter of fact...what?"

"I did some detective work." She smiled broadly. "The man she was having an affair with is named Stark Stabler."

Crawford barely reacted. "Well, thank you, Ms. Pine."

"Are you going to arrest him?" Holly elbowed him playfully. "Maybe I get some reward money?"

It was her little ha-ha.

Crawford shook his head. "Sorry, there's no reward money."

She smiled. "I was just kidding."

"And, Ms. Pine, we actually know about Mr. Stabler" —her face dropped— "but thanks anyway."

She frowned, and Crawford saw her tube tan crack a hair. "Well, I guess I wasn't too helpful."

"I appreciate the effort anyway," Crawford said reaching for his wallet. "If you have any more thoughts in the future" —he handed her a card— "why don't you just email them to me? It'll be easier than coming all the way here."

She smiled, fluttering her fake lashes. "Oh, it was no problem. I loved seeing where you work."

Fuuuccckkk.

ELEVEN

Crawford tried to get past Ott's cubicle without getting spotted, but Ott knew his walk.

"Hey, Charlie, so how'd it go with Holly? She serve up a case-buster for you?"

Crawford just kept walking but heard Ott's chair scrape on the floor.

Ott followed him back to his office. Crawford turned to him. "Put a lid on the Holly shit, huh?"

Ott laughed. "Aw, don't be so sensitive. Not everyone can have their very own stalker. I just wanted to tell you about my calls to the names on Stabler's list. The guys from the Poinciana. I just knocked off two and made four earlier."

"Yeah, and?"

"Stabler was definitely at the Poinciana, and he definitely was on the range and putting green. One guy saw him tee off and two guys saw him in the bar. But—and seems like a pretty big *but*—nobody remembers actually seeing him on the golf course after he teed off."

"Good work," Crawford said. "So, seems like he's got himself a flimsy alibi."

"Not only that," Ott said, "three of them commented they thought it strange that Stabler was playing by himself. He usually plays in two regular foursomes, and none of 'em ever saw him play solo."

Crawford was nodding. "So his alibi just went from flimsy to shaky."

"Yeah, it was like he realized he needed one, so, spur-of-the moment, he went to the Poinciana and made himself as visible as possible."

"The problem is, the guy can have no alibi at all but it doesn't matter if we got nothing solid on him," Crawford said.

Ott nodded. "Yeah, good point."

"I got an idea, though," Crawford said. "I'm gonna take a drive over to the love nest and see if any of those keys from Mimi Taylor's condo fit. I got an appointment with the judge to get a warrant to search the place."

"Good thinkin'," Ott said. "We're getting to be regulars at the judge's chambers."

El Cid is one of the most desirable locations in West Palm Beach. As the crow flies, it's less than a thousand yards to Palm Beach—just over the Intracoastal—but millions of dollars apart in terms of real estate prices. The house at 317 Granada Road was a small white stucco—singularly lacking in curb appeal. In Palm Beach it would have gone for a million five; here, you could pick it up for a mere five hundred thousand.

The third key Crawford tried unlocked the front door. It was light and sunny inside and looked like it had been completely renovated recently. There was no foyer or entranceway, you just walked straight into the living room, which had brightly polished red oak floors. Crawford put on his vinyl gloves and walked through the entire house. It had three bedrooms and three baths, all of them, including the master, small. It looked as though someone had spent an afternoon in Pottery Barn and Williams-Sonoma—Crawford's guess was Mimi Taylor—charging up a bunch of things on Stark Stabler's credit card then called it day. There were almost no personal possessions in the entire house, and the closets contained a minimal amount of clothing. It looked exactly like what it was — a place where two people went, knocked back a few cocktails, then had sex.

Crawford was about to leave, when he opened a coat closet to the left of the front door. In it was a six-foot-tall fiberglass golf bag carrier on wheels. Crawford's first thought was that Mimi Taylor's body could easily have fit in it.

With room to spare.

TWELVE

It got better.

Crawford opened the golf bag carrier and saw down at the bottom a woman's pearl earring. He took out his iPhone and took a few photos, first of the golf bag carrier itself, then of the earring at the bottom. Then he had a thought and walked into the kitchen. He opened drawers until he found what he was looking for: a yellow box of small plastic trash bags. He took one, went back to the closet, knelt down, picked up the earring, and placed it in the bag.

Then he put the plastic bag in his jacket pocket, pulled out his phone, and dialed a number he had dialed hundreds of times before. It went straight to voice mail.

"Hi, this is Dominica. Leave a message and I'll get back to you as soon as I can."

"Hey, Dominica, it's Charlie," he said. "I need to speak to you. Call me as soon as you can."

He went and got back into his Crown Vic and pounded the steering wheel, excited that he may finally have had a break in the case. He drove back to the station and went straight to where the CSEU—Crime Scene Evidence Unit—cubicles were. Dominica was not there, so he left her a note to call him. Then he went to Ott's cubicle.

"Check this out," Crawford said to Ott, who was on his computer.

"Whatcha got, bro?"

Crawford handed Ott the four photos he'd taken at 317 Granada. "Found this in a coat closet at the love nest."

Ott studied them closely. "Holy shit, man, so you're thinking our boy Stark moved Mimi Taylor's body in this thing?"

"Could be," Crawford said. "And I'm guessing that earring belonged to her. I'm trying to track down Dominica to see if Mimi Taylor was wearing the mate to this one when she got killed."

Ott high-fived Crawford. "Good goin', man. 'Bout time we got movin' on this sucker."

Crawford smiled. "Well, it helps I got you poking holes in the guy's alibi."

Crawford saw Norm Rutledge's office door open and the great man walk out. Rutledge's title was Director of Public Safety, though he, Crawford, and Ott still referred to his position as Police Chief, since Director of Public Safety had the ring of a glorified crossing guard. Rutledge had steered relatively clear of Crawford and Ott on the Taylor case so far, which was exactly the way they liked it.

He walked over to them. "Hey, boys, you're lookin' awful happy," Rutledge said. "You get laid or something?"

That was the second-worst thing about Rutledge. His sense of humor. The worst thing was when he'd meddle in their cases and float lame theories about their homicides.

"No such luck," Crawford said. "But we may be getting somewhere on Taylor."

Rutledge gave them the double thumbs-up. That was the third-worst thing about him. The lame gestures. "So, let's hear."

Crawford went through the case blow-by-blow, with Ott occasionally interjecting and Rutledge doing his double thumbs-up thing once more. Just as Crawford wrapped it up by showing Rutledge the photos of the earring, he looked up and saw Dominica McCarthy walk in. Dominica had big brown eyes, high cheekbones, a bouncy full head of hair, and a figure everyone agreed was in the top tenth of one percent in Florida and quite possibly the world.

"Hey, guys," she said.

"There you are," Crawford said, taking the plastic bag out of his pocket. "Just one quick question." He held up the bag. "Does this earring match one you found on Mimi Taylor?"

Dominica looked at it and shook her head. "Sorry, Charlie, but she was wearing two gold studs."

"Wait, are you sure?" Crawford asked.

"Yeah, I'm sure," Dominica said, pulling out her iPhone. "Got shots of 'em right here."

The three men crowded around as Dominica scrolled through photos taken in the master bath at the house on North Lake Way the day of the murder. "See," Dominica said, pointing to a close-up of Mimi Taylor's head.

"Shit," Crawford muttered.

Rutledge cocked his head. "Well, it looks like that case you thought you had wrapped up might need a little bit more work."

Crawford had once calculated that in about forty percent of his conversations with Rutledge he'd had the overwhelming urge to cold-cock the man.

THIRTEEN

IT WAS BACK TO SQUARE ONE.

Saturday morning, and Mimi Taylor's funeral was in forty-five minutes.

You'd expect that Palm Beach billionaires and millionaires would object to having their final resting place be in West Palm Beach, but, fact was, Palm Beach had no cemeteries. So, Margaret M. (Mimi) Taylor was being buried at Woodlawn Cemetery across the Intracoastal in West Palm. There was, however, in Crawford's opinion, nothing the least bit shabby about Woodlawn. You drove in through a massively impressive stone archway with the words *THAT WHICH IS SO UNIVERSAL AS DEATH MUST BE A BLESSING* carved into it. Some might take issue with that sentiment, which had been variously attributed to German philosopher Johann Schiller, the eighteenth-century satirist Jonathan Swift, and even Henry Flagler, who originally owned the cemetery land back when it was a pineapple field. What is known for sure is that in 1914, Flagler gave the Woodlawn property to the city of West Palm Beach.

Others buried where Mimi Taylor was about to be interred included a woman who had confessed to murdering her married lover. Her name was Lena Clarke, and she'd been the West Palm Beach postmistress. When in court for the murder trial, she claimed to have been, in a previous life, a resident in the Garden of Eden when the solar system was created, as well as—much later on—the Egyptian goddess Isis. She did a two-year stint at Chattahoochee State Hospital for the Insane before returning to West Palm Beach to sort mail again and teach Sunday school at the Congregational church.

But the best-known couple to have a tombstone at Woodlawn were Judge Curtis Chillingworth and his wife, Marjorie. There are no bodies beneath their shared tombstone because the couple was kidnapped, taken on a boat out to sea, wrapped in weights, then flung over the side. Five years after the heinous crime occurred, one of the killers bragged about the murders to a friend and it surfaced that he and another man had been hired by another judge to kill the couple. The other judge was the kingpin in a local moonshine racket and feared being exposed by Judge Chillingworth.

So, Mimi Taylor was far from the first murder victim in Woodlawn's history.

The funeral party was small. Corinne Taylor sat with an older male friend whom Crawford and Ott couldn't identify. There were a number of women in their thirties, forties, and fifties, some of whom Crawford remembered from their meetings at the various real estate agencies. His rough count was that there were twenty to twenty-five women, most of them agents, with Rose Clarke being one of the attendees. Rose gave Crawford and Ott a little hand wave. Arthur Lang, the manager of the Sotheby's office where Mimi Taylor worked, had worn a shocking-pink tie, which Crawford considered somewhat inappropriate.

Quickly catching Crawford and Ott's attention was a man sitting in the back row and clearly moved by the occasion. He was wearing a fashionable blue suit and burgundy tie and dabbed occasionally at his eyes with a handkerchief. He had sandy-brown hair, watery blue eyes and a tan that would have made George Hamilton (not to mention, Holly Pine) envious.

Ott and Crawford were sitting at the other end of the back row. Ott leaned into Crawford. "Any clue who he might be?"

Crawford shook his head. "We'll find out."

As they expected, Stark Stabler was not in attendance.

At the end of the short ceremony, Crawford and Ott waited as people payed their respects to Corinne Taylor. One of the last ones to do so was the man in the blue suit. He started to give Corinne a hug, but she made no move to hug him back, so he awkwardly pulled back and shook her hand. They spoke for less than a minute, he doing most of the talking. Then two women, one of whom Crawford remembered from the Douglas Elliman meeting, approached and expressed their condolences to Corinne. The older man who had sat with Mimi's mother gave Corinne a kiss on the cheek and slowly walked away. Finally, it was Crawford and Ott's turn. They took a few steps toward her.

"Hello, Mrs. Taylor," Crawford said, shaking her hand. "It was a very nice ceremony. Again, my condolences."

"And mine too," Ott said, shaking her hand.

"Thank you both for coming," she said, then got right to business. "Anything so far?"

"We have several possibilities we're working on," Crawford said. "Mrs. Taylor, if you would tell us who the last man you spoke to is, please?"

"Oh, that's my friend, Mark Chase. He lives up in Vero Beach."

"And before him, the younger man in the blue suit?"

Corinne Taylor's smile faded. "Oh, that's Lowell. Lowell Grey. The playboy, remember? As many polo ponies as girlfriends?"

"Right, I remember."

"He told me how sorry he was, then said he had been thinking about trying to get back together with Mimi, but..."

"What did you say to him, Mrs. Taylor?" Ott asked.

"I just said something innocuous like, 'That's nice,'" Corinne said. "Then he asked me something kind of strange."

"What was that?"

"He asked if I had a key to Mimi's condo. Said he had left a paddleboard there and wanted to get it."

"Why did you think that was strange?" Ott asked.

"Well, because he had six months to get it, while Mimi was alive," Corinne said. "Why didn't he get it then?"

Crawford glanced at Ott, who, judging by his expression, seemed to think that was a good question too. "Did he say where it was? The paddleboard?"

"Out on her balcony," Corinne said.

"He seemed kind of broken up," Crawford said.

"Or maybe that was just Lowell being dramatic. I've seen it before." Corinne sighed. "Well, I think I'm going to spend some time with my daughter alone now."

Crawford and Ott said goodbye and got into the Crown Vic for the ride back to the station.

"What are you gonna do now?" Ott asked as they crossed the north bridge.

"Thought I'd drop in on Stabler again," Crawford said. "Ask him about that earring."

Ott nodded. They drove in silence for a few moments. "Also, how do you s'pose he was going to explain to his wife where the hundred grand went that he was going to give Mimi?"

"Good question. Like I said before, he could have made that whole thing up," Crawford said. "Right after him... Lowell Grey."

Ott nodded. "I agree. That paddleboard thing?"

"Yeah," Crawford said, nodding. "Like the lady said, a little strange."

Crawford tapped his fingers on the console. "Tell you what occurred to me...maybe he wants to get into Mimi's condo for something other than his paddleboard."

Ott nodded. "I buy that. Especially since it seems he forgot about the paddleboard until now. Want me to give him a call?"

"Sure. I'll swing by Stabler's house and ask him a few questions," Crawford said. "You try to set up an interview with Grey."

"You got it," Ott said. "He and I can compare notes about polo."

Crawford pulled into Stark Stabler's parking court and parked between a Mercedes S550 and a Porsche Cayenne.

The unsmiling Asian woman in the blue uniform answered the door again. She didn't hide her frown when she saw Crawford. When he told her he wanted to see Stabler, she walked away without a word.

Two minutes later, Stark Stabler appeared.

"How 'bout a little walk, Mr. Stabler?" Crawford said, turning and walking back down the steps.

Stabler followed him. "Anything but sitting in that car of yours again."

"You got something against American cars?" Crawford asked, eyeing the Mercedes and Porsche bookending the Vic.

"Thing smelled like a pile of jockstraps in a goddamn locker room."

Crawford caught Stabler's eye. "Probably 'cause it's had a few criminals sit in it over the years."

They walked another ten yards, and Crawford stopped, reached into his pocket and took out his iPhone. He scrolled down to a photo of the earring in the golf bag carrier and showed it to Stabler.

"Whose is this?" he asked.

Stabler squinted. "Oh, shit. My wife's been looking everywhere for that."

"How would it end up in the bag carrier?"

Stabler shrugged. "'Cause we both used it," he said. "She went on a ladies' weekend down to Casa de Campo two months ago."

"Where's that?"

"The Dominican Republic."

Crawford looked down at Stabler's green rubber Crocs and found them unbefitting of a former Davis Cup tennis player. "My question is"— his eyes wandered back to Stabler's face— "what was your bag carrier doing at 327 Granada?"

"I took it there straight from the airport a couple of weeks ago," Stabler said.

"Where were you?"

"In Nassau. A place called Lyford Cay."

"Then what? You took your clubs over to the Poinciana and left them there?"

"Exactly."

Crawford nodded and shot another look down at Stabler's Crocs. He noticed his left foot was dirty. Definitely not a good look for someone who'd gotten to the semifinals at Wimbledon. His eyes drifted back to Stabler's face and his pencil-thin mustache. It had looked fine on the old-time actor David Niven. But Stabler was no David Niven.

"You like art, Mr. Stabler?" Crawford asked.

"What kind of a question is that?"

"Just curious."

Stabler thought for a second. "Not really," he said. "Norman Rockwell a little."

"How 'bout Modigliani?"

"Who?"

Crawford eyed him for a tell. Was he playing dumb or just...dumb?

He glanced over at the Crown Vic between the two expensive German cars. "I think I should inform you you're a suspect in the murder of Mimi Taylor. So, don't be going on any fancy golf trips."

"You gotta be kidding," Stabler said, a bead of sweat rolled down his forehead. "I told you I was at the Poin—"

"I heard you," Crawford said. "The question is, did you play a full eighteen or cut it short?"

FOURTEEN

Crawford's cell phone rang as he was pulling out of the driveway of Stark Stabler's house. He fished it out of his pocket and looked down at the display. Ott.

"What's up?"

"So, here's a coincidence for you," Ott said.

"Tell me."

"I'm driving down Worth Avenue and I get near the end and I look up to see these two sign-installers putting up a new sign on a shop. Guess what it's for?"

"I don't know? A Walmart?"

Ott laughed. "Yeah, about as likely as a Home Depot. No, it says Lowell Grey Gallery."

"No shit."

"Yeah, so I parked and looked through the window. There was this young woman and guy in there putting up paintings but no Lowell. So I knocked on the door, and the girl opens it and tell me it's not opening 'til Tuesday. I told her I was looking for Lowell Grey and she goes, 'Oh, that's my dad. I just came down from DC to help him with the installation.' She explained that Lowell's having a big opening cocktail party tomorrow night. He's expecting like three hundred people to show up for it."

"Well, well," Crawford said. "What kind of art did they have?"

"From what I could tell, real abstract stuff. Like that artist who puts up a canvas and throws shit at it."

"Can't say I know who that is, Mort."

"Yeah, you do. The guy who shoots a paintball gun at his canvases."

"No clue who you're talking about."

"Well, anyway, the paintings are colorful, I'll say that for them," Ott said. "So, the daughter told me she expected Lowell back in a few minutes."

"Where are you now?"

"Back out in the car."

"Okay, so I'm ten minutes from there. Meet you outside the gallery. What's the address?"

"It's 318 Worth. You can't miss it, sign guys are still out there with their crane."

"See you in a few."

Lowell Grey was still wearing the blue pants from the blue suit he'd worn at Mimi Taylor's funeral. He also still wore the crisp button-down shirt, though he had rolled up the sleeves.

Crawford knocked on the gallery door. Ott was right beside him.

This time the gallery namesake opened the door himself. "Sorry, fellas, we don't open until Tuesday. Wait, didn't I see you at Mimi Taylor's funeral this morning?"

"Yes, you did," Crawford said. "My name is Detective Crawford, and this is Detective Ott, Palm Beach Police Department. We're working on the Mimi Taylor homicide. Could we speak to you, please?"

"Ah, yes, sure," Grey said, opening the door further. "Come on in." Pointing to the young couple, "That's my daughter, Melissa."

"Yes, we met," Ott said, as Melissa, clad in black spandex, waved.

"And that's Todd," Grey said, pointing to a man in blue jeans and a blue-and-white sports shirt. "The brains behind the operation."

Todd, on a ladder, smiled and waved too.

"We can go in the back and talk," Grey said.

They followed him into a room that had two brand-new white leather contemporary sofas facing each other with a chrome-and-glass table in between. On three sides of the room were paintings leaning against the walls. "Sorry about the mess," Grey said. "Kind of a last-minute scramble around here."

"We understand," Crawford said. "Mr. Grey, we know you're busy, so we'll try to make this brief...we have some questions about you and Mimi Taylor."

"Well, ask away."

"Okay, our understanding was that you and Ms. Taylor broke up six months ago and that you were the one who initiated it."

"Yes, that's pretty accurate."

"But we observed you at the funeral, and you clearly were upset, so—"

"You wondered what was up?"

"Well, yes."

"Basically, I screwed up," Grey said. "I should have never ended it. I met another woman and was temporarily...smitten. Head over heels. Infatuated, really. It was ridiculous. She was—" he lowered his voice "—younger than my daughter, and it lasted about five minutes. But when I realized the error of my ways, it was too late, Mimi was already seeing that odious bore Stark Stabler."

Crawford didn't need to know why he called Stark Stabler an "odious bore" but agreed.

"Mr. Grey," Ott cut in, "Mrs. Taylor mentioned that you asked her if you could borrow a key to get into Mimi Taylor's condo and get a paddleboard of yours."

Grey slipped his brown loafers off with his heels and put his feet up on the glass-topped table. The blue socks had pairs of crossed polo mallets sprinkled on them.

"Yes," Grey said finally, "I've been getting a little squishy in my core" —he grabbed a fold of skin at his stomach— "and figured I better get back out on the water."

"Gotcha," Ott said.

"So, have you always been interested in art, Mr. Grey?" Crawford asked.

Grey chuckled. "I'll level with you," he said. "Back when I lived up in New York, it was a good way to impress women. Start talking about Caravaggio this, or Basquiat that, women eat that shit up. I always used to ask 'em if they wanted to go to the galleries down in Chelsea on our first date. Get 'em thinking I was a real connoisseur, you know. Gagosian this, Acquavella that."

Crawford leaned forward. "I could be wrong, Mr. Grey, but isn't the Acquavella gallery on the Upper East Side?"

Grey looked dumbstruck.

"Charlie used to live up in New York," Ott explained.

"Wherever it was," Grey said, "women love a guy who can talk the talk."

Crawford decided to lob it in there. See how Grey would react. "What's your opinion of Modigliani?"

Crawford didn't notice a flinch or a hesitation.

"I like him. Talk about a guy who gave all his subjects the longest damned necks."

He wasn't wrong.

"There was one," Crawford said, "*Reclining Nude,* that got a hundred and seventy million at auction a couple years back."

"I remember reading about that," Grey said, not reacting to the painting's name. "My paintings here go for a little less than that. Case you were thinking about putting one on your living room wall."

"I'm not sure I have a wall big enough for these," Crawford said, then abruptly changed the subject. "Mr. Grey, where were you last Thursday between twelve noon and two o'clock?"

It didn't seem to dawn on Grey what he was being asked at first. Then, "Wait, a minute, you don't—"

"Everybody we talk to gets asked that question," Crawford said, putting up his hand.

Grey didn't look insulted but instead pointed to his face. "See this golden tan?" he said. "I was out at my pool. Gotta look good for my opening."

"With anyone?" Ott asked.

"Nope. Solo."

"Did anyone see you there? A pool cleaner. A gardener maybe?" Ott asked.

Grey shook his head. "You don't really think—"

"Gotta ask," Ott said.

Grey shrugged.

There was nothing more they needed to ask.

"Well, thanks for your time, Mr. Grey," Crawford said, getting to his feet. "Maybe we could do you a favor..."

"What's that?" Grey asked.

"We have a key to Mimi Taylor's condo," Crawford said. "If you want, you could stop by our station at 345 South County when you want to pick up your paddleboard."

"Hey, that's really nice of you," Grey said, suddenly casual. "You find anything helpful there?"

"No, not really," Crawford said.

"Well, that's too bad," Grey said, slipping back into his loafers. "So, I might swing by your station tomorrow or the next day."

"Just give us a call before," Crawford said, shaking Grey's hand and handing him a card. "And good luck with the opening."

Ott nodded, and they walked out into the gallery, waving goodbye to Melissa and Todd. Then they went outside and onto the sidewalk.

"What did you think?" Crawford asked.

"He didn't react much when you asked about Modigliani and mentioned the specific painting."

"Yeah, I know."

Ott reached the car and hit the clicker. "What was the plan when you offered him the key to Mimi Taylor's condo?" he asked. "I could see something shifty going on in your brain."

Crawford laughed. "I was thinking there might be something there that we didn't spot that he wants. And not a paddleboard. I'm thinking about getting the boys at Sun-Tech to install a few cameras."

A big smile spread across Ott's face, and he gave Crawford a fist bump. "Always something up your sleeve, bro."

"And if Grey doesn't take that paddleboard, maybe I'll give it a go." He grabbed a fold of skin on his stomach. "Getting a little squishy in my core, don't ya know."

FIFTEEN

THE DRY-ERASE BOARD HUNG VERTICALLY FACING CRAWFORD and his desk. Ott was standing next to it with an orange Expo low-odor marker in hand. The board was four feet high and three feet wide, and there was plenty of room to write the names of suspects and people to be interviewed.

Under *Suspects*, Ott, who had by far the better handwriting, had written Art Nunan, Johnny Cotton, Stark Stabler, and Lowell Grey. Buddy Lester had not been included on the list because both Crawford and Ott had found him convincing when he'd told them he'd never been to Palm Beach.

Ott had gone to the Palm Beach Kennel Club and found two men who said that Art Nunan was at the dog track when the murder took place. But, one admitted to drinking a lot that day and, under pressure from Ott, the second one said Nunan gave him ten bucks to say he was there at the time.

Johnny Cotton, who had been working close to the murder scene when it happened, made for a dark horse suspect because of his convincing lack of art knowledge. But, maybe more importantly, he had a very tight window between when his fellow landscapers went to get lunch and when they returned twenty minutes later. Still they weren't ruling him out.

Both Crawford and Ott agreed that Stabler and Grey were their primaries at this point.

Crawford took his cell phone out of his pocket. "Just had a thought," he said to Ott, dialing the phone.

"Hey, Rose, it's Charlie," he said. "Mind if I put you on speaker? I got Mort here, so keep it clean."

"Yeah, none of the usual bawdy stuff," Ott said.

"I'll try."

"We need to ask you about Lowell Grey," Crawford said.

"Didn't I mention him to you before?" Rose asked.

"Yes. 'Too much money and too much time to screw around' were your exact words."

"That about says it," Rose said. "And now he's going into the gallery business."

"That's what we wanted to talk to you about," Crawford said. "He doesn't exactly strike me as a dedicated art lover."

There was a pause at the other end. "Here's all you need to know about Lowell Grey, the man's a dilettante. He probably knows enough about art to tell the difference between a van Gogh and a Warhol, but that's about it. Just like he probably knows the difference between a polo pony and a cow...but that's about it."

Ott laughed.

"Just sayin'," Rose said. "Though I did hear that the man might have some unusual sexual proclivities."

"What's a proclivity?" Ott asked.

Rose laughed. "So Charlie taught you how to play dumb too, huh, Mort?"

"Nah, it comes natural."

"But what's with his opening a gallery?" Crawford asked.

"His latest fad," Rose said. "He's got some young guy who's going to run it and do all the heavy lifting. Lowell gets to bloviate about *his gallery* at cocktail parties. He's a forty-five-year-old guy who thinks he's still got to impress women."

"I'm a fifty-one-year-old guy who can't," Ott said wistfully.

"You're doing just fine, Mort," Rose said.

"He said he was trying to get back together with Mimi Taylor," said Crawford.

"I don't know anything about that," Rose said.

"You ever hear about him mistreating women, anything like that?" asked Ott.

"There was something...a long time ago," Rose said. "Up in New York, I think."

Crawford leaned forward in his chair. "What happened?"

"I remember it was in *Page Six*" —the famous gossip column in the *New York Post*. "It was like something inspired by that Marquis de Sade weirdo."

"Really?" Crawford said. "Be a little more specific?"

"Sorry," Rose said. "I can't. Can't you delve back into the annals of *Page Six*?"

Crawford already knew that was a job he was going to foist off on Ott. "What else, Rose?"

"He's really vain."

"I can see his tan's pretty important to him," Crawford said. "What else?"

"Oh, Jesus, where do I start?" Rose said. "Well, for one thing, he posts his workout schedule on Facebook. Like who would possibly care? And speaking of Facebook, he's the king of selfies. All these stupid poses...like that *Zoolander* guy."

"All right, Rose," Crawford said. "As always a fountain of knowledge on a myriad of subjects."

"Are you cutting me off just when I was getting rolling?"

"Much as we'd like to sit around and shoot the breeze with you—"

"I know, I know, you got a murder to solve."

"Yes, but thanks for everything," Crawford said.

"Yeah, thanks, Rose," Ott said.

"You're always welcome. Bye, boys." She clicked off.

"Piece of work, huh?" Crawford said.

"Piece," Ott said.

OTT WENT AND LOOKED INTO THE *PAGE SIX* STORY ABOUT Lowell Grey. A half hour later he came back and had a copy of the story with a date handwritten on it of 3/14/2011.

"Back when you were a wee lad, Charlie," Ott said.

"That was a couple years before I left," Crawford said, referring to his stint in the NYPD.

"But you didn't hang with Lowell and the gang who, it turns out, were getting it on with a bunch of lady wrestlers."

"What?"

Ott handed him the copy of the *Page Six* article. "Can't make this shit up."

Crawford started reading it. *Men from prominent families and posh boarding school backgrounds have recently found amusement far from their exclusive athletic and social clubs on Park Avenue. A group of young financiers, bankers, and ad executives are known to have regularly frequented a decidedly un-tony Lower East Side spot called 98 Lady Wrestlers (the number apparently refers to the address at 98 Broome Street, as opposed to the number of wrestlers in the enterprise). The main feature of the club's activities is to wrestle naked with the women wrestlers, some of whom were reported to weigh in excess of 250 pounds. Apparently, the men were rarely victorious, which according to one participant, the polo player Lowell Grey, was 'what made it such a hoot.'*

It went on for another paragraph, but that was enough for Crawford.

Ott saw the look on his partner's face. "Exactly," he said. "What the *fuck*, right?"

Crawford was shaking his head in confusion. "Yeah, I mean... wrestling with naked women who weigh twice as much as you? I mean, why in God's name would that be a fun source of entertainment?" He exhaled, still shaking his head. "I always thought these guys just played a mean game of squash."

SIXTEEN

THE NEXT MORNING AT MIMI TAYLOR'S CONDO, CRAWFORD MET up with a man he'd worked with before, Mel of Sun-Tech Systems. The only instructions he gave Mel, who was very good at what he did, was to put an "eye" on the whole apartment and hide the cameras well. Mel, who was not much for conversation, nodded and started working.

In the meantime, Crawford first checked to see if there was, in fact, a paddleboard on Mimi Taylor's balcony. There was. Perhaps that really was the reason Lowell Grey wanted to get into her condo. Or not.

Next, he spent an hour and twenty minutes going over every square inch of the twelve-hundred-square-foot space. He even went through every book in Mimi Taylor's four shelves of books, having once found a note inside a book that was key to solving a murder.

While he was on his iPad checking emails at the kitchen table, Mel came up behind him.

"Okay, Charlie, time to play hide 'n seek."

Crawford went from room to room and finally spotted a camera peeking up over a piece of cove molding. "You'd have to be looking for it to see it," Crawford said. "This guy's not gonna be. Great work as always, Mel."

CRAWFORD FIGURED HE'D KILL TWO BIRDS WITH ONE STONE. For one thing, he missed Dominica McCarthy. Of course, he had the power to remedy that situation. Like dial his cell phone and ask her out for a drink. Or dinner. Or both. Nothing difficult about that. Nothing except the fact that the charge of "Mr. Noncommittal" had recently been hurled at him and the possible truth to the allegation had shaken him up a little.

Maybe it was the failure of his fourteen-year marriage in New York—or what he referred to as eight and a half years of marital bliss and five and a half years of pure, unadulterated hell. It was a subject he tended not to speak about with anyone. The prospect of failing again had put the fear of God in him. At one point in the last year, he had actually thought about asking Dominica to marry him. Well, more accurately, he had floated a trial balloon and had actually gotten what appeared to be the green light...but then he'd just kind of chickened out.

Aside from the personal, Dominica was, professionally, a damn good person to bounce ideas off of. Maybe it was the female perspective. Maybe it was simply because she was really smart. In any case, with both the personal and professional in mind, he decided to head down to where the crime scene evidence techs were located in the Palm Beach Police building.

And there—looking like a million bucks—she was. The first thing you noticed was her dark complexion, then the pronounced cheekbones, which made her cheeks look sunken, then her dazzling green eyes.

She looked up from her computer and smiled. "Well, hello, Charlie."

"Well, hello, Dominica. What's new in your world?"

"Not much. Where you at on Taylor?"

"That's part of the reason I came to see you."

"And the other part?"

"Just to be in your orbit."

"That's very sweet, Charlie."

"That's what they call me, Sweet Charlie."

"Or sometimes, Inscrutable Charlie."

"Only you call me that," Crawford said. "So I want to tell you about my suspects, then I want you to tell me who you think did it."

She swung her chair around to face him. "Okay, I love games like this."

Crawford told her about Art Nunan, Johnny Cotton, Stark Stabler, and Lowell Grey and everything he had on each one of them.

"That guy Grey hit on me once," Dominica said matter-of-factly when Crawford mentioned him last. "I was at Green's for lunch with Cato, and he just came right up to us." She lowered her voice into the tone of an oblivious male. "'Hello, ladies, my name's Lowell Grey and I'd love to join you.'"

"He's not shy, I'll give him that," Crawford said.

"No, but he's pretty damn boring and—oh, Jesus—so full of himself."

Crawford nodded his assent. "Okay, so that's my subject lineup. Whodunit?"

"Well, so you got two rich guys and two career criminals, and from what you said, none of 'em have much for alibis."

"Correction. They think they have good alibis. However, Ott and I think they suck."

"I agree. Well, so out of all of them, I'd say Stabler has the best motive."

"To kill Mimi Taylor so she doesn't tell his wife, you mean?"

Dominica nodded. "First of all, he's got a lot to lose if his wife dumps him. Plus, if he kills Mimi, he doesn't have to give her the hundred thou."

Crawford nodded.

"But, and it's a big but, we don't know what motives the others might have. Like maybe Mimi Taylor walked into the house when that guy Johnny Cotton was burglarizing it on his lunch break. Or maybe Mimi was going to reveal something about Grey. Or maybe, I don't know, maybe she got into a poker game with Art Nunan down at the dog track...lost money and wouldn't pay him."

Crawford laughed. "Okay, the first two were pretty good. That last one's lame."

"Yeah, I know, but point is, you don't know what motives the other three might have had."

"Or," Crawford said, shifting from one foot to the other, "maybe they didn't have any motive it all."

"You mean—"

"I mean, just a random killer or a serial killer. Just killed to kill."

Dominica shrugged. "There's always that, I guess."

"Okay, so I'll ask you again, who's my guy?"

"I don't know, they all look pretty good."

"That's not the answer I was looking for."

"A little lesson in life, Charlie," Dominica said with an expression rife with the mysteries of the universe. "You don't always get the answer you're looking for."

Crawford cocked his head. "What's that supposed to mean?"

A shrug. "I don't know. Whatever you want it to." She paused for a moment. "I will say this, I think it's a hell of a lot more unlikely that career criminals like Cotton and Nunan would have a clue who Mogigliano—as Mort calls him—is than Stabler or Grey."

"Except Stabler claimed he never heard of him," Crawford said, pausing a moment. "Okay, so even though you fell short of solving my homicide, you still get a nice dinner. How about Willie's?"

"I love Willie's. When?"

"Tonight."

Dominica laughed. "Sweet Charlie...Inscrutable Charlie...add to that, Last-Minute Charlie."

Crawford walked into his office as his cell phone rang.

It was Lowell Grey.

"Hey, Charlie. It's Lowell." Like there was only one Lowell in the universe. "I wanted to take you up on your offer to get that key to Mimi's condo and pick up my paddleboard."

"Sure. When did you want to go down there?"

"Is now okay?"

He was glad he'd gotten Mel in there first thing in the morning.

"Ah, sure. Come on by. I'm at the station now."

"Be there in five."

Crawford looked at his watch. It was 11:50. He walked out to the reception area and waited for Grey. He planned to go get a sandwich after he gave Grey the key, then monitor Grey's activities in the condo via his iPad. Mel—tech wiz that he was—had hooked up the cameras at Mimi Taylor's apartment in such a way that the live footage would be transmitted straight to Crawford's iPad.

A few minutes later, Lowell Grey walked into the station wearing Bermuda shorts, tasseled loafers with no socks, and a moss green sports shirt with the logo of the Poinciana Club on it.

"Thanks," he said, taking the key. "I'll be back in forty-five minutes."

"No rush," Crawford said. "If I'm not here when you get back, just leave it at the desk."

Grey walked out, and Crawford went around to the back of the building and got into his car. He'd decided that he'd follow Grey down to the south end of Palm Beach and monitor what Grey did in Mimi Taylor's condo from her old parking lot.

It took him just under fifteen minutes to get there. He parked between a van and a Mini and clicked on his computer just in time to catch Grey walk in the front door to Mimi Taylor's condo. Grey went straight to the balcony and approached his paddleboard, then turned and went back inside empty-handed.

He beelined straight for the kitchen, then to the refrigerator and opened the door. Grabbing a Heineken like Ott, maybe? Crawford watched as Grey reached into either the crisper drawer or the chill drawer. He lifted up something with his left hand—it looked like a flat box of breakfast sausages, Crawford thought—then, with his other hand, picked up something that had been underneath the box. As Grey tucked it under his arm, Crawford couldn't make out what it was, except it was flat and rectangular. Then Grey went back out to the porch, grabbed the paddleboard with his other hand, hefted it so it was parallel to the floor, and headed toward the door.

Crawford opened the front door of the Crown Vic, got out, and walked toward Mimi Taylor's building. Instead of going inside to the lobby, he waited outside.

A few minutes passed, then Lowell Grey walked out, paddleboard in one hand, the mysterious bundle tucked up under his left armpit. He spotted Crawford, and his smile slid off his face.

"Charlie," he said. "Wh-what are you doing here?"

"I just have one question for you."

Grey turned to his side to hide the bundle from Crawford's view.

Crawford pointed. "The question is, what's that?"

Grey was frozen.

"What do you have there?" Crawford asked again. "That thing under your arm you're trying not to let me see."

"Oh, this," Grey said, pulling out the bundle. "Just a DVD I left there."

Crawford stepped into Grey's space. "That you kept in the refrigerator?"

Grey frowned. "How did you—"

"Cameras," Crawford said. "I got a warrant to have them installed, if you'd like to see it."

"No, that's okay." Grey didn't look happy.

"What's the DVD of?" Crawford asked. "This warrant says I can appropriate anything you took out of Ms. Taylor's condo."

"It's just a DVD."

"I can see that. But of what?"

Grey sighed long and painfully, and his tan seemed to fade one shade.

"What's on the DVD?" Crawford asked again.

"Just, ah, me and Mimi."

Crawford knew it was not Grey and Mimi Taylor taking a moonlit walk on the beach. Or playing tennis. He put out his hand. "I'm going to need to appropriate that from you as it may be relevant to my investigation of Ms. Taylor's murder."

Grey suddenly looked like a little boy who was about to have a good cry. "Why are you doing this to me? I didn't kill Mimi. I told you, I was at my pool when it happened. Plus, you can ask anyone, I'd never hurt a fly."

Crawford raised his hand. "I need to take it from you."

A lone bead of sweat went racing down Grey's face and dropped to the pavement.

"Hand it over," Crawford said, more forcefully. "I'll return it to you if I determine it's not something we consider relevant."

"You won't, trust me."

"Mr. Grey."

"You promise you won't let anyone else see it?"

"Just me and my partner."

Grey finally handed it to him. "Please get it back to me as soon as possible."

Crawford wasn't going to make any promises. "Thank you, I'll be in touch."

Crawford turned and walked away. He got to his car and looked back.

Grey hadn't moved.

It must be one hell of a DVD, thought Crawford.

"Wow, I can see why he didn't want anybody to see it," Ott said, after watching the first minute of the DVD.

They were in Crawford's office.

Crawford recognized that it had been filmed in Mimi Taylor's living room. The film opened up on a shot of Mimi wearing a black leather bikini bottom, nipple clamps, a Zorro-like mask, and looking very self-conscious. It seemed as if a camera had been placed in a stationary position. On one of the bookshelves, Crawford guessed.

"These things really hurt," Mimi said to the camera.

"You get used to them," an off-camera Lowell Grey assured her.

"I don't think so," Mimi responded, as a black-leather-clad Grey strode into the picture.

Crawford and Ott couldn't help laughing. Over both his shoulders were leather straps that went all the way down to his groin area where they connected with a leather jockstrap that had two black leather bands that went around his hips. Around his neck was a dog collar with sharp studs and in his right hand a whip with four short strands of leather.

"He's not really going to use that thing, is he?" Ott said.

"Jesus, spare us," Crawford said.

And at that Grey took a few steps toward Mimi and snapped the short whip.

"Ow!" Mimi cried. "How in God's name is this supposed to be fun?"

"I didn't say fun," Grey said. "It's just supposed to enhance the sexual experience."

"Where'd he get that shit from?" Ott asked.

"I don't know why we can't just do it the regular way," Mimi protested.

"Because it was getting to be the same old, same old," Grey said and snapped his short whip a little harder this time.

"Ow, goddammit! That really hurt!" Mimi took a step back. "Why don't I do it to you if you think it's so much fun?"

"Because I'm the slave master," Grey said.

Mimi put her hands on her naked hip. "Oh, Jesus, Lowell, *really*?"

"And I want you down on your knees," Grey said and cracked the whip again.

"All right, enough," Mimi said. "I've had it with your silly game. I'm going to go change. I'm not a goddamn dog or your slave or whatever it is you want me to be."

Mimi Taylor walked out of the picture and presumably to her bedroom.

Lowell Grey sighed as Crawford had seen him do earlier and muttered under his breath, "Just when it was getting good."

Ott turned to Crawford. "You ever get into any shit like that, Charlie?"

"Not for a couple years," Crawford deadpanned.

Ott's eyes lit up. "Really, you did?"

Crawford smiled and shook his head.

Ott looked disappointed. "I'll admit it," he said, "sex with the same woman can get a little old after a while, but I don't get trying to spice it up with shit like that."

Crawford leaned back in his chair and put his hands behind his head. "Maybe you should look at it from the woman's point of view," he said. "It goes both ways, bro."

SEVENTEEN

WILLIE'S WAS A BURGER JOINT BUT ACCORDING TO MANY, THE best burger joint in southern Florida. It was located just off of Clematis in a little hole-in-a-wall, one-story building, which was half Willie's and half Nat's Tats.

Crawford had a half-finished beer mug in front of him, and Dominica had a glass of rosé.

"I never knew you were so trendy," Crawford said.

"What do you mean?"

He pointed at her wine. "You used to drink pinot grigio, then you jumped ship. Everyone says rosé is what the 'trendies' drink these days."

"Catch up, Charlie, it's been around for years."

Crawford shrugged. "Shows you what I know," he said then lowered his voice. "So, I want to ask you about something."

"Okay. Ask away?"

"How would you feel about a little B and D?"

Dominica frowned. "What?"

"Bondage and discipline."

"Yeah, I know what it stands for, but are you serious?"

Crawford kept a straight face. "Yeah, I went to see that new *Fifty Shades of Grey* movie—"

"Get out of here? You saw that?"

"Yeah, *Fifty Shades Freed.* Those two actors in it get pretty...creative."

Dominica shook her head as the burgers showed up. "I just can't see you going to that. Bet you were the only guy in the theater."

"There were a couple of others."

"Yeah, I'll bet. Wearing raincoats."

Crawford laughed as Dominica took a bite. "So, you're avoiding my question."

"Which is what?" Dominica asked.

"Well, I went to this site called Candyman," Crawford said, holding up his hand for the waiter. "And it had these leather outfits that were pretty racy. There was one police costume that was unlike anything I've ever seen the boys down at the station wear. A pair of handcuffs hangin' off—" He couldn't keep a straight face anymore and burst out laughing.

Dominica slapped his arm and started laughing too. "You jerk, I couldn't tell whether you were serious or not. What made you launch into that whole thing?"

"I don't know. Just thought I'd mess with you a little."

"You didn't really see that movie, did you?"

He shook his head.

"You're bad," Dominica said with a smile as the waiter came up to them.

"A couple more, please," Crawford said, gesturing to their drinks.

DOMINICA'S APARTMENT WAS CLOSER TO WILLIE'S, SO THAT'S where they had ended up.

Crawford kissed Dominica as he rolled off her onto the other side of the bed. He was more than a little out of breath, and his naked body glistened with sweat.

"Sometimes I worry about having a heart attack with you," he said.

She shushed him with a finger on his lips.

He spoke through the finger. "You don't suppose that would've been more fun with a little spanking or something?"

Dominica brought her other arm around Crawford's shoulder, leaned over, and kissed him. "Couldn't have been better with anything."

EIGHTEEN

Crawford drove the twenty blocks to his apartment building, took a shower, dressed, and walked the few blocks to Dunkin' Donuts. His favorite server, Jeanelle, had moved on to greater challenges—Costco, he was told—so he placed his usual order with a young Hispanic-looking man who had an alert, ready smile.

"Two blueberry donuts with a medium extra-dark," Crawford said and added, "just one shot of milk." He hadn't needed to add the "one shot" with Jeanelle, as she had his coffee down to a science. Crawford was pretty particular about his coffee. He wanted just enough milk to change the color from black to dark brown.

Crawford picked up his order, then stuffed two bucks in the tip jar and headed to his table over in the corner. Problem was, a couple with two kids were sitting at it. He mentally shrugged—how were they to know it was his table?—and sat at the one next to it. Just as he did, his cell phone rang. It was the number of the police station.

"Crawford," he said.

"Charlie," said the dispatcher. "Got a bad one at Dunbar. Number 1-7-1."

"Thanks. I'm on my way." He put the lid on his coffee and the remaining donut back in the bag and headed for the door.

NUMBER 171 DUNBAR WAS A WELL-PROPORTIONED, TWO-STORY, white Spanish stucco house that had five blue-and-whites parked haphazardly on the street along with four unmarked cars, one of which Crawford recognized as Ott's Buick Regal. On the lawn was a small, discreet for sale sign. A uniform was stringing crime scene tape along the front of the house while curious neighbors huddled in little packs on the street and sidewalks to either side.

Crawford got out of his car, nodded to the uniform, and went into the house. He saw the body right away. There was a wide stairway straight ahead through the large entrance foyer. At the bottom of the stairway lay a naked woman. Ott was off to the right of the body, taking a picture with his iPhone, his leather notebook tucked under his arm.

Crawford approached Ott, who lowered the phone and turned to him. "Hey, man," Ott said. "You ever take any French back in high school?"

Crawford looked down at the body and saw four words hand-lettered on her stomach that seemed to have been written with a red marker. *Nu descendent un escalier*, it said. He got closer and realized the message had been scrawled in lipstick.

Crawford pointed to the stairs. "Means 'nude descending a stairway.' There's a famous painting by that name."

Ott shook his head. "I'm guessing the way this woman descended was more like being thrown down the stairs."

"She pretty busted up?"

Ott nodded. "Yeah, a broken arm, ribs, you name it."

Crawford shook his head in sympathy. "So, we got the art angle again," he said. "*Reclining Nude*, now this."

Ott nodded. "And a real estate agent vic at a house that's a listing of hers."

Crawford nodded.

"Just like Mimi Taylor," Ott said. "Her name's Mattie Priest, works at Linda A. Gary Real Estate. She was found by a cleaning lady at just past ten thirty."

Crawford nodded and flicked his head in the direction of Medical Examiner Bob Hawes, who was hunched down over the body. "You talk to him yet?" Crawford asked.

"Yeah, 'carotid thrombosis' in his lingo; 'strangulation' in ours."

"So, what do you think?" Crawford asked.

"Best guess is it happened upstairs, then she either fell or was thrown down the stairs. Pretty sure thrown."

There were four people clustered around Mattie Priest's body: Hawes and three crime scene techs. Crawford decided to question them later, once they'd had time to gather more evidence.

"You been upstairs?" Crawford asked.

"Nah, just got here five minutes ago. I was about to go up."

"Let's check it out."

Ott nodded and they stepped around Hawes and the techs and went up the stairs, keeping an eye out for clues along the way. Putting on vinyl gloves, they first went into a bedroom that appeared to be the master. It had his-and-her bathrooms and his-and-her walk-in closets. Nothing was in the closets or bathrooms. Everything was scrupulously clean and orderly and nothing caught Crawford's or Ott's eye. To be sure not to miss anything, Crawford crouched down and looked under the king-size bed.

Nothing.

Then they went into another bedroom. It was about half the size of the master and featured only one bath but an extra-large closet. Crawford walked over to the bed and pointed at the bedspread. It was rumpled and had a depression in it.

Ott nodded. "Someone either sat on it or lay down."

Crawford nodded, walked around the bed and saw women's

clothes scattered on the carpet—a black silk skirt and a white collared shirt. On top of them were white panties and a white bra. Crawford crouched down and saw shoes just under the bed.

Ott followed him and pulled out his iPhone. He took several shots from above, looking down, then several more from a lower angle.

"If she was stripping, probably would have put her clothes on that," Crawford said, pointing to a beige-colored chaise just a few feet away.

Ott nodded. "So, I'm guessing someone told her to strip, and she just dropped her clothes."

"But no obvious signs of consensual sex or rape," Crawford said. "The bed would be more messed up."

Ott nodded. "Yeah, I agree." He took a few shots of the bed. "Unless it was a stand-up."

Crawford put his hand on his chin. "Looks like a guy was either with her or surprised her here. Told her to take her clothes off, strangled her, then threw her down the stairs. Seems like a pretty strange MO to me."

"I hear you, but I wouldn't rule out rape so fast," Ott said. "Just 'cause that wasn't the case with Taylor."

"What do you think about a copycat?" Crawford asked.

"I was thinking about that," Ott said. "Thing is, we did a pretty good job keeping a lid on the Taylor scene. The *Reclining Nude* art thing never got into the papers or TV news, as far as I know."

"Yeah, well, Red Noland knew about it. You know how it is... details like that never get totally suppressed. Somebody's always telling somebody."

Ott nodded. "But in my experience, copycats are more *Law & Order* than real life. When was the last time you saw one?"

"Good question. Back when I first started out, actually. Sixteen years ago, to be exact. Turned out, it wasn't really a copycat after all. Just looked like one."

"I rest my case."

They went through the rest of the upstairs but didn't find anything. Just a spotless house that probably had a cleaning person come every day.

"Let's go to her office," Crawford said. "See if we can find out what her schedule was this morning."

They walked down the grand stairway, and Crawford caught Bob Hawes's eye.

"You gonna be here a while?" Crawford asked.

"Couple of hours anyway," Hawes said.

"We'll be back."

Hawes nodded.

Crawford turned to Sheila Stallings, one of the CSEUs. "Her clothes are upstairs in the bedroom with blue wallpaper. We're guessing that's where she was strangled."

"Thanks," Stallings said.

The office for Linda A. Gary Real Estate was located at 201 Worth Avenue, just a short distance from where the Lowell Grey Gallery was soon to open.

Crawford asked to speak to Linda Gary, but she was out showing a house, so he asked if there was an office manager on duty. There was. A woman by the name of Nancy Anselmo.

She had a glass-walled office that looked out over the agents' cubicles. A woman who appeared to be in her mid-forties, Anselmo had short blonde hair and a businesslike air about her. She also looked apprehensive about being visited by two Palm Beach Police detectives.

Crawford and Ott remained standing in her office. "Let me get right to the point," said Crawford. "I'm sorry to tell you, but your agent Mattie Priest was killed a few hours ago at 217 Dunbar Road."

Her face blanched and she instinctively covered her mouth. "Oh my God," she said. "Oh my God," she said again.

"My partner and I both express our condolences," Crawford said. "As I'm sure you can appreciate, we need to move as quick as possible to find the killer and have a few questions."

"Of course, I understand," Nancy said. "I just...I'm so shocked. And, oh God, less than a week after what happened to Mimi Taylor."

Crawford and Ott nodded. "Our first question is, is it possible to find out if Ms. Priest was showing the house on Dunbar this morning? And if so, to whom?"

"We're a pretty small shop, so I know how most of the agents handle their schedules," Anselmo said. "I'm pretty sure Mattie had her showing schedule on her computer."

"Would it be possible to take a look at her computer?" Ott asked.

"Sure," Anselmo said, "if it's on. But I don't have her password or anything."

"Understand," Crawford said. "Do you know whether Ms. Priest had a family?"

"She was married." She exhaled. "Oh, poor Ted—but she didn't have kids."

"Does her husband work, do you know?"

"Yes, he's an attorney at Moulton Cohen," Anselmo said.

As Crawford continued to ask questions, Ott looked up the number of the law firm she mentioned.

"So if you'd take us to Ms. Priest's desk..." Crawford gestured with a tilt of his head.

Anselmo nodded and led them out of her office, into the cubicle area.

They caught a break in that Mattie Priest's MacBook Air computer was not only on but on her calendar page.

Her first appointment of the day was at 9:00. It said simply *Ann and Troy Price*, no location. It also had a phone number next to it. Crawford recognized the area code as a Los Angeles one. Later in the day she had two more appointments: two o'clock at 230 Barton and four o'clock at 102 Caribbean.

Obviously, she would not be making either one of those.

NINETEEN

Before Crawford and Ott left the Linda A. Gary Real Estate office, they asked Nancy Anselmo whom Mattie Priest was closest to in the office. Anselmo gave them two names and explained that the woman who really knew her best was Sylvia McInerny, her partner.

"You mean they worked together as a team?" Ott asked.

"Exactly," Anselmo said. "They've been together as long as I can remember."

"Is she here now?" Crawford asked.

"Yes, right over there," Anselmo said, pointing to a woman who was on the phone and gesturing with one hand.

Crawford asked Anselmo to request that Sylvia McInerny come into the conference room since there were so many agents sitting within a close radius of her. He felt that her reaction might set off a chain of shock and emotional reactions.

After McInerny's initial jolting reaction about her partner's death, she collapsed into a chair and began to sob. She said over and over about how Mattie's husband was going to be "devastated," "crushed," and "destroyed." Nancy Anselmo helped calm her down, but it was clear Sylvia McInerny had lost a very dear friend.

"Ms. McInerny," Crawford, who remained standing, said, "could I ask what you know about Troy and Ann Price, the couple your partner was meeting at 217 Dunbar Road?"

"Well, I knew them pretty well since Mattie and I have been working with them for about a year."

"Why so long?" Crawford asked.

"That's not even that long," McInerny said. "Sometimes we work with buyers three or four years until they actually buy."

Nancy Anselmo nodded.

"I noticed they have a Los Angeles phone number," Crawford said.

McInerny nodded. "You don't recognize the name?"

Crawford glanced at Ott, who showed no reaction. Ott was a lot more knowledgeable about pop culture and celebrities than he.

"Who are they?" Crawford asked.

McInerny leaned forward and dropped her voice. "Troy Price was head of Alpha10 Studio. He quit after he was charged with harassment and sexual assault. It was a big story right after Harvey Weinstein."

Ott nodded. "I remember. The woman who accused him was the daughter of a famous actor, right?"

McInerny nodded.

Crawford glanced over at Ott, who was working his iPhone, Googling Troy Price, no doubt.

"On another subject, did Ms. Priest ever express any fears about anyone? Or mention anyone she might have had a run-in with before?"

McInerny's eyes shot to Anselmo's. "Mattie? Never. Everyone loved Mattie. I doubt she ever had a real enemy in her entire life."

Nancy Anselmo nodded. "Some people in this business create enemies. Mattie would have rather lost a deal than antagonize someone. She was also scrupulously honest, which I can't say about everyone in real estate."

"I have to ask this, though it may be uncomfortable," Crawford said. "Were you aware of any extramarital affairs or anything at all like that? Especially anything recent or within the last couple of years?"

"Mattie and I have been partners for fourteen years, and I can guarantee you she never strayed once," McInerny said. "And because she was pretty, there were plenty of men who made advances. But she never showed the slightest interest."

"Did she ever happen to mention that Troy Price might have... made advances?"

McInerny hesitated. "Well, as a matter of fact, she did," she said softly. "It was before the whole thing came out in the news about him. Mattie had had lunch with Troy and Ann—Ta-boo, I seem to remember—and they had a bottle or two of wine, then went and looked at houses. She told me Ann was in the kitchen and she and Troy had just walked into the master bedroom. Mattie told me he said to her, 'If I buy this place, will you join me here when Ann's on the golf course?'"

"Really?" Crawford said. "Was that the only time?"

McInerny sighed. "No, there were others. But Mattie just kept ignoring him or else laughed it off."

"Like, what else did he say?"

"One time he got pretty graphic."

"About what?"

McInerny's face flushed to a matador-cape red, then she glanced at Nancy Anselmo. "I'd rather not say."

Ott handed her a card. "How about this, just email what he said, would you?"

McInerny looked a little relieved. "Okay," she said, as she wrote some numbers on the back of her card. "Here's Troy's number."

"Thanks," Crawford said. "Ladies, I think that will do it for now.

Again, our deepest condolences for your loss. She sounds like she was a really nice woman."

"She was," McInerny said, and Anselmo nodded.

Crawford and Ott walked out of the conference room with the two women. Crawford could see by the looks of the other agents that they knew something was up.

Crawford walked out the front door onto the Worth Avenue sidewalk. "This guy Price sounds like a real sleazebag."

Ott waggled his eyebrows. "Let's go find out."

TWENTY

On the way back to the station, Crawford dialed Troy Price's number.

He got a recording. "This is Troy. I'm either on the golf course or shooting a picture and can't be bothered. Leave a message."

Another reason not to like the guy, Crawford thought. "Call me please, Mr. Price. This is Detective Crawford, Palm Beach Police." He left his phone number and turned to Ott. "Sounds like another all-star asshole."

"Why? What—"

"Just listen," Crawford hit redial and handed Ott his phone.

Ott listened, then started shaking his head. "Yup," he concurred.

It was Ott's turn to do the death notification. He and Crawford were headed in different directions and would be leaving the station in separate cars — Ott on his way to the law firm where Mattie Priest's husband worked and Crawford back up to the crime scene on Dunbar Road.

Ott walked up to the reception desk at the Moulton Cohen law firm, ID'd himself, and said he needed to see Ted Priest right away. The receptionist looked alarmed and said he was meeting with a client. Ott said it was critical that he see him as soon as possible.

The receptionist called Priest, spoke to him, then told Ott she'd lead him back to Priest's office.

Priest, a nice-looking man in a grey, pin-striped suit looked uneasy. It was a look Ott had seen too many times before. The look of someone who could only imagine the worst reasons why a detective had suddenly shown up out of nowhere in his life.

Ott asked Ted Priest to sit down, then seated himself and told him what had happened. *Oh my God* was the most frequent reaction when a loved one got the news, followed closely by something like *No, no, that can't be.* Ted Priest said both things in the same sentence. Ott told him how sorry he was for his loss a second time, then went quiet for a few moments. As Priest held his face in his hands, Ott decided to ask him a soft question. Whether his wife, or he, had any enemies or anyone who he thought might do harm to either of them. Priest's answer was even more emphatic than Nancy Anselmo's and Sylvia McInerny's. No, Mattie was incapable of getting anyone angry at her, let alone making enemies.

Ott gave Priest a card, asked for his number, and said either he or his partner would be in touch. He didn't want to burden the poor man with a million questions now. It was time for him to be allowed to start grieving. Police questions could wait a day or two.

But Priest had his own questions. He asked Ott if he thought it was the same killer as the one who murdered the real estate agent last week. Ott said it was too early to tell but that it was probably a good chance it was the same person.

Ted Priest looked out his window for a few moments and didn't say anything. Finally, he volunteered that he had a premonition that morning that something bad was going to happen. He cut himself shaving, he said, then he bumped his coffee mug with his elbow while he was reading the newspaper and it shattered on the floor. He hadn't had a day start out like that in a long time.

Ott knew it was time to go.

Crawford took the short drive over to Dunbar Road and again noticed the discreet sign. Linda A. Gary Real Estate. Below it was the name, Mattie Priest, then her number.

Crawford flashed to Rose Clarke and felt a rare spike of fear chill his spine. He needed to warn her after this visit, tell her she should not only be very careful about being alone in houses but also carry a can of pepper spray at all times. Maybe even get a pistol. But then he remembered her going off on an anti-gun diatribe and lighting into the NRA after the mass school shooting in Parkland, just down the road.

He walked into the house and saw that nothing much had changed except Bob Hawes had stripped down to a white T-shirt that was sweat-stained and gamey-looking. Mattie Priest also had a sheet that covered everything but her face.

"You get him yet?" Hawes asked Crawford.

Crawford shook his head. "Was it rape this time?"

Hawes shook his head back at him. "Which leads me to believe the same guy did both."

"Yeah, well, there's the art thing too," Crawford said.

"The art thing, the no-rape thing, the real estate-agent thing," Hawes said. "Hey, by the way, Charlie, I'm impressed you *parlez-vous* the *français*."

Crawford ignored the comment and glanced over at Sheila Stallings. "Anything upstairs? You get anything from her clothes?"

"Nope," Stallings said. "But the lipstick in her purse matches the writing on her body."

Crawford nodded. "Figures. You'll let me know if you find something else?"

Stallings nodded.

Crawford was eager to talk to Troy Price. As well as reinterview numbers two, three, four, and five on his suspect list: Stark Stabler, Lowell Grey, Johnny Cotton, and Art Nunan. The question was, would they have better alibis than the last time?

He called Mattie Priest's partner, Sylvia McInerny, who answered on the first ring.

"Hi, Ms. McInerny, it's Detective Crawford again. I was wondering if you knew where Mr. and Mrs. Price stay when they're here in Palm Beach?"

"The Chesterfield," McInerny said. "They always get a suite. He always says it's got this 'old Hollywood retro' feel to it. I never really understood what he meant by that. Or how he even knows anything about *old Hollywood*. I mean, he's like, forty."

The Chesterfield was all the answer Crawford needed.

He thanked her and headed to the hotel at 363 Cocoanut Row.

The man at the desk told him that Mr. and Mrs. Price had just taken their dog for a walk down by the marina. Probably wouldn't be long, he added.

Crawford sat on a brown leather couch in the reception area and picked up a *Town & Country* magazine. He started leafing through it and stopped at an article featuring the town of Lake Forest, Illinois. Somewhere back in his previous life he remembered that Lake Forest was to Chicago what Greenwich, Connecticut, was to New York City. An expensive suburb where successful financiers, $1,000-an-hour lawyers, and captains of industry lived. Then he saw the name Roger Fentress in the caption of one photo. The shot was of a preppy-looking man in his mid- to late thirties, brown hair with a little grey on the side, horn-rimmed glasses, and a tweed jacket. Next to him—and in front of a classic white-brick colonial—stood a tall, slender woman with dirty-blonde hair and high cheekbones. To her right were two boys, early teens and both chips off the old block.

The woman—Diana Jennings was her name twenty years back—had been Crawford's first love in college. Diana was from a small town in Colorado and was a competitive skier who'd been .034 seconds from making the Olympics. They were freshmen together, class of 2001, and had dated from halfway through their freshman year until the end of sophomore year. Then, in the fall of 1999, Crawford, twenty at the time, had taken a year abroad in Florence, Italy, and had met and fallen madly in love with a twenty-six-year-old Italian newspaper reporter he met in a bar. To his credit, Crawford had written Diana and told her what had happened. Diana, apparently confident it was a romance that would run out of steam, waited months expecting to hear that it was a flash-in-the-pan romance.

But four months later, Crawford was still going strong with Ginevra, so Diana finally accepted an invitation to go to a fraternity party with Crawford's former roommate Roger Fentress.

The *Town & Country* article described Roger Fentress as a "wunderkind fund manager" not to mention a "scratch golfer" and a man with "reputedly the largest wine collection in Illinois." When he and Crawford were roommates, the only wine they'd known about was Charles Shaw Napa, also known as Two-Buck Chuck.

"Yo," said the voice to Crawford's side, "you the detective?"

Crawford had been a thousand miles away. He snapped out of his reverie. "Are you Mr. Price?"

The man was short, had a shaved head, watery blue eyes and a considerable paunch. Crawford was thinking small-town CPA, not perfidious studio head.

"Yeah, Troy Price," he said. "The man over there said you're looking for me."

Crawford saw an attractive woman in a short skirt and blue polo shirt with a popped collar behind Price.

Crawford got to his feet. "I'm a homicide detective with the Palm Beach Police Department." His instinct was to shake Price's hand, but he didn't feel like it.

"This is my wife, Ann," Price said. She merely nodded suspiciously. "What's this about?"

Crawford put his hand on his chin. "I understand you both had an appointment with Mattie Priest this morning. Was it to see a house at 217 Dunbar?"

"Yeah, but only I went," Price said.

He had Crawford's full attention now. "Why was that?"

Ann Price took a step forward. "I felt sort of crappy," she said. "We figured if Troy liked it, we'd go back together."

Crawford nodded and turned to Price. "Mattie Priest was murdered this morning. Her body was found at the house on Dunbar Road."

"Jesus, you're kidding," Price said as his wife covered her mouth with both hands and her eyes widened.

"That is so horrible," Ann Price said. "Oh my God."

Crawford nodded again. "How long were you at the house, Mr. Price?"

"Um, not long," Price said. "I knew right away it wasn't for us. We want the master on the ground floor. Tell you the truth, I was kind of pissed at Mattie."

"Why?"

"Because we had made it really clear where we wanted the master." He shook his head and glanced down. "I'm just so shocked... the poor woman."

Though the man's priorities were clearly out of whack, his reaction to Mattie's death struck Crawford as genuine. "When you say, 'not long,' how long? Ten, fifteen minutes?"

"Yes, that's about right."

"Then where did you go?"

"Back here." Price shrugged and smiled. "I had a sick wife to attend to."

"So, you were back here by nine thirty?"

"At the latest." Price's expression changed. "Wait a minute, you're not—"

"Just routine questions, Mr. Price," Crawford said. "Did you notice anything unusual when you went through the house?"

"Like what?"

"Oh, I don't know, the house was pretty immaculate, maybe something that was out of place?"

"I don't know exactly what that means, but no."

Crawford ran his hand through his hair. "What about...did you see anyone on the property when you were there? A pool man, a gardener, anyone at all?"

"You know what," Price said. "I did see a guy there. Out of a side window. Looked like a workman, and I didn't think anything of it."

"Can you describe him?"

"Dressed in dark clothes. Brownish hair, maybe around forty to forty-five. My age."

"Did you see him doing anything? Some kind of work, I mean?"

"No, he just walked by a side window," Price said. "I saw him for, literally, three seconds."

Crawford made a mental note to call Mattie Priest's partner, Sylvia.

"Okay, I appreciate you taking the time to answer my questions." He handed Price a card. "If you think of anything else that might be helpful, please give a call."

Price took out his wallet and put Crawford's card in it. Then he took out some money. They looked to be hundred-dollar bills.

"Detective," Price said, taking a step closer to Crawford and dropping his voice, "I really don't need to read in the paper that I was at that house. I have a few...issues at the moment." He handed Crawford five crisp hundred-dollar bills.

Crawford held up his hand. "Mr. Price, I don't take money... except from my ATM machine." He gave him a curt nod and walked out of the Chesterfield.

TWENTY-ONE

BACK IN HIS CAR ON COCOANUT ROW, CRAWFORD DIALED Mattie Priest's partner.

"Hi, Ms. McInerny, it's Detective Crawford again. I just have a quick question. Did you or Ms. Priest happen to have a man come wash the windows at the Dunbar house yesterday morning?"

She didn't hesitate. "No, neither of us did."

So much for Crawford's Diego Andujar theory. "Okay, thanks, that's all I wanted to know." Then he had a thought. "Would you email me a list of all the people that worked at the Dunbar house. Pool men, landscapers, cleaning people, a caretaker, if there is one."

"Sure," McInerny said. "Your email is on your card?"

"Yes. Thank you." He clicked off.

He drove back to the station and went to Ott's cubicle.

Ott, on his computer, looked up when he heard the familiar footsteps. "S'up, bro?"

"How'd it go with Priest's husband?"

"Oh, you know, the usual."

"He have any idea who could have done it?"

"Nah, not a clue," Ott said. "I kept the questions to a minimum. Figured I'd circle back tomorrow or Tuesday."

Crawford nodded. "Let's go back to the board, figure out where to go next." He was referring to the dry-erase board opposite his desk in his office.

They walked back there together and assumed their positions: Ott with the orange marker in hand since Crawford's handwriting was close to illegible and Crawford in his chair looking on.

On the board, it said Art Nunan, Johnny Cotton, Stark Stabler, and Lowell Grey under the word *Suspects*.

"Add Troy Price," Crawford said.

"You met up with him?"

Crawford nodded. "Yup."

"And is he an all-world—"

"He tried to bribe me to keep his name out of the paper."

"So that would be affirmative."

Crawford nodded again. "He was all right, up to that point."

"How much?"

"Five hundred."

"That would have been enough for me."

Crawford laughed. "So, who do you want to talk to? To check alibis for Priest?"

"I'm sick of Lowell Grey. How 'bout I do Stabler and Johnny Rotten."

Crawford laughed again. "All right. I'll do the other two."

"How 'bout Troy Price's timeline?" Ott asked, orange marker at the ready.

"Well, first off, he went there without his wife."

Ott got a hungry look in his eyes.

"She said she wasn't feeling well, and he says he was only there for ten minutes. So, to answer your question, Price was at 217 Dunbar from nine to nine ten or so, then back to the Chesterfield, where they're staying, by nine thirty. He also said he saw a guy there. Through a window. Dressed in dark clothes, brown hair, around forty. Said he looked like a workman. My first thought was Diego Andujar, but I checked and they hadn't hired him—or anyone—to do the windows. My second thought was Cotton, but his hair's not exactly dark. I'm thinking of getting Price to describe the guy he saw to the sketch artist."

"Good idea," Ott said. "Any chance he might have just dreamed him up on the spot?"

"Maybe."

"What's your gut on the guy?"

Crawford shrugged. "My gut's been a little off lately. But offhand I'd say it's a long way from sexually harassing women to strangling them and throwing them down a staircase. By the way, Hawes said no rape again."

"He's a hundred percent on that?"

"Yup."

Ott started nodding slowly. "In my experience, Hawes's hundred percent is another guy's seventy-five percent."

"He can't screw up a rape kit."

"You'd be surprised," Ott said.

"So, based on what Mattie Priest's friend, Sylvia McInerny, told me about Troy Price propositioning Priest when his wife was in the next room, I'm wondering if that's what he had in mind when he went to the house this morning."

Ott perked up. "You didn't tell me that."

"Just found out a little while ago," Crawford said. "Mattie was showing Price the master bedroom of some house when his wife was down in the kitchen, and Price lowers his voice and says something like, 'Maybe you and me spend a little time here when Ann's out on the golf course.'"

"What a schmuck," Ott said. "He really said that?"

"Yeah, you believe it?" Crawford said. "I think these Hollywood clowns think they can do whatever the hell they want. Hopefully, the Me Too Movement'll change it."

"Hopefully," Ott said. "But in the meantime, we got this Price jackass. So, play it out. You're thinking he might have propositioned her, she said no, he got rough, ripped off her clothes?"

"Thing is, that all takes time," Crawford said. "If, in fact, he got back to the Chesterfield at nine thirty, I don't see how he would have time to, one, take her clothes off, or get her to strip; two, strangle her; three, throw her down the stairs; and four, stage her body and write those words in French."

Ott shrugged. "I don't know...as you went through the list, I could see it taking no more than ten, fifteen, minutes. I don't think it's a time issue."

Crawford was silent for a moment. "Maybe you're right," he said.

"So, what do we do about him?"

"I saw a security camera at the Chesterfield," Crawford said. "I'm going to go there and see if it shows exactly what time Price came back."

"Good idea," Ott said, holding up a list. "Going back to Noland's suspect list, I think we've been through everyone on it."

"Yeah, and everyone but Nunan and Cotton are in the clear."

Ott nodded, then looked back at the board, capping and uncapping his marker. "You didn't have any others who were possibles, did you?"

"Nope. Not a one," Crawford said. "So, first things first, let's go find the four before they have a lotta time to work on their stories, then meet back here and go over what we've come up with."

Ott nodded. "I'm hoping it's Price."

"Why?"

"'Cause I hate ugly little guys who abuse women."

"Just ugly little guys?"

Ott shook his head. "All guys who do."

Right after Ott walked out, Crawford dialed his phone. He called Red Noland and asked him if he could borrow his sketch artist. The Palm Beach Police Department was too small to have one on its payroll, so West Palm had generously provided the services of their guy, Ronnie Waite, several times in the past. Crawford's problem with sketch artists' renderings were that unless someone had really distinctive facial characteristics—like a tattoo or a wine-colored birthmark—then the sketches all tended to look generic. But, still, it was worth a shot.

Red Noland said it would be fine if Crawford borrowed Waite, so Crawford called Waite directly and left a message asking him to call him back.

Crawford's second call was to Troy Price. He got his cheesy recording again. "Mr. Price, it's Detective Crawford. Expect a call from a man name Ronnie Waite. He does police sketches, and I'd like to have you describe the man you saw on the Dunbar Road property to him. Thank you."

Crawford's third call was to Rose Clarke.

"Hello, Charlie," Rose said.

"Hey, Rose," Crawford said. "I'm sure you heard about Mattie Priest."

Rose exhaled. "I sure have. What's going on, Charlie? It's getting really scary around here, you know?"

"I know. I just want you to be very careful. If you have to go show a house, go with another agent. And make sure none of the buyers you take around are sketchy." He was remembering the trailer-park couple she had told him about.

"I don't really want to show at all," Rose said. "I mean, that was so brutal what happened to Mattie."

"What did you hear happened?" Crawford asked.

"That someone hanged her then threw her down the stairs."

Exaggerations could be expected, Crawford knew. It was Palm Beach, hyperbole capital of the western hemisphere.

"Just for the record, that's only half true. She didn't get hanged, but she was strangled."

"Still, who wants to go into a house when some psycho might be hiding in a closet. Know what I mean?"

"Yeah, I do. Have you heard anything at all that might be helpful?"

"What haven't I heard is more like it. It just happened, and the rumor mill is churning."

"Where are you now?"

"Home," Rose said.

"Can I come over? You can tell me about what you've heard."

"Sure. Join me for cocktail hour."

Rose lived in a house that could comfortably fit a family of six. Six bedrooms, seven baths, a half-million-dollar infinity-edge pool and a commodious pool house, where Crawford had let himself be seduced by Rose before, and one of the most spectacular views of the ocean in Palm Beach.

She welcomed him at the door with a kiss and a Sierra Nevada Torpedo, his beer of choice.

The kiss he received happily, but he held up his hand to the beer. "You trying to get me drunk or something?" he said, smiling. "Some other time."

"Oh, sorry, I forgot, Charlie the Boy Scout is on the job." Rose raised a drink that looked like a Bloody Mary. "Me, I'm done for the day."

She walked toward her living room, and Crawford followed her.

He smelled her perfume and watched her walk—more like her undulating sway—which was as sexy as always. Her back and bare shoulders were hard and muscular, not an ounce of fat anywhere. She walked into the living room, sat down on one side of a snow-white couch and patted the seat next to her.

It was a temptation he didn't need to wrestle with at the moment. "I'm just going to sit here," he said, indicating the love seat opposite her.

"Aww," Rose said, pouting her lips the way only she did.

"So tell me about what you've heard."

"You know how it works. If it's just a whisper, it gets blown up to a full-scale scandal. If an unmarried couple are dancing a little too close, they're dry-humping on the dance floor."

"Dry-humping?"

"You know." She laughed. "Well, maybe you don't." She tittered. "Anyway, the first suspect is Boysie Johnson."

"That's a name?"

"Yeah, I don't know what his real name is, but he's the heir to some fortune. I forget which. So, in his entire life Boysie has never had a job. Except riding around on his rusty old Schwinn bike picking up cans."

"Wait. What?"

Rose shrugged. "He spends his whole day riding around picking up cans, then I guess he takes them somewhere and gets, whatever-it-is, a nickel for every can. On a good day, he maybe makes six or seven bucks, then he goes home to his parents' twenty-million-dollar-house on the Intracoastal."

"I think I've seen this guy," Crawford said. "Always wears like a blue T-shirt, dark hair, around my age or a little older."

"You're a young thirty-eight, Charlie. He's an old thirty."

"But still lives with his parents?"

"Uh-huh, and what I heard was he couldn't find enough cans in Palm Beach 'cause—well, you know—'cause the streets are so free of human refuse that he ended up going over to the greener pastures of down-market West Palm."

"Where the refuse is plentiful."

"You would know..." She winked and sipped her drink.

The man was a match to Troy Price's description of the man he had seen. "What are his parents' names?"

"Boyd and Naomi Johnson. Address is 1191 North Lake Way."

"What else do you know about Boysie?"

Rose leaned back in the couch. "I remember hearing something about him burning down a dormitory at his boarding school up in Connecticut."

"Really?"

"That was a long time ago," Rose said. "But I think he did a little time in a nuthouse for that."

"I think I'll have a talk with him."

"I would."

"Who else?"

Rose cracked a wide smile. "Well, this next one is probably a reach."

"I've had murderers be a reach before."

Rose took another sip of her Bloody Mary. "Okay, so the man's name is Rodney Bowman and, for lack of better words, he's a flasher. Or was, until he stopped getting invited anywhere."

Crawford shook his head and chuckled. "Is there any kind of deviant Palm Beach isn't represented by?"

Rose laughed. "That's a very good question, and I'd say the answer is no. Anyway, Rodney was a man everyone liked. Had a good sense of humor, kind of a practical joker, played a good game of bridge, I heard. A staple on the cocktail circuit. Then all of a sudden there were these reports of him flashing women. But discreetly. At first, anyway."

"How in God's name is something like that ever discreet?"

"Well, like he'd do it really fast. Where you'd say to yourself, did I really see that, or did I just have one too many?"

Crawford shrugged. "Okay, if you say so."

"Then one time—" Rose started chuckling. "Sorry, this isn't really funny, but it kind of is."

"I'm afraid to ask, what happened?"

"So, it was at a cocktail party for the Bladder Cancer Advocacy Network, and the way I heard it was Rodney went into the men's room and came out with his...*thing* out and both his pants pockets pulled out—"

"You gotta be—"

Rose shook her head. "Went up to this group of horrified women and said, 'This is my impression of an African bush elephant.'"

Crawford felt he had now—without a doubt—heard it all. "That's true? That really happened?"

Rose nodded. "After that he was kind of banned from the cocktail and charity ball circuit. I haven't seen him in a couple of years."

Crawford shook his head. "That's the most bizarre thing I've ever heard. Not sure he sounds like a serial killer, though. What's he look like?"

"Tall, grey hair, a droopy mustache, sixty-five or so," Rose said.

He didn't fit Troy Price's description, but he still was worth looking into. Crawford decided to put him on his interview list.

"Thanks...I almost hate to ask. Anybody else?"

"No, not really. I still hear Stark Stabler's name come up. Except I don't know if he's got any connection to Mattie."

Crawford figured he knew practically everything there was to know about Stark Stabler. He stood up. "Rose, as always it's been eye-opening."

"Just trying to do my job as your number one confidential informant."

"And a hell of a job you're doing," Crawford said. "As soon as I get a little spare time, let's grab dinner."

Rose got to her feet. "That's what I was hoping to hear."

He gave her a kiss on the cheek. "You smell great, by the way."

She kissed him back. "So do you." She sniffed. "Pure testosterone."

TWENTY-TWO

Crawford went straight from Rose's house to Lowell Grey's. Needless to say, Grey was eager to get his S & M amateur hour DVD back. Crawford had a very difficult time making eye contact with Grey as the man put forth yet another flimsy alibi. One that couldn't be confirmed by anyone else. He had woken up, done ten laps in his pool, had some breakfast, then read the paper. At 9:30 he had turned on the TV to see how the stock market was doing. Then at 10:30 he had gone over to his gallery to make final preparations for the opening.

Johnny Cotton's alibi was better. He and the other men in the Luxury Landscaping crew had cleaned up two houses on the north end of Palm Beach between nine and twelve that morning. Cotton claimed to be working side by side with the other three men the entire time. In what appeared to be a shot at Crawford, Cotton asked whether the mailman, whom Crawford had invented, had identified Cotton as being at the house where Mimi Taylor had been killed. Crawford told him that the mailman wasn't able to make a positive ID and couldn't be sure. Cotton just nodded his head, smirked and said, "Uh-huh, I see."

When they rendezvoused later in Crawford's office, Ott caught him up on Stark Stabler and Art Nunan, whom he was now referring to as "the dog track dude." According to Ott, Stark Stabler was starting to get pretty aggressive and threatening to go to his lawyer about how he was being harassed by Crawford and Ott. Ott, who had never been very accomplished at mollifying people, told Crawford he started to tell him to go fuck himself but bit his tongue and suggested instead that he "do what he thought best." Crawford gave him kudos for his uncharacteristic show of self-restraint then listened to him describe Stabler's alibi.

Stabler said that he had been out late the night before and had a lot to drink, so he slept in. Ott had asked him, "Until what time?" To which Stabler replied, "Just past eleven."

"Jesus, are you kidding?" Crawford said. "I haven't slept that late since the all-night keggers in college."

"Keggers? Christ, you went to Dartmouth. I thought you guys sat around and drank martinis."

"Are you kidding? It's in New Hampshire. We had a still in back of the dorm. Sheep for dates."

Ott chuckled. "Sounds like fun."

Truth was, hearing about Lowell Grey's and Stark Stabler's mornings made Crawford a little envious. Particularly Grey's. Wake up when you wake up instead of when the alarm goes off, take a nice swim followed by a leisurely breakfast, then peruse the paper, check to see how your stocks are doing. Not that he had any stocks, but hell, what was not to like about that?

Crawford told Ott about going to the Chesterfield Hotel, seeing a security camera aimed at the front door, and asking the manager if he could see tape from that morning between 9:15 and 9:45. The manager was cooperative and—sure enough—it showed Troy Price coming through the Chesterfield's front door at exactly 9:32. Crawford had him replay it a few times, paying particular attention to whether Price looked mussed up or had the expression of man either distressed or anxious. His face simply looked vacuous.

Then he told Ott about the two men Rose had mentioned, Boysie Johnson and Rodney Bowman.

Ott started shaking his head halfway through and didn't stop. "Did it ever occur to you," he said when Crawford had finished, "that we live in the twilight zone? I mean, shit, a guy with his dong out pretending he's an elephant. How many cocktails do you have to have to think that's a good look?"

Ott made Crawford promise that he'd take him along when he went to see Rodney Bowman, saying, "One thing I've never had a chance to do in my long, distinguished career is interview a flasher before."

Crawford went to the internet phone directory and found a number for Bowman.

He dialed the number and a woman answered. He wasn't expecting that, having figured that Bowman would be single.

"Yes, my name is Detective Crawford," he said, "Palm Beach Police, is Mr. Bowman there, please?"

"Ah, yes, he is. But he's taking a nap at the moment."

"When do you think he'll be up?"

"I would say a half an hour or so."

"Okay, me and my partner will stop by to see him in an hour."

"O-kay."

"Thank you."

Crawford clicked off and turned to Ott. "Sorry, gotta wait an hour."

Ott stood up. "Good. That'll give me time to see what I can come up with on my two other mutts."

Frances, the woman from the reception desk, poked her head into Crawford's office. "Knock, knock?"

Crawford craned his neck. "Hey, Franny, what's up?"

She held up a sheet of paper. "I got a sketch from that West Palm sketch guy."

She handed it to Crawford.

"Thanks." He took it as Ott leaned forward to have a look.

"You're welcome," Frances said, walking toward the door.

"Looks like any old white man in his thirties," Ott said.

"Kinda looks like Brennan," Crawford said, referring to a uniform cop.

"Or one of the trainers at my gym," Ott said.

"A little like a young Rutledge," Crawford said.

Ott shook his head. "Worthless."

Crawford tossed it in his trash can.

Crawford rang the doorbell of the one-story ranch house at 223 Sanford Avenue. A few moments later, a heavyset black woman came to the door.

"Hello, I'm Detective Crawford. I called earlier. This is my partner, Detective Ott."

Ott nodded.

The woman smiled. "I'm Mr. Bowman's caregiver, Jonetta. Come right in. He's watching one of his shows."

They followed her into the living room.

They saw all they needed to see. A man hooked up to a dialysis machine who seemed absorbed in a TV show that Crawford was ninety percent sure was *The Flintstones* based on hearing the unforgettable voice of one of his boyhood idols, Barney Rubble.

Crawford tried to head Jonetta off at the pass. "We don't need..." But it was too late. She had already gotten Rodney Bowman's attention.

He looked up and smiled. "Hey, fellas," Bowman said. "Did you fix the filter?"

Crawford glanced at Jonetta.

"He thinks you're the pool repairmen," she murmured.

Crawford glanced out the window at the backyard and stage-whispered back, "But there's no pool."

Jonetta nodded. "I know, but I think there was at his last house."

Crawford nodded and turned to Bowman. "Hi, Mr. Bowman," he said. "Yes, we just installed it, and you've got a ten-year guarantee on it."

"Well, thanks, boys," he said, then glanced at Ott. "You fellas always do such nice work."

Ott nodded and flashed him a thumbs-up. "We aim to please."

THEY WERE IN THE CAR, HEADED BACK TO THE STATION. "You can usually take Rose's tips to the bank," Ott said.

"Yeah," said Crawford. "I think a fair amount of time's passed since Ol' Rodney's stint as the elephant man."

TWENTY-THREE

Crawford had called and spoken to the mother of Boysie Johnson and made an appointment to stop by and see her son at 6:30 that night. After that, he had another appointment with Troy Price at the Chesterfield. It was set for 7:15, and Ott was going to go along. After that, Crawford was going to call it a day.

The Johnson house was a really ugly Mediterranean. Mainly because it was chocolate brown with fire-engine red trim. Crawford thought the function of Arcom, or the Architectural Commission, the "aesthetic police" as Rose called them, was to crack down on bad taste in Palm Beach houses. Apparently, they had missed one.

Mrs. Johnson met Crawford at the door. She had one of those faces that looked as if it had long since forgotten how to smile.

"What is this about, Detective?" she asked when Crawford identified himself.

Crawford decided to waste a smile on her. "I just need to speak to your son about a matter."

"Did you think that was an answer?" she shot back.

"I would like to ask him where he was this morning."

"Where he always is," Mrs. Johnson said.

"Could I speak to him, please, Mrs. Johnson?"

Her long, dramatic sigh communicated the message that neither she nor her son had time for whatever lame, inconsequential nonsense Crawford was there to discuss.

"Come in," she said. "I'll go get him." She pointed. "Go in that room over there."

It was a small study that looked like it should be in a monastery.

A few moments later, a man walked in. He was as Rose had described him. Dark hair, looked to be around forty but shorter than Crawford expected. And he had an abnormally large head. He had inherited his mother's smile, which was to say his expression was blank.

"Hello, Boysie—"

"My son's name is Boyd Junior; he's not called that anymore."

"Okay. Hello, Boyd Junior," Crawford said. "I'll just be needing a minute of your time. How about we sit?"

Boysie looked at his mother. She gave a quick nod.

Crawford and Boysie sat, while his mother stayed standing. Hovering was more like it.

"I'd like to know where you were this morning. Could you tell me, please?"

Crawford saw that there was clearly something off about the man, as if he were concentrating really hard trying to understand the simple question. Drug burnout was his first theory.

"Well, I went to my job like I do every day."

Crawford wondered if he was referring to something other than picking up cans.

"Your job, can you tell me what it is?"

"I go find cans and get money for them."

Nope.

"And where do you do that?"

"Mainly in West Palm Beach."

"And how do you get there?"

"My bike, over the north bridge."

"So you go down North Lake Way, then over the north bridge?"

"Yup. Uh-huh."

"Which means you go past Dunbar Road."

Mrs. Johnson put her hands on her hips. "What are you implying?"

A little spittle had gathered at the corner of her mouth.

Crawford put up his hands. "I'm not implying anything, Mrs. Johnson. I'm just asking your son a few questions." He turned back to Boysie. "Do you know where Dunbar Road is?"

Boysie shook his head. His mother's tone had clearly made him agitated.

"Did you stop anywhere before you went over the north bridge this morning?"

"No, of course, he didn't." Mrs. Johnson shot him hateful eyes. "That's not his routine."

"I asked your son."

Boysie looked extremely anxious. "No, I never get off my bike, except to get cans. Bottles sometimes."

Crawford nodded, leaned forward, and patted Boysie's arm. "It's okay—"

"Don't you dare touch my son," Mrs. Johnson said.

Ignoring her tone, he smiled at Boysie. "Just one last question, are you okay?"

Boysie nodded. He had the look of a dog that had been kicked a lot when it was a puppy.

Crawford noticed he had a watch. "What time do you leave here in the morning?"

"Seven thirty on the dot. Every morning," Boysie said with pride.

Crawford had heard all he needed to hear. Aside from concluding that Boysie was a highly unlikely murderer, there were several cameras on the north bridge where he could see when Boysie crossed into West Palm Beach and when he returned later that day. He planned to foist off the job of studying that day's tapes on a uniform he had used for similar jobs in the past.

He stood up and thanked Boysie and Mrs. Johnson.

Boysie said, "You're welcome." His mother didn't say a thing.

Crawford and Ott's reception at the Chesterfield Hotel wasn't any more welcoming than the one Crawford had just had at the Johnson home.

"I thought we did this before," Troy Price said, as Crawford and Ott sat opposite him in the expensively appointed Chesterfield reception area. "I told you what happened, you checked it out, end of story."

"We need an exact timeline," Crawford said. "You got to the house on Dunbar at nine and at nine thirty-two you entered the Chesterfield lobby. It's exactly five and a half minutes from there to here, going the speed limit, which leaves you twenty-seven minutes to tell Mattie Priest again you weren't interested in a house with a master on the second floor."

"Probably could tell her that a couple hundred times in twenty-seven minutes," Ott chimed in.

Price shook his head and sneered. "So, you brought along your comedian partner, huh?"

Crawford tapped a table next to him with his hand. "Mr. Price, tell us what happened from when you first walked in the front door of the house until you got back in your car to take the five-and-a-half-minute ride back here."

Price sighed. "Okay, I said hello to Mattie, then went into the living room, checked it out, then the dining room—ditto—then the kitchen and the pantry."

"And how long did that take?" Crawford asked. "Ballpark?"

"Oh, about five minutes."

"Thought you said the whole thing took you five minutes."

"Hey, I wasn't checking my watch every two seconds."

"Then what?"

"I went from the kitchen to the maid's room and bath in the back."

"Okay, that's what, another...minute?"

"Like I said, I wasn't timing it."

"Then where'd you go?" Ott got back into the act.

"Upstairs."

"Why'd you go upstairs if you knew there was no master bedroom on the first floor?" Ott asked.

Price started to blink. "'Cause I figured, what the hell, I was there, might as well look around a little."

"Okay, so it takes you fifteen seconds to get up the stairway. Now you've got twenty minutes unaccounted for."

"There were a lot of bedrooms up there."

"So you spent twenty minutes up there, then left?" Crawford asked.

"No, not that long."

"Remember, you told me you were at the house for five minutes," Crawford said.

"Okay, I was a little off."

"A little?" Ott said.

Crawford leaned close to Price. "I got a theory, Mr. Price," he said. "I think you were trying to seduce Mattie Priest. Talk her into having sex with you upstairs."

"Yeah, and she said no," Ott said. "So maybe you lost it. Your big ass ego shattered. Shot down by a lowly real estate agent."

Price's fists tightened and his face turned crimson. "Who the fuck are you?" he growled. "You clowns have no fuckin' idea who you're dealing with."

Price looked like he was fighting an urge to haul off and slug Ott.

"Oh, yeah, I do," Ott said. "A guy who propositions women when his wife is in the next room. I mean, pretty bush league, my friend."

Price started to get up, but Crawford reached over, put his hand above his knee and pushed down. "Hold on a second. We're not done here," he said. "Did you touch that woman? Lay a hand on her at all?"

Price was still hot. "Of course, I didn't, it was early in the morning."

Crawford and Ott looked at each other quizzically.

"What's that got to do with anything?" Crawford asked. "Just so you know, we're getting latent finger and palm prints later today from her clothes."

"Yeah, so in case you want to change your tune, better do it now," Ott said.

"I'm not doing anything of the kind," Price said, getting up, unimpeded by Crawford this time. "If you really are getting fingerprints, you'll find none of 'em are mine."

"Okay, Mr. Price, well thank you for your time," Crawford said. "And, not that we don't trust you, but we're going to need you to stop by our station tomorrow to be fingerprinted."

Price rolled his eyes. "It'll have to be day after tomorrow."

"Why?"

"I got a bunch of conference calls and a golf game."

Crawford shot a glance at Ott, then back to Price. "This is a priority."

"The hell it is," Price said.

"Tell you what," Crawford said. "You're not at our station by twelve, I'm sending a detail of uniform cops to find you."

Ott had to get his licks in. "So, please, don't make 'em drag you off the golf course kicking and screaming."

TWENTY-FOUR

Crawford was frustrated as hell. He had spent way too many days and hours to be where he was. Which, in a word, was nowhere. There was nothing else to do except go back over and dig down deeper into the suspects he had. He remembered something that had caught his interest about Stark Stabler in Wikipedia, but then he had been interrupted by a phone call and had never gotten back to it. The gist of it was that Stabler had been defaulted in the doubles final of a big tournament. He clicked back on to Wikipedia and read the profile again. It was the French Open back in 1990, and Crawford did the math and figured Stabler was twenty-eight years old and hadn't won a major up to that point.

He called up the relevant Wikipedia page and read it carefully. The cryptic explanation in the article read, "Stabler and his doubles partner, Dennis McKinley, were defaulted on the eve of the final for reasons that remain unclear." That was the problem with Wikipedia, you didn't always get the full story. And sometimes their facts were a little off. Nevertheless, the story piqued Crawford's interest. The only problem was he couldn't exactly call Paris and, using his limited French, try to get to the bottom of it. So instead he Googled the

USTA—the United States Tennis Association—and actually found a telephone number for their headquarters in White Plains, New York.

A woman answered. He identified himself, said he was a tennis fan. "I'm curious about a men's doubles match at the French Open and was hoping I could get some information about it."

"I might be able to help you," the woman said.

"The thing is, the match was played twenty-eight years ago," Crawford said. "Well, actually it *wasn't* played...but it was supposed to have been."

"I'm not sure I understand."

"Does the name Stark Stabler mean anything to you?"

"Sorry, sir, it doesn't, but there's someone here who might be able to help," she said. "His name is Bill Torrey. He's kind of our tennis historian."

"Yes, I'd like to speak to him if he has a few minutes."

"I'm looking at him across the office right now," she said. "Let me put you on hold for a second."

"Sure. Thank you very much."

A few moments passed, then a voice. "Hello, this is Bill, can I help you?"

"I hope so," Crawford said. "My name is Charlie Crawford, I'm a detective in Palm Beach, Florida, and I'm looking into something."

"Okay. What do you need to know?"

"Do you remember a player named Stark Stabler?"

"Absolutely. Great backhand, so-so forehand, a hundred-mile-an-hour serve back when that was really fast. Married a rich woman."

"That's the guy," Crawford said. "So, my question is this, back in 1990, he and his partner, Dennis McKinley, were in the finals of the French Open—"

"But got defaulted."

"Yeah, exactly, so I just wondered if you knew why."

There was silence at the other end for a few moments. Then. "Yes, there was some scandal involving a woman player, I think."

"Scandal? What do you mean?"

"I don't remember the exact circumstances," Torrey said. "But I know who would know."

"Who is that?"

"Dennis McKinley," Torrey said. "That was his one big shot to win a major. He was kind of a journeyman player. He never got to a final again. I heard he wanted to kill Stabler."

"So whatever the issue was, McKinley wasn't involved."

"No, as I remember, whatever the issue was, it just had to do with Stabler," Torrey said. "Come to think of it, Dennis ended up being a club pro. Somewhere down near you. Delray, I think."

Crawford was dying to find out what happened. "I'd really like to talk to him."

"I don't remember what the club's name is off the top of my head, but I can find out."

Crawford gave him his number and fifteen minutes later Torrey called back with the name of the club and its phone number.

Crawford looked at his watch, thinking that maybe he'd just take the twenty-minute ride down to Delray Beach. But he decided against it, figuring he'd get the same answer in a phone call. He called the number.

Dennis McKinley was on the court giving a lesson, so Crawford asked the employee if she could ask McKinley to call him back.

He glanced out his window as he thought about what to do next. His thoughts were interrupted by leaden footsteps he hadn't heard in a while. It was Norm Rutledge, his boss, and right behind him, grimacing slightly, was Mort Ott.

"We need to talk," Rutledge said.

"Okay," Crawford said, as Rutledge started to sit down.

"Hey, that's my chair," Ott said. "It's molded to my ass by now."

Rutledge flashed him the stink-eye but sat in the other chair.

"What's the subject, Norm?" Crawford asked.

"Dead real estate agents," Rutledge said succinctly. "They're not good for the local economy."

"Keep going," Crawford said.

"I've had a bunch of calls from all the usual suspects," Rutledge said.

"Let me guess," Crawford said. "That would be the mayor, the head of the town council...and, ah, the Rotary guy?"

"Yup, and a few others've checked in," Rutledge said. "Like the president of the Palm Beach Board of Realtors."

Crawford hated to ask what he or she had to say, so he didn't.

"This guy named Shaw and his board members want to have a meeting with us," Rutledge said. "He feels that there should be a cop present when agents show houses from now on."

"What? That's crazy."

"His suggestion was that a cop didn't need to actually be with the agent as they show a house—that would be a little distracting—but maybe be outside or on the porch or something. You know, just a presence."

Crawford glanced over at Ott, who was being uncharacteristically silent.

"Norm, you gotta be fucking kidding," Crawford said. "Last time I checked there were something like a thousand agents—full- or part-time—in Palm Beach. So let's say one shows a house every day, no, let's just say every other day. That means we need to have guys go to five hundred showings a day."

Rutledge's blank look made it clear he hadn't done the math. "That's just what the guy suggested."

Ott leaned into Rutledge. "Well, then he's smokin' some really good shit. Tell him to go hire a bunch of rent-a-cops or something. Our uniforms got way better things to do with their time."

"You know, Ott," Rutledge said. "Maybe you should try looking at it from their point of view. They've had two of their agents brutally murdered."

"I'm aware of that, Norm. We were at the scenes," Ott said. "Hey, I feel bad, obviously, for the vics and their families. It's just that suggestion is crazy. You got money in the budget to pay for a hundred more uniforms?"

"'Course not, but you need to hear some of the shit I'm hearing," Rutledge said. "The mayor told me there hasn't been one sale in the last four days. Not only are agents scared, but so are buyers. We really don't need people thinking Palm Beach is a goddamn war zone. Why don't you just get the killer...like today?"

Crawford could see by Ott's look that he was thinking about responding with one of his quaint expressions like, *Yeah, and why don't you pull a rabbit out of your ass.* But he held his tongue. Crawford was impressed by his partner's second display of self-control.

Crawford glanced at Rutledge. "We understand your concern, Norm. We're doing everything we can."

Rutledge nodded. "If you understand my concern then you'll understand that's hardly the answer I was looking for. Hey look, I know this armed guards for real estate agents thing is a shitty idea. But I need you to meet with this Board of Realtors guy just to appease him."

Ott rolled his eyes, and Crawford did a slow version of counting to ten. "Okay, Norm, we'll see the guy, but how 'bout we keep it short?"

"There's actually going to be three of them. The president and two others," Rutledge said.

Crawford sighed. "Clusterfuck, huh?"

"Maybe you guys could refrain from rolling your eyes and saying fuck every third word when you meet with 'em."

"Maybe, maybe not," Ott said.

Rutledge stood up. "Well, thank you for being your usual thoughtful and reasonable selves."

Crawford raised his eyebrows. Ott was usually the one who went heavy on the sarcasm. "You're very welcome, Norm," he said.

Rutledge walked out, and Ott stayed seated.

"Can't say I was surprised," Ott said.

"Yeah, I was kind of expecting something like that."

"Can you imagine us being on real estate-showing detail?" Ott got a funny look in his eyes. "Now, if we got a piece of the commission, that would be a whole different story."

"I get them being freaked out about all this—" Crawford stopped to answer his cell phone. "Hello."

"Hi, Charlie, it's Holly."

Holly? Oh, right.

"Yes, hi, Ms. Pine," Crawford said, rolling his eyes at Ott.

Ott, who had stood up to leave, was sticking around now.

"I was wondering if you'd do me a big favor," she said then added, "But there's a reward that goes with it."

"What's that, Ms. Pine?"

Not in this lifetime would he ever be calling her Holly.

"I'm showing a house to a man I've never met before. He called me on a sign at my listing on Kawama. I was hoping you'd be there. Maybe just in your car or something, so he sees you. Afterward, for your effort, I'll buy you a drink at HMF" —whatever and wherever HMF was— "that bar at The Breakers."

"I'm sorry," Crawford said, "but me and my partner are flat-out at the moment. Why don't you take along another agent with you?"

"It won't take long, I promise. I'll be in and out in fifteen minutes. Then you can get your reward. I figure you for a Jack Daniels kind of man."

He couldn't stand Jack Daniels.

"Thank you, Ms. Pine, but I just can't make it," he said. "But, good luck, I hope you sell it."

She sighed. "Okay, thanks."

He clicked off and his phone rang again.

It was a number he didn't recognize. He decided to take it anyway. "Hello."

"Hello, Detective, this is Dennis McKinley. You called and left a message?"

"Oh, yes, thank you for calling me back." Ott stood up, gave a wave and walked out. "I'm curious about an incident that occurred a long time ago in your tennis career. When you and your partner Stark Stabler were defaulted in the finals of the French Open."

McKinley groaned. "Yeah, what about it?"

"What was the reason for the default? My understanding is that it had to do with something Stabler did?"

"Damn right it did," McKinley said. "Like trying to knock down Laura Stubbs's front door."

The name was vaguely familiar to Crawford. "She was a tennis player, right?"

"Yeah, she had just lost in the semis there."

"Can you tell me exactly what happened, please?"

"Uh, okay. Stabler had a bottle of wine at dinner and somehow got it into his head to pay Laura a visit in the middle of the night. He pounded on her door 'til she opened up, then he started groping her. She fought him off and finally forced him to leave."

"So there was no rape or anything?"

"Everything but," McKinley said. "She woke up the tournament director in the middle of the night and told him what happened, and that was it for us. Instant default. My big chance, up in smoke. I coulda killed the bastard. Never spoke to him again."

"Can't say I blame you," Crawford said. "Were there any other incidents that you know of involving Stabler?"

"You know what, Detective?" McKinley said. "After what happened that night I never wanted to hear another goddamn thing about Stark Stabler."

"I get it. Well, thank you, Mr. McKinley, I really appreciate your time. I won't keep you any longer."

"You're welcome," McKinley said. "If you happen to see that dirtbag, be sure and give him my worst."

TWENTY-FIVE

Crawford beelined down to Ott's office. Ott was on his computer.

"I just heard a good story about Stark Stabler," Crawford said.

Ott leaned back in his chair and put his hands behind his neck. "I'm all ears."

At the end, Crawford asked Ott to look up a name on his internet phone directory. The name was Sally Stabler.

Ott actually found two numbers. One looked like a landline, the other a cell.

Crawford dialed the cell number and a woman answered. He clicked on speakerphone.

"Mrs. Stabler?"

"Yes, who's this?"

"My name is Detective Crawford, Palm Beach Police, and I would like to come see you as soon as possible."

She laughed. "That's going to be a little difficult since I'm on a chairlift out in Montana."

"Skiing?"

"Yes, Detective, that's what you do on a chairlift...they take you up a mountain so you can ski down it." He could see she and Stabler deserved each other. "Why are you calling me, anyway?"

"So, you were not in Palm Beach yesterday morning?"

"No, I was two thousand miles away. I asked you what this is about."

"A local matter," Crawford said. "Thank you very much, Mrs. Stabler."

He clicked off before she could ask anything else. "What a complete pain in the ass."

Ott laughed. "What...did you think Stabler'd be married to a rich, hot babe with a sparkling personality?"

THEY WERE IN STABLER'S LIVING ROOM, WHICH, THOUGH bright and cheery, looked as though it had been decorated by someone in the 1950s. It also was the home of two parrots who liked to talk. But their vocabularies were limited. The red one seemed to have two phrases that it alternated between "Here, kitty, kitty" and "That's what she said." The blue one just burst out laughing every minute or so. It was more like a cackle, and something told Crawford that the bird might be imitating Sally Stabler's laugh.

"Gotta tell you," Ott was saying to Stabler, "the way you made it sound, I figured your wife was with you yesterday morning."

Stabler frowned. "I never said that."

"No, you never did," said Ott. "But that was the impression I got."

"Well, that's your problem."

Crawford glanced away from the blue parrot to Stabler. "And your problem, Mr. Stabler, is you don't have an alibi. I want to ask you about something that happened a long time ago."

Stabler did a combination sigh and groan.

"The night before you were to play in the doubles final at the French Open back in 1990—"

"Jesus Christ, that's ancient history. Why don't we talk about when I was in kindergarten?"

Crawford ignored him. "You assaulted a woman named Laura Stubbs that night."

"The hell I did," Stabler said. "She came on to me at dinner."

"Did Mattie Priest ever come on to you?" Ott asked.

"I barely knew the woman," Stabler said.

Ott started tapping the coffee table next to him. "When I talked to you before, you implied you didn't know her at all."

"Like I just said, I barely knew her."

"Which is way different from not knowing her at all," Ott said. "Which is what you clearly implied."

Stabler sighed. "Do you have a tape recording of our conversation, Detective?"

Crawford glanced at Ott and could see his partner getting sick of the verbal sparring. He noticed a vein in Ott's forehead that stuck out when he got angry.

"So, you have absolutely no alibi, is what you're telling us," Crawford said. "And you're also telling us that you got defaulted from the final of the French Open because Laura Stubbs 'came on to' you."

"What the hell does something that happened a million years ago have to do with anything?"

"Glad you asked," Crawford said. "Because what happened then is similar to what happened to Mimi Taylor and Mattie Priest. It's called a pattern."

"Difference is," Ott said, "They didn't live to tell about it."

"That whole thing over there was a put-up job because two French guys were in the finals against us, and the tournament director was French."

"'Put-up job,' huh?" Crawford said. "So you're saying the French Open is a rigged deal. Is that it?"

Stabler did his sigh-groan combo again. "I'm saying I'm getting really sick of you two harassing me every five minutes."

Crawford leaned closer to Stabler and lowered his voice. "I'll be perfectly honest with you, that really doesn't concern us much. See, we're trying to solve two brutal murders and, as far as a suspect goes, you check a lot of the boxes."

"I don't give a damn if I check a thousand boxes. I had nothing to do with either one. And you don't have one goddamn shred of evidence."

Crawford's eyes flicked around the room. "I've been admiring your art collection." He pointed. "That one over there, who's the artist?"

"I don't know. It's my wife's collection. I just know that one's a Chagall." He pointed to the wall behind Crawford and Ott.

Crawford and Ott turned and looked at it. "Very nice," Crawford said then pointed to the wall to his left. "And that one, I'm pretty sure, is a Modigliani."

Stabler turned to it. "I wouldn't know," he said. Then to Crawford, "How's a cop know about art?"

Crawford eyed the man and decided to answer the question with a question. "How's a married man know so many single women?"

Stabler leaned forward. "Okay, that does it," he said. "Right after you leave here, I'm going to call my attorney and direct him to initiate a lawsuit for police harassment." He stood up. "So, why don't you get the hell out of here, so I can make that call."

Neither Crawford nor Ott moved. "Have at it, Mr. Stabler," Crawford said. "And as your attorney will no doubt inform you, my partner and I are just doing our jobs."

The blue parrot in its cage ten feet away started squawking. "Just doing our jobs. Just doing our jobs." Then it added, "Here, kitty, kitty...that's what she said."

TWENTY-SIX

Stark Stabler, Lowell Grey, Troy Price, Art Nunan... dubious, unlikely, long shot, nah. That was how Crawford had them sized up after good hard reexaminations. Which was not to say that none of them could have done it. Because he hadn't ruled out any of them yet. That left Johnny Cotton. And even though Ott seemed to have written him off as a suspect, Crawford was not so sure. His gut, which had been a long way from batting a thousand lately, was hinting that the ex-con might just be an artful con man.

He had gotten the names and addresses of the other landscapers on Cotton's crew, so rather than interview them in Cotton's presence he wanted to wait until they were done for the day. Not have Cotton listen in to the conversation.

It was a little past five when he dialed one of them. Enrique Diaz. Diaz answered.

"Mr. Diaz, this is Detective Crawford. We met earlier," he said. "Are you alone at the moment?"

"Yes."

"Good. I just wanted to ask you a question. Was Johnny Cotton with you and your crew the entire morning today?"

A long pause. "Yes," Diaz said finally.

"You're sure about that?"

"Yes," Diaz said.

"Okay, well, thank you. Do me a favor and don't mention this conversation to Cotton."

"Okay," Diaz said.

Crawford clicked off, figuring the first words out of Diaz's mouth the next morning would be "Hey, Johnny, guess who called me last night?"

He dialed a black guy on the crew named Lincoln Jones.

Jones answered right away.

"Mr. Jones, this is Detective Crawford from this morning. Are you by yourself?"

"Yeah, I am. Why?"

"I just have a quick question for you," Crawford said. "Was Johnny Cotton with you and your crew the whole morning the day that woman was killed?"

No hesitation. "Yeah, except the coffee run."

"Wait? He went and got coffee?"

"Yeah, it was his turn."

"And how long was he gone?"

"Oh, you know, half hour. Maybe a little more. Hang on, come to think of it, it was closer to forty-five minutes. I 'member him saying he had to wait for the drawbridge when we got on his ass 'cause it took so long."

"So, the bridge..." Crawford said. "Meaning he went over to West Palm to get the coffee?"

"Yeah, Dunkin' Donuts on Clematis."

Crawford knew it well. "How'd he seem when he got back?"

"What d'you mean, how'd he seem?"

It was kind of a clunky question. "I mean, any different than usual? Was he any more keyed up than usual?"

"Keyed up?"

"You know, nervous, excited?"

"Nah, dude just seemed like he always did. I dint notice nothin' out of the ordinary."

"You didn't see any cuts or anything on his face, did you?"

"Nah, nothin'."

"Okay. Well, thanks. I'd appreciate it if you didn't mention we had this conversation."

"You got it."

Forty-five minutes? One of the landscaping jobs was five minutes from the house on Dunbar. The other one...even closer.

This was headline news.

TWENTY-SEVEN

The real estate agent was ten minutes late for her appointment. She was surprised that her buyer's car wasn't parked in the driveway. She got out of her car, unlocked the house and went around and did what she always did, checking to see that everything was nice and clean. It also meant making sure there were no dead bugs on the white Carrera marble countertops or that any green chameleons whose cheeks puff out like basketballs weren't scurrying around inside.

Another five minutes went by and still no buyer, which wasn't particularly upsetting because she had plenty of customers who treated a house showing as if it were a cocktail party: you were invited to come at seven but didn't arrive until seven thirty.

She went into the kitchen to get a glass of Pellegrino. She had bought several bottles when she first got the listing and had one bottle left in the fridge. She opened it, took out the bottle, and went to get a glass in a cabinet next to the butler's pantry. She reached up and got a glass and as she did felt a hand grab her shoulder roughly and pull her into him. With one hand, he held her tight and with the other, he put something over her mouth. Then with both hands he pulled it tight. *Duct tape.*

The man was half a foot taller than she and had what appeared to be a nylon stocking over his head. She noticed a rip in it just below his nose. She tried to scream but nothing came out.

Without saying a word, he started ripping her clothes off. First, her blue silk blouse. He grabbed both sides and pulled, and the buttons went flying. Then with one hand, he reached for her bra right above her left breast. He tugged it and the clasp broke, leaving her bare-breasted.

With an arm around her shoulder, he reached down and put his other hand inside the front of her skirt. He yanked the skirt hard, and it ripped up the entire front. He let the skirt fall to the floor then tore off her panties.

She was completely naked now.

He put his hands around her neck and started choking her. She could feel his thumbs pressing into her windpipe—the pain and the lack of oxygen combining to create a blinding terror as she struggled to free herself. As her vision began to tunnel and consciousness slipped away, she suddenly heard the most wonderful sound possible, the unmistakable crunching sound of car tires on the Chattahoochee pebble driveway.

In that instant, the attacker released his grip and fled from the kitchen.

THE DISPATCHER CALLED CRAWFORD FIRST. WHEN HER CALL went to voice mail, she called Ott and reached him.

Then Ott called Crawford and got him. "Charlie," he said. "Holly Pine's at Good Sam." Good Samaritan Hospital in West Palm Beach. "She was assaulted at that house she was showing."

"Oh, Jesus," Crawford said. "Is she all right?"

"I think so. Apparently, she's conscious. Probably sedated. I guess someone showed up in the middle of the assault and scared the guy off."

"Let's go there right now," Crawford said. "You doin' anything?"

"I was, but this is more important. See you there in ten?"

"Make it fifteen," Crawford said.

Crawford did a quick internet search for florists that were open late and found one. A torrent of guilt washed over him like a ten-foot wave. However bad off Holly Pine was—physically or psychically—it was on him. It was true that Palm Beach's finest were not in the business of providing armed guards for real estate agents, but he could have found time to do it just that one time.

Then he thought about the optics. How it would look if word got out that Holly Pine had asked him to accompany her because she was suspicious about a guy who had contacted her to see a house? In two words, *not good*. In three words, *really, really, bad*.

So, to try to assuage his guilt he bought a dozen roses for her. Just after he handed the salesperson his credit card, he wondered if Holly Pine would infer that this was a romantic gesture on his part.

Stop, he told himself as he signed his name. That was of absolutely no importance whatsoever.

Then he wondered whether Holly Pine would even welcome him or the flowers. She might, with good reason, look upon him as someone who failed to prevent her assault. She might even harbor hostility toward him. Well, if so, he'd have to get beyond that because she might well hold the key to the identity of the killer.

Holly Pine's room at Good Samaritan Hospital was like all the other hospital rooms Crawford had ever stayed in or visited. A white tile floor, fluorescent lighting, a curtain on a track that surrounded the bed, and a few bad landscape prints that were screwed into the walls.

She lay in bed with a *Marie Claire* magazine in her lap. On first glimpse, all Crawford could see that looked different about her was that her neck was a fierce red in color. She had no apparent bruises or black eyes and was able to muster a stoical smile as he handed her the bouquet of roses in a glass vase.

"Thank you," she said, her tone weaker than usual.

"How are you feeling?" Crawford asked as Ott stood by his side.

"I'm okay," Pine said. "The shock has worn off. Nothing even remotely like that has ever happened to me before." Then, looking at the roses, "They're so beautiful."

Crawford nodded. "It's the least I could do. I just want to tell you how sorry I am I didn't go with you to that house. Especially since you told me you were distrustful of this man. I should have made the time and, again, I am very sorry."

"That's okay, I know it's not part of your job description. It was a little like asking you to help a little old lady cross the street. Not that I'm a little old lady or anything," Pine said, smiling. "I just had this premonition, I guess you'd call it. Which is why I asked you."

Wow. On top of having gone through the whole terrifying ordeal, Holly Pine was going to be understanding. How bad was she—totally unintentionally—going to make him feel?

Ott took a step toward her bed. "Ms. Pine, can we ask you some questions, please?"

"Of course," Pine said. "But will you please stop with the 'Ms. Pine'?"

Ott nodded. "Okay, Holly. If you would please start at the beginning?"

"Sure." She took a deep breath.

"Take your time," Crawford said. "We're in no rush."

She took a few more deep breaths. "This is not easy. So...I got to the house on Kawama five minutes late but didn't see a car in the driveway. So, I unlocked the front door and went in. I turned on all the lights so it was nice and bright. I tried not to think about what happened to Mimi and Mattie. 'It's just another showing,' I kept saying to myself. Then, as I always do, I went through every room to make sure everything looked inviting."

"When you do that, what are you looking for?" Crawford asked.

"Just to make sure there aren't any surprises. Like, one time I found a dead cockroach on a pillow in the master. Yuck. Another time, I found a snake, very much alive, in a laundry room."

Ott smiled. "Something like that might tend to be a deal-killer. So, everything looked all right."

"Yes, everything was fine until I walked into the kitchen to get a glass of water."

Then she told them about the frightening attack and how she managed to struggle back into her shredded clothing before the other agent walked into the house.

"She had come to preview the house," Pine said. "She came by our office to pick up a key earlier in the day."

"Preview it," Ott asked. "What exactly does that mean?"

Crawford knew because Rose Clarke had explained it to him once.

"She was going to show it tomorrow," Pine said, "and wanted to see it first. That way she'd know all the good things about the house and could point them out."

"Did you notice anything else about the man aside from him being six feet tall or so and strong?"

Pine thought for a second. "Yes, his smell. It was like he lived in a dumpster."

Crawford shrugged. "Maybe he does."

Except that would rule out Stark Stabler, who smelled like he drenched himself in expensive aftershave every morning.

"I mean, really bad," Pine added.

"What else can you tell us about him?" Crawford asked.

Holly Pine glanced out the window then back to Crawford. "The whole thing took less than a minute, I think. I can't think of anything else."

"Well, thank you very much for letting us come see you," Crawford said.

"Yes, we really appreciate it," Ott added.

"Make you a deal," Crawford said, getting to his feet. "One of us will be there at any showing you have until we solve this thing."

Pine held out her hand. "Deal. Though I may take a few days off from showing."

Crawford walked up to her bed and shook her hand. "Can't say I blame you."

Ott shook her hand. "We'll even go in before you show to make sure there're no snakes in the house."

Holly managed a pained chuckle.

"Speak for yourself," Crawford said. "Snakes scare the hell out of me."

TWENTY-EIGHT

It was just past eight at night. Crawford had gone back to the station, and Ott had gone home.

The first thing Crawford did was call Dominica McCarthy.

"Hi, Charlie," she said. "Long time no—"

"I got a big favor to ask," he said.

"So, I see I got the all-business Charlie, as opposed to good-time Charlie."

Crawford laughed. "Yeah, 'fraid so," he said. "I need you to go to a house on Kawama and see if you can lift a print."

"The real estate agent killer?"

"Yeah, he went after number three, but someone showed up when he was right in the middle of it."

"Jesus, is she all right?"

"Yeah, but if it had been three minutes later... Anyway, I went there and saw that he jimmied open a living room window," Crawford said. "The address is 207 Kawama. Place is open now."

"I'm on my way."

"Thanks. I owe you."

"What's new?"

Crawford clicked off and looked out his window at the full moon.

Crawford had a theory about the real estate agent killer. But then, he always had theories. That was a detective's stock in trade. History had shown that about twenty percent of his theories panned out. But that didn't stop him from having them.

He turned on his computer, went to Google and clicked on Malpaso Correctional Institution, also known as Malpaso Max. He scrolled down until something caught his attention.

It said: *In 1999, Malpaso instituted the Art in Prison program, which includes creative writing, poetry, visual arts, dance, drama and music. The program continues to this day and has expanded to include yoga, meditation and horticulture. A substantial portion of the prison population has been involved in the program.*

It was as if the words "visual arts" were in red flashing lights. It went on to explain that outside artists volunteered to come several days a week to teach the inmates in various fields. Crawford next Googled "Art in Prison" and found several eye-opening articles. One told about a Malpaso inmate named Bruce Moller, serving twenty-one years to life for murder, who created a sculpture inspired by Ernest Hemingway's book *The Old Man and the Sea*. It depicted a bearded fisherman hooking a huge marlin as his boat is being buffeted by eight-foot waves.

The article explained how the piece was fashioned from materials allowed in the prison's restricted environment. The papier-mâché waves were a mix of floor wax and toilet paper. The boat is made from the back of a writing tablet cut into pieces. The oars were carved from Popsicle sticks from the canteen; the sail was snipped from a sheet. The fishing line was a broken string from a guitar class. It was an impressive piece of sculpture that, Crawford felt, wouldn't have been out of place in a Soho gallery.

Another article mentioned that there was a website called Prison Art where you could buy art made in various prisons throughout the country. Crawford went to it and found hundreds of pages of everything from charcoal sketches to richly colored oil paintings. He knew he'd need at least a whole day to go through all of it. Some of it was amateurish, and anybody could have done it, but much of it was really good.

At the end of one article, he read the following quote. "*We artists are indestructible: even in prison or in a concentration camp. I would be almighty in my own world of art, even if I had to paint my pictures with my wet tongue on the dusty floor of my cell.*"

Pablo Picasso had said that fifty years ago.

TWENTY-NINE

Crawford was in his office at five a.m. He hadn't been able to sleep much with all that was bouncing around in his head. He wanted to go through the thousands of paintings on the Prison Art website. He had a good idea what he was looking for but was fully aware that it might also just be a big waste of time. When Ott rolled in a little after eight, Crawford was still looking at photos of paintings.

He explained his theory to Ott, who thought it had merit, then called the number for the Malpaso Correctional Institution, a state prison in northern Florida. He was put on hold for five minutes then disconnected. He called back and was told nobody was available to help him. Something told Crawford that this was typical of a phone call to a prison. He called back at nine, and, after speaking to three different people, was finally connected to the assistant warden, a man named Henry Bostwick. Crawford identified himself and said that he was working on a murder case in Palm Beach. Then he started asking questions about Malpaso's art program.

"Yeah, keeps 'em busy," Bostwick said. "Supposed to be good for building self-esteem, they tell me, plus good for depression. Between you and me, I don't give a fuck whether they're depressed or not as long as they're not stirring up trouble."

Crawford figured that was probably a pretty typical attitude of prison officials. He asked Bostwick how the program worked.

"Well, for the art program there are three volunteers who come here during the week. As I understand it, one of them teaches them about art. You know, history and shit. Gives them like slide shows of paintings and sculpture, then discusses it all. The other two are actual painters, so they try to teach the prisoners how to draw, or paint, or do sculpture, whatever the hell. I've seen some of their stuff, and it's pretty damn good. Some of it, though, my dog coulda done."

"So, I'm guessing," Crawford said, "they see slides of paintings, and some of 'em try to paint in a style similar to ones they like."

Bostwick didn't respond right away. "Never thought about it, to tell you the truth, but I guess so. Probably like anything. You see someone do something good and you try to copy it, right? Like me trying to swing a golf club like Tiger Woods." Bostwick chuckled. "Hasn't exactly worked out the way I hoped."

"Would you mind if I spoke to the art teachers there?" Crawford asked.

"Me? No, not at all," Bostwick said. "I don't have their names and numbers handy. But I could call you back with that."

"That would be great," Crawford said. "I'd really appreciate it."

"Why you interested in all this?" Bostwick asked.

"Got a couple murders down here. One of my suspects did time there."

An hour later, just when Crawford was about to call Bostwick back, Bostwick called him.

"Thanks for getting back to me," Crawford said.

"Yeah, no problem. Here's what I found out. Just two of the art teachers come here now. One of them stopped coming about a month ago. Nobody seems to know exactly why she quit 'cause she had been the one who'd taught here the longest. Anyway, here are the names and numbers of the other two."

Crawford wrote down the information, thanked the assistant warden, and clicked off.

The first name was Martin Sanchez. Crawford dialed his number, but the call went to voice mail and he left a message.

The second name was Sasha Estes, and she answered. He told her why he was calling.

Specifically, that he was interested in a former inmate named Johnny Cotton and wondered if she knew if he had been involved in the art program there. Estes explained she was one of the ones who instructed the inmates on how to paint. She said she was familiar with Cotton's name but didn't remember having any personal contact with him. He asked her a few more questions, thanked her, and hung up.

Twenty minutes later, Martin Sanchez called back.

"Yeah," he said. "Johnny was one of my best students. He loved Impressionism and Cubism and a lot of twentieth-century French painters."

So, Ott and he had been conned, Cotton pretending to be clueless about art.

"Cubism?" Crawford thought back to his old college course. "Would that be Marcel Duchamp by any chance?"

"Sure would. Along with Picasso, Braque, Léger, Cézanne...a pretty long list."

"What about Modigliani?"

"No, he wasn't a Cubist. He was Italian by birth but spent most of his time painting in Paris."

"What was your impression of Cotton, Mr. Sanchez?"

Sanchez thought for a second. "Smart. Very smart. But here's the thing with all the inmates at Malpaso, they're always on their best behavior with me. The art program is about all they got. Otherwise it's just four walls. So, they really don't want to blow it."

"But when you say smart, how so, exactly?"

"I mean if he saw a slide just once, he'd memorize it. Not just that but take in every little detail and never forget it. So, if I were his teacher and I was giving him a grade, he'd get an A-plus. He'd be my prodigy. It's too bad Luna Jacobs isn't around anymore, I'm sure she could give you some good insights."

"Who is she?"

"She and Sasha used to teach together. Then one day Luna didn't show up. I never really found out why she quit. I don't know if anyone knew why. I asked, and what I heard was that she had moved away all of a sudden."

"So, she was Cotton's teacher?"

"Yes." Sanchez was silent for a few moments. "And you didn't hear this from me, but I heard there might have been a little thing between 'em."

"Define 'little thing,' please."

"How 'bout a *workplace romance*," Sanchez said. "He had a way about him that I could see would be attractive to women."

Crawford had to search for the right words for his next question. "This workplace romance between Luna Jacobs and Johnny Cotton... is there anyway something like that ever goes beyond a teacher-student relationship?"

"You mean sexual?"

"Yes."

"If they were creative enough. And those two were *very* creative."

"But Malpaso doesn't have anything like conjugal visits."

"Oh my God, no way."

Crawford wondered if there might be a spare closet or bathroom off of the art space.

"My last question is about the slides you showed," Crawford said. "Was one of them, by any chance, Duchamp's *Nude Descending a Staircase?*"

"Sure was. That's one of my favorites."

"And how about Modigliani's *Reclining Nude?*"

Sanchez paused. "I'm thinking that may have been before Cotton was in my class."

"But still, he could have seen it in an art book or something, right?"

"Absolutely," Sanchez said. "By the way, I saw that sold a few years back for over a hundred and fifty million."

"A hundred seventy million four hundred fifty thousand, to be exact."

Sanchez laughed. "You know your stuff."

"Not really," Crawford said as he looked at where Malpaso was located on the map on his computer. About a two-hour drive north.

"Well, Mr. Sanchez, I really appreciate your time and the information," Crawford said. "I may head up your way. If I do, maybe we can meet. Or, if not, I might just give you another call."

"Sure. Anytime."

"Okay, thanks again."

Crawford went straight to Ott's cubicle and told him about his conversation with Sasha Estes and Martin Sanchez.

"I sure bought his dumb act," Ott said. "Sounds like our guy."

"Looks it. Problem is we got no evidence. Nothing to hang him on," Crawford said. "I think I'm gonna take a little run up to Malpaso, see what I can dig up."

"Want me to come?"

"As much as I relish your scintillating car conversation, we both don't need to go. Stay here and find out whatever else you can about Cotton."

"I'm on it," Ott said and his voice suddenly took on a relieved tone. "Christ, I hope this means we don't have to take any more shit from that dirtball Stabler."

THIRTY

Crawford took I-95 north up to Melbourne and followed his GPS from there. Malpaso Correctional was out in cow country. Way out there.

He called assistant warden Henry Bostwick after he got onto I-95 and asked if he could meet with him and get access to the prison-art workshop. Bostwick said that would be fine and volunteered to get him a visitor's pass for the Art in Prison program. Crawford guessed that Bostwick probably had a fairly dull job, with every day being like the one before, so maybe he actually relished the idea of a new face coming for a visit.

Five minutes after he spoke to Bostwick, he got a call on his cell. He looked at the display. Dominica.

"I was just about to call you," he said.

"I lifted a bunch of prints from that pantry and the kitchen," Dominica said.

"All different?"

"Yup. Seven different people."

"I'll have the ones from my ex-con sent over to you."

"Sounds good."

"Match 'em up, will ya?"

"I'll do my best."

Just before he reached Malpaso, he called Bostwick again and said he was almost there. Bostwick met him at the front entrance of the prison, asked him to surrender his Sig Sauer P226 pistol, and ushered him through the metal detector.

"You guys ever have any prison breaks here?" Crawford asked, making conversation.

"Had a riot once," Bostwick said. "That was a bad day."

"I'll bet," Crawford said.

"Nobody got killed. Bunch of injuries, though."

They walked past a long row of cells, which ran for at least the length of a football field. At the end of it was a solid steel door. Bostwick took out a ring of keys, selected one, put it in the keyhole, and opened the door. It opened into a large room with paintings and various other art media. Ten men in blue uniforms were painting; a small, birdlike woman stood behind a man who had a painting on an easel.

"Hi, Sasha," Bostwick said as they approached her. "Got a fella here who wants to check out your little operation."

Sasha Estes smiled and walked over to the two men. "I've never heard of it referred to as a little operation before."

"Hey, Sasha," Crawford stepped forward and put his hand out. "I'm Charlie Crawford, detective with the Palm Beach Police Department. We spoke earlier."

"Oh, yes," Estes said, shaking his hand. "Welcome to the masterpiece studio, formerly Cellblock D."

Crawford looked around. "Pretty nice space," he said, glancing at the inmates. The first one he observed didn't appear to have one square inch of skin that wasn't covered in tattoos. Another one was missing a front tooth. A third one had ear, nose, eyelid and lip piercings. But all of them seemed to be absorbed in their projects. Two of them had glanced over at Crawford and Bostwick, but the rest seemed disinterested.

"It suits its purpose," Sasha said. "Marty Sanchez told me he spoke to you."

"Yes, he was very helpful," Crawford said. "I don't want to take you away from your work too long, but I have a few more questions, if you don't mind."

"Yes, sure," Sasha said. "What would you like to know?"

He didn't want their conversation overheard. "If we could just step over this way, please." Away from the inmate artists.

"Oh, sure," Sasha said, following him.

"My questions mainly have to do with your colleague, Luna Jacobs."

Henry Bostwick tapped the floor with his foot. "Well, I'm gonna leave you two to talk." Then, turning to Crawford, "How 'bout I come back in a half hour or so?"

"Yeah, that would be good. Thanks."

Bostwick nodded and walked away.

Crawford smiled at Sasha. "So, were you and Ms. Jacobs close at all?"

Sasha folded her arms on her chest. "Fairly close," she said. "I mean we were fellow artists in this vast cultural wasteland of central Florida."

"Why did Ms. Jacobs stop coming here, do you know?"

"I have no clue," Sasha said. "She never said a thing to me about it. It was a pretty big surprise. I mean, one day she just never showed up. Never told anybody anything. Not me, not Marty, not anybody in the prison."

"And did you contact her?"

"That was the weird thing. I must have called her five times on her cell. Left a bunch of messages, and she never called back."

"But in the past, she had? Returned your calls, I mean."

"Yeah, always."

"Do you know if anything was going on in her personal life where she might have wanted to leave town all of a sudden?"

"I don't think she had much of a personal life. Just her painting and coming here. She got a lot of satisfaction helping the guys here."

Crawford glanced over at three men doing a wall-size mural, then back to Sasha, and lowered his voice. "Do you know anything about her having a relationship with an inmate?"

Crawford thought he saw an inmate subtly lean in their direction.

"You mean Johnny Cotton?" she asked softly.

Crawford nodded.

"She mentioned something to me. But wouldn't tell me his name even though I had a pretty good idea who. I'm not sure why she didn't want to tell me his name. She described him as having a 'gentle soul.'" Sasha laughed. "Really? From what I understand he brutally murdered a woman."

Crawford noticed the full-body-tattoo man, sitting ten feet away, glance over.

"So that's it. She just disappeared," Crawford said. "Do you know the exact date? When you last saw her, I mean."

Estes pulled an iPhone out of her blue jean front pocket. "Yes, I can tell you. Hang on a sec," she said scrolling to the calendar. "Oh, wait. I don't need to look. I remember. It was February fifteenth. The day after Valentine's Day. Just over a month ago."

Crawford nodded. "Well, thank you, Ms. Estes. That is very helpful."

She shrugged. "That's it? That's all the questions you have?"

"Yes, I think so. If I think of any more, I know how to reach you."

"Well, you have some time 'til Henry comes back. You want an art lesson in the meantime?" She pointed at the three men doing the mural. "Or those guys need a fourth."

"Thanks, but even stick figures are a big challenge for me," Crawford said. "Maybe I'll just wander around. Check out the guys' work."

Sasha gestured expansively at the room "Be my guest."

Crawford walked over to the tattooed man, who he suspected

might have been eavesdropping. He looked at his easel, where a remarkably realistic pen-and-ink drawing of two men wielding knives — shivs, in prison parlance—were slashing at each other in the prison yard. Behind them in a tower above, a guard was looking down and aiming a rifle. Slightly behind the two prisoners, three more guards advanced cautiously toward them, pistols drawn.

Something told Crawford that the man was working from memory. Either a scene he had actually seen, or one that another prisoner had described in vivid detail.

The man turned to Crawford. "You like it?"

"Yeah, you're good, man."

The man smiled and shrugged. "But the world will never know."

"Put it on that website. Prison Art."

"I did that once," the man said. "Guy offered me five bucks for something I spent two months on. Fuck that."

Crawford studied it closely. "How much you want for it?"

"It ain't done, man."

"I can see that. When it's done, how much you want?"

"Two hundred bucks."

Crawford reached for his wallet to see what he had. Six twenties, a ten and a five.

"I'll give you a hundred now and a hundred when it's done."

The man's tattooed face lit up. "Fo' real?"

Crawford reached for the money then wondered whether inmates were allowed to take cash. "Make like I'm shaking your hand," Crawford said under his breath, as he took out the five twenties.

They shook hands, and Crawford palmed the man the hundred dollars.

Then he handed him his card. "Let me know when it's done. I'll send you the other hundred and some money to cover shipping."

The tat man smiled at him. "I don't know a lot of cops into art."

"Who said I was a cop?"

"Come on, man, cons can always tell," the man said, moving his head closer. "I'll give you a freebie."

"What's that?"

"Johnny Cotton was about as much a 'gentle soul' as Ted fuckin' Bundy."

"You knew him?"

"Yeah." He paused to search for the right words. "And to know him...was to hate him."

THIRTY-ONE

Henry Bostwick showed up a few minutes later. Crawford thanked the tattooed inmate, who had told him his name was Jack Lamb, and Sasha Estes again, then let Bostwick lead him out of the art room.

Crawford turned to Bostwick as they walked past the long row of cells. "Can I find out the exact date of Johnny Cotton's release?"

"Sure, that's easy," Bostwick said.

They walked into an office, where Bostwick asked a woman about Cotton's release date. She came back a few minutes later and said, "February fifteenth."

Crawford turned to Bostwick. "That was the last day Luna Jacobs came to work."

"No shit," Bostwick said. "That's a coincidence."

"I doubt it," Crawford said. "Can we also find out where she lived?"

"Yeah, we probably have that somewhere in the records." Bostwick asked the woman at the desk, "Can you look up the home address of one of the women who worked in the art program, please?"

"Sure, what's her name?"

"Luna Jacobs. She worked here a long time."

It turned out that information was in another office, but after a while they were able to locate it.

Luna Jacobs's address was 1522 Spruce Road in Melbourne.

"If she moved away, she probably sold the place," Bostwick said. "Or maybe she leased it and the lease expired."

"*If* she moved away," Crawford said. "Want to take a little drive, Henry?"

"Let's go," Bostwick said.

They drove in separate cars to the beige, ranch-style house on Spruce Road. There was a black Taurus in the driveway that clearly hadn't been washed in a while. It had leaves all over it and a dead palm frond on the trunk.

Bostwick pulled in behind the car. Crawford parked on the street and walked up to Bostwick.

"You don't happen to know what Luna Jacobs drove, do you?" Crawford asked.

Bostwick shook his head. "No clue."

They walked up to the front porch and Bostwick pressed the doorbell.

They waited a minute and he pressed it again.

Still nobody came.

Crawford walked up to a window, shaded his eyes, and looked in. It was a small, neat living room. All four walls were covered with art. It was like Jack Lamb's tattooed face, except covered with watercolors, charcoal sketches, pen-and-ink drawings and oils.

"I don't see anything," Crawford said. He stepped off the porch and went to the house's mailbox. It was stuffed with letters, flyers, and a few magazines and had no room left to squeeze anything else in it. He figured the mailman had given up.

Crawford walked around the side of the house as Bostwick pounded on the door again.

Crawford was looking for a window that wasn't locked but found none. He went around the back. No luck. Then he went to the last side of the house and found a window that hadn't been locked.

He pulled out a pair of vinyl gloves from his pocket and pushed the window up. It stuck stubbornly, but he finally forced it up an inch or two. Then he put both hands under it and shoved it up a foot.

The stench that came pouring out almost knocked Crawford off his feet.

THIRTY-TWO

Henry Bostwick didn't step foot into the house because of the smell. In terms of grisliness, it was a close runner-up to a homicide Crawford had caught back in New York's Hell's Kitchen. There, a body was found in an abandoned building where it had been festering for months, the man's pet dog's remains next to him. A noose hung from a rafter above what was left of the man.

The only way the authorities could confirm that the badly decomposed body was Luna Jacobs was because her sister, who lived in Orlando and drove down later that day, ID'd her. She recognized an old family ring and a watch that she and her husband had given her sister as a Christmas present a few years back.

Crawford stuck around long enough to find out from the Melbourne medical examiner what he already suspected, that there was absolutely no way to determine the cause of death. He called both Sasha Estes and Martin Sanchez and gave them the news. Sasha was particularly broken up. "Oh my God, no wonder she never called back," she said. "I feel so terrible now, never checking her house. It just never dawned on me."

Crawford consoled her as best as he could. Then he spoke to the local homicide detectives and told them what he knew, that his primary suspect in the death of Luna Jacobs was a former inmate at Malpaso named Johnny Cotton. The same day Cotton was released was almost surely the same day he killed Jacobs.

Crawford was less than impressed by the reaction of the two local detectives who caught the case. One of them introduced himself as Glen Steyer, but neither seemed interested in Crawford's conclusions on the case. In fact, they seemed like types who talked more than they listened and who assumed they were five steps ahead of him.

Crawford went to the neighbors on either side of Jacobs's house and to three houses across the street and showed them his photo of Cotton. He asked them if they had seen the man in the picture approximately a month ago. None of them had. There was nothing more he could do. He went back into Luna Jacobs's house and suggested to one of the homicide detectives that he check to see if a security camera in a nearby commercial area had picked up an image of Cotton at the time of Luna Jacobs's death. The detective thanked him, but Crawford got the sense he'd never bother.

Crawford called Ott and told him the whole story.

"You had yourself a productive day, Charlie."

"Productive, but nothing that's gonna hang Cotton."

"You want me to go pick him up?"

"For what?"

"Suspicion of murder. Four to be exact," Ott said. "Then we sit him down and good-cop/bad-cop the shit out of him. Drag a confession out of him. I don't give a fuck if it takes ten hours."

"It's a good thought," Crawford said. "But this guy is gonna be real tough to crack, guarantee you."

"Yeah, but we got him lying to us. Not telling us about his little forty-five-minute coffee break."

"Yeah? So? He just says, 'Oops, sorry, I forgot.'"

Ott was quiet for a few moments. "I don't know, there's gotta be something we can do."

"I know what you mean, but my sense is we don't take him in 'til we got him dead to rights," Crawford said. "What we definitely gotta do, though, is put a tail on him. Make sure he doesn't kill again."

"If we can find him," Ott said.

"Yeah."

"Might be a big *if*."

"I know."

Ott sighed. "Okay, man, where you now?"

"About ready to hit the road."

"You gonna be ridin' with Neil again?" Ott asked.

Shortly after Crawford and Ott teamed up, they had taken a road trip on a case, and Crawford had slipped in a CD of Neil Young's greatest hits.

"You like the whiner, huh?" Ott had asked at the time.

"*The whiner*? What are you talking about?"

"Half his songs, sound like he's whining instead of singing."

"I'm guessing you're not a fan?"

"No, I'm actually a huge fan," Ott had said with a shrug.

"So I guess you like whining, then?"

"I guess I do."

They had just listened for a while until the song "Old Man" came on.

After it was over, Ott turned to Crawford. "You know the story on that song?"

"Yeah, something about a guy at a ranch Neil bought."

"Close," Ott said. "So, Neil, at the tender age of twenty-four bought this ranch and inherited this guy as its caretaker. He's the old man in the song. I think the guy was, max, forty years old."

They listened to a few more songs as they motored north on the turnpike.

Then came Young's "Heart of Gold."

"What's his obsession with age, anyway?" Ott asked.

"You mean the refrain?"

"Yeah, '*...and I'm gettin' old.*' I mean, dude was twenty-seven when he wrote that. Fuck, when I was twenty-seven, I'd just started shaving."

THIRTY-THREE

The meeting with the three people from the Board of Realtors was scheduled to take place in Norm Rutledge's office. Crawford swung by Ott's cubicle about ten minutes late.

"We really don't need this bullshit," Crawford mumbled.

"I hear you," Ott said. "Not with Cotton on the loose."

They went into Rutledge's office. Two men and a woman were waiting for them. The woman he knew well. Surprise, surprise, it was none other than Rose Clarke.

Crawford smiled and nodded at Rose, who smiled back.

Rutledge made an ostentatious show of looking at this watch and casting a frown at Crawford.

"Sorry we're late," Crawford said.

Rutledge looked at one of the men, then gestured at his detectives. "So, this is Detective Crawford and Detective Ott," he said. "And fellas, this is Dennis Shaw, head of the Board of Realtors, and David Crane and—I think you know—Ms. Clarke."

A lot of nodding, shaking hands, and nice to meet you's. Just for the hell of it, Crawford shook Rose's hand.

"This is a first," Rose said under her breath.

Crawford smiled.

Rutledge had brought extra chairs into his office for the meeting. They all sat down. "All right," he said. "At this point I'm just going to turn the meeting over to Mr. Shaw."

Shaw, a balding man with a drooping blue bow tie, nodded at Rutledge. "Thank you. So, gentlemen, and Rose, we all know why we're here today. We've got a crisis of epic proportions in Palm Beach. Customers who are canceling appointments, agents who are fearing for their lives, and a market which right now is dead in the water. And because of that we are here now to ask you what you're doing about it. More specifically, when you're going to catch the murderer."

Crawford glanced at Ott, then Rutledge, then Shaw. "Well, Mr. Shaw, of course there's no answer to that. My partner and I have been focused exclusively on the case since Mimi Taylor's murder as have numerous crime scene techs and many others."

"I can also volunteer this," Rutledge said. "In the four years that Detective Crawford and Detective Ott have led our homicide division, they have solved every case they have worked on."

"Thank you, Chief, Detective Crawford. That's all very reassuring, but all we care about is the last two. The ones that involve our slain agents."

"I understand that, Mr. Shaw," Crawford said, "and at this point we have a number of solid suspects."

"Well, if you do," Shaw said, "why don't you go and arrest the one who did it and make our community safe again?"

Crawford glanced over at Ott. "The reason is," Ott said, "we don't have enough evidence to do that. We're confident we'll get to that point, but we haven't gotten there yet."

Everyone had spoken except Rose. "I'm in a funny position here," she said, "because on one hand I represent the board, but on the other hand Detective Crawford and Detective Ott are good friends of mine. I know very well how professional they always are and how hard they work at their jobs" —she caught Crawford's eye, then Ott's

— "and I'm just hoping you guys are close to taking someone in. I've never seen it this bad out there."

Crawford and Ott both nodded.

Crane, a man with a double chin and sweat on his forehead, tapped his fingers on Rutledge's desk. "Rose, that nice little declaration of support for the detectives is all very good, but is it possible that it is motivated by personal feelings?"

Everybody in the office knew what he meant.

Rose gave him a look like she wanted to give him a toe to the nuts. Her mouth opened as if she were ready to light into him. But—just like that—she changed her expression and smiled ear to ear. "Thank you, David, but everyone here except for you, and possibly Chief Rutledge, knows me well enough to know that I would never let a personal friendship get in the way of doing my job."

"Well," Shaw said to Crawford, "I don't think we need to belabor this. We've expressed our feelings, and I just hope you're not treating our concerns lightly."

"Mr. Shaw, let me say this," Rutledge said, his hands joined as if in prayer, "we recognize that the real estate industry is one of the primary engines of commerce in Palm Beach and, because of that, it's critical that we work together harmoniously."

Crawford suppressed a groan, hearing for the umpteenth time the world-champion suck-up side of Rutledge.

With nothing left to be said, everyone shook hands again and said their goodbyes. Rose, however, who could get away with whatever she wanted since she was indisputably the best in the business, gave Ott a kiss on the cheek and Crawford a kiss on the lips and made sure David Crane saw it.

THIRTY-FOUR

"Fucking asshole," Rose said under her breath, referring to her colleague David Crane.

Shaw and Crane had left Rutledge's office and Rose, Crawford and Ott were walking back to Crawford's office.

"Why, Rose," Crawford said, his hand covering his mouth in faux shock, "that's so unladylike of you."

"Yeah, well, that douchebag deserves it."

"Know what I always say?" Ott said.

"What's that?" Rose asked.

"Don't ever trust a guy in a blue bow tie."

"Or any bow tie," Rose said.

Ott bumped fists with her as they sat in Crawford's office.

Crawford put a foot up on his desk. Then Ott did. Then Rose did.

All three laughed.

Rose leaned forward. "So, *are* you close?"

"You know we can't go into specifics," Crawford said. "But I hope so."

Rose sighed. "That makes two of us."

Crawford's cell phone rang. He looked down at the display. It was Dominica.

He looked up at Rose. "Your friend Dominica."

"Give her my love."

Crawford clicked on. "Rose says to give you her love."

"What, are you two having a nooner or something?"

"Very funny. What's up?"

"It's a positive match," Dominica said. "One of those prints from the Kawama house kitchen matched Johnny Cotton's."

Crawford's leg slid off his desk, and he sat upright. "You're kidding."

"Nope. No question about it."

He turned to Ott. "Positive ID on Cotton with the fingerprints at the Kawama house."

Ott stood. "Let's go get the bastard."

Crawford was looking at Rose as he spoke into the phone. "Thanks, you're my hero."

Rose shrugged. "What did I do?"

I meant Dominica, Crawford mouthed.

"Nice," Dominica said in his ear. "You can't tell us apart now."

"It's a little confusing," he said.

"Okay, well, I gotta go," Dominica said. "You and Rose have fun."

"It's business," Crawford said.

"Yeah, your favorite kind, monkey business." She hung up.

Crawford stood and smiled at Rose. "Okay, we gotta run."

She cocked her head. "Sure you're straight on who I am?"

"Very funny. And, yes, I'm sure."

Ott had called Luxury Landscaping to find out where Johnny Cotton's crew was working. It was either at a house on Seminole or Emerald, according to the woman answering the company phone.

It turned out to be Seminole. Ott drove them to the address and found three cars parked there. One of them, a white Caprice, looked familiar to Crawford. Then he realized it was the same car one of the Melbourne homicide cops was driving.

"Might have a clusterfuck here," Crawford warned.

"What do you mean?" Ott asked as they exited the car.

Crawford pointed at the Caprice. "I think that's a guy from Melbourne PD."

"Oh, shit," Ott said as they walked around the house to the backyard.

Crawford groaned when he saw the Melbourne homicide detective Glen Steyer getting in Johnny Cotton's face and, no doubt, talking tough. The other three landscapers were off in a corner of the backyard, blowing leaves and pruning trees, trying not to stare but doing a poor job of it.

Crawford and Ott walked up to Steyer, who glanced over at them. "Hey, Glen, what are you doing down here?"

"What do you think? Asking my suspect here a few questions."

"And what do you think of his answers?"

Steyer gave a sarcastic laugh. "He says he has no idea where Luna Jacobs lived. That he never saw her except when he was in art class at Malpaso."

"Did you expect him to say he went to her house on Spruce Road and strangled her?"

"Think this shit is funny?" Steyer said.

"No, but I think you driving down here was a big waste of time," Crawford said. "Where'd he say he went after he got out of Malpaso?"

"Some restaurant. Had himself a nice steak dinner."

At that moment, a woman came out of a door in the back of the house; her eyes went from cop to cop to cop to ex-con. "What's going on back here? Who are all you people?"

"We're police, ma'am. Palm Beach Police Department," Crawford said. "We won't be here long."

"Police? Why?"

Ott gave her his best smile in an attempt to appease her. "It relates to a case of ours, ma'am."

She wasn't appeased. "Well, make it quick. I'm about to have friends over for lunch."

The three cops nodded, and the woman walked away.

Glen Steyer took a step toward Johnny Cotton. "I'm taking you in."

"For what?" Cotton shot back.

"Suspicion of murder."

Crawford moved closer to Steyer and lowered his voice. "Don't be an idiot, Glen, you got nothin'." Before the detective could speak, Crawford turned to Cotton. "What were you doing at 207 Kawama Road the other night?"

"I wasn't at 207 Kawama Road the other night," Cotton said.

"Then how come a fingerprint of yours was there?"

Cotton cocked his head. "Since when do fingerprints have time stamps on them? I probably went there for an open house or something."

Ott laughed. "You make it a habit of going to open houses in Palm Beach?"

"Matter of fact, I do. You got a problem with that, Detective? There any law says I can't go to open houses here?"

Ott took a step closer to Cotton. "Don't fuck with us, Cotton. What were you doing there?"

Cotton shrugged. "Just seeing how the other half lives. Hey, you never know when you're gonna hit the lotto. I want to be ready to spend my millions when my ship comes in."

Ott glanced at Crawford then back to Cotton. "Guess you think you're a pretty slick act, don't you?"

"I just think I'm a simple landscaper trying to do my job," he said. "But you cops keep coming around, harassing the shit out of me."

Crawford motioned to Ott to step away from Cotton, out of earshot.

Glen Steyer took a step toward them.

Crawford put up a hand. "Not you."

Steyer looked like his feelings were hurt as Crawford and Ott retreated.

"We ain't got shit here, you know," Crawford said quietly.

"Yeah, but talk about circumstantial," Ott said. "I mean, the fact that he was working a few doors down from where Mimi Taylor got killed. The fact that he got out of prison the same day the art teacher got killed. His fingerprints at the house where Holly Pine got assaulted."

Crawford pondered for a second then shook his head. "Prosecutor wouldn't touch it. Not enough meat for a jury."

"You don't think so?"

Crawford shook his head.

Ott sighed then muttered, "Motherfucker."

Crawford turned and went over to Glen Steyer. "You can take him in, but he'll be out in five minutes."

Steyer was silent. He'd clearly reached the same conclusion.

Crawford turned to Cotton. "Sorry to bother you, Johnny. You can go back to your weeds."

THIRTY-FIVE

Before the day was over, Crawford and Ott, not to mention the Palm Beach Police Department, were sued for a million dollars.

What happened was the owner of the house on Seminole Avenue called up Luxury Landscaping and complained that they had in their employ someone who was either a criminal or a "person of interest." (She actually used that phrase, apparently being a *CSI* or *Law & Order* fan.) The woman was then connected to the manager, who, in order not to lose a customer, said he'd immediately take the man off the job. The manager then drove over to the house on Seminole and, on the spot, fired Johnny Cotton.

Cotton went straight to a law firm, his contention being that he was constantly being harassed and that, because of certain cops' actions, had lost his job. An ambitious young lawyer decided to take the case. He arrived at the million-dollar lawsuit figure by computing what Johnny Cotton would lose in wages if he never worked again, plus court costs. Not only that, he was well aware of the fact that the town of Palm Beach had a lot of money in its coffers.

So, by the end of the day, Crawford and Ott had both been served.

Crawford shook his head. "This guy doesn't know when to quit," he said to Ott, who was sitting in his office.

Crawford heard the unmistakable thudding footsteps of Norm Rutledge getting closer. "Oh, fuck."

And then, there he was in all his sartorial splendor. A shiny brown suit from either the dacron or rayon family, paired with a resplendent orange-and-avocado-green tie.

"What the fuck is going on?" Rutledge bellowed, his eyes going from Crawford to Ott.

"That bullshit lawsuit, you mean?" Crawford asked.

"Yeah, of course that's what I mean. And lemme tell ya, the mayor doesn't think it's bullshit. He ran it by the town attorney, who thinks the guy's got a case."

"Doesn't matter," Crawford said. "It'll go away when we take the guy in."

"And just when is that gonna happen?"

"Soon."

Rutledge never sat down when he stopped by on his surprise visits. He just paced, dropped his bombs, and left.

"And there's another thing." Rutledge apparently had multiple warheads.

"What's that?" Ott asked, his tone leery.

"You're off the hook on this one, Ott," Rutledge said, turning to Crawford with a glare. "What's with that real estate agent who got assaulted? Asking you to go with her 'cause she had a customer she was worried about?"

"Where'd you hear that?" Crawford asked

"Where do you think?" Rutledge said. "It seems we didn't impress Shaw and Crane of the Board of Realtors. They don't think we're doing everything in our power to get the killer. That guy Shaw said that the local news might want to know how we" —his eyes drilling into Crawford's— "meaning *you*, failed to protect a woman who specifically requested help."

"That's such bullshit," Ott leapt to Crawford's defense. "We all agreed there was no way in hell we could run around to every house showing without hiring a hundred new guys."

"That seems to be your mantra these days, Ott. Bullshit this, bullshit that." Rutledge turned back to Crawford. "I suggest you talk to that guy Shaw. Try to appease him."

"What do you want me to do, Norm? Get down on my hands and knees and beg him not to go to the media?" Crawford asked.

"Actually, that's the first good idea you've had all week," Rutledge said. "You don't seem to be taking this seriously enough for what it can do to us—i.e., give us a huge black eye. How 'bout getting a little proactive, head this thing off at the pass."

Crawford did his variation on counting to ten, which he had used in the past with Rutledge. He glanced out his window and counted the birds sitting on a limb of a big banyan tree.

Then he shot Rutledge a look. "Okay, Norm," he said. "Duly noted."

"What the hell's that mean?"

"I'll do something about it. What the hell else do you want me to say?"

Rutledge nodded, smiled, and headed to the door. "In case I haven't made myself clear, Crawford, that's an order."

He walked out without another word.

Crawford took out his cell phone and started dialing.

"Who you calling?"

"Rose."

She answered. "Hello, Charlie."

"We need to talk. How 'bout lunch?"

"You're on."

They decided on a place and time and Crawford clicked off.

"Let me guess," Ott said. "You're going to get her to exercise her feminine wiles to, as Rutledge would say, 'head this off at the pass.'"

Crawford nodded. "Yeah, I really don't need the local press up my ass. Remember how much it distracted us on Ward Jaynes," he said, referring to their first case together in Palm Beach.

"Yeah, sure do. Every time they stuck their noses in, we made news we didn't wanna make."

Crawford nodded. "I gotta get this behind us so we can quit fuckin' around and concentrate on Cotton."

"Amen."

CRAWFORD HAD TWO GO-TO'S. ONE, OF COURSE, WAS MOOKIE'S, the cop bar in a seedy part of West Palm Beach, where no self-respecting Palm Beach cop would ever think to plop his ass down on a barstool. The other was Green's Pharmacy, which, despite the name, served the best hamburgers in Palm Beach, not to mention six or seven things on its breakfast menu, which—as the cliché goes—were *to die for*.

He was on his way to Green's at 151 North County Road. It wasn't far from the station, but there were a few rights and lefts on the way there. And every time he made a turn, he noticed a small black Japanese car—he wasn't sure whether it was a Toyota or a Honda—made the same turn. So, he pulled over to the side, and, sure enough, the little black car pulled over to the side fifty feet behind him. After a few moments, he accelerated, and the little black car accelerated. He thought about doing a U-turn to get a look at the driver but vetoed it because the car's windshield was tinted coal-mine black; no doubt the side windows would be too.

As he approached Green's, he pulled into a metered space without hitting his blinker and glanced over at the little black car. It kept going straight; as he suspected, its side windows were as black as its rear window. He wondered how the driver could see the road, or anything else for that matter.

He walked into Green's as he watched the car continue up North County.

Rose was at one end of the luncheonette, chatting up a waitress named Millie.

The waitress winked at him as he approached. "Hey, lover boy."

Crawford was in a cranky mood. Mainly because of Norm Rutledge but also because of the sudden appearance of the mysterious Japanese car. "Why do you call me that?" he asked Millie wearily.

"Oh, you know," she said.

"No, I don't know."

"Hello, lover boy," Rose chimed in.

Crawford shook his head and scowled. "How 'bout Charlie?" he fumed. "That's my name. Charlie."

Millie smiled and glanced back at Rose. "The lo-cal platter?"

Rose nodded. "Pretty predictable, huh?"

Millie looked at Crawford. "I'm guessing a bacon cheeseburger and a mushroom burger?"

He nodded. "Yup."

"Why don't you get that all in one?" Rose asked.

"I'll tell you why. Because I'm a growing boy, and I need my three thousand calories a day."

"Three? You're supposed to only have two thousand."

"What's a thousand measly calories?"

Rose nodded. "Okay, Charlie, what is it you need to know?"

"I need to know a lot, but that's not what I need most," Crawford said. "I need you to rein in that dipshit Shaw."

"What did he do now?"

"It's not what he did, it's what he's threatening to do," Crawford said. "Did you hear about Holly Pine asking me to—"

"Go along with her on a showing?" Rose cut in.

"Yes, exactly. Then what happened, unfortunately happened. So Shaw, who apparently thinks me and Ott are sitting on our hands, threatened to go to the *Post* and tell them about the incident. He seems to think that threats will get us to work harder. Like if we don't have the killer in jail five minutes from now—"

Rose put a hand on Crawford's arm. "I can get him to chill."

"You sure?"

"Yes, or at least buy you some time," Rose said. "He prides himself on being a 'man of action' and sometimes does stuff before thinking it through. I'll take care of it."

Crawford put his hand on hers. "Thanks, I appreciate it. I really don't need that distraction."

He looked out the window onto North County Road and saw the little black Japanese car double-parked in front of the front door of Green's. His first instinct was to run outside and confront whoever it was.

Rose looked to where he was still looking. "What are you looking at?"

He kept his eyes on the car. "A guy who I think's been following me."

"You mean, like a tail?"

He glanced at Rose and chuckled. "Yeah, exactly."

"Well, why don't you run the plate, find out who it is?"

"I love it when you talk cop-talk."

She leaned across the table and kissed his cheek.

Crawford pulled out his iPhone and scrolled down to where he had already written down the license plate number. "Just for the record, it's Florida number REM441."

Rose smiled. "Oh, you already got it?"

Crawford nodded. "Yeah, despite what your compadre Dennis Shaw thinks, I been doin' this a while."

THIRTY-SIX

Crawford was not surprised to find that the license plate belonged to one John R. Cotton. He knew that if he had chased after him, he probably wouldn't have caught him. In addition to running the plate with the DMV, he asked for and received Cotton's latest home address. He lived in Lake Worth. Crawford decided to pay him an immediate visit.

He filled in Ott, and together they headed down to the town some called Lake Worthless. Cotton's house was on a street by the name of Royal Palm Drive. The street name was a lot fancier than the small ranch with yellow shutters, one of which was hanging on for dear life. The house didn't have a garage, and there was no car in the driveway.

Ott pulled in the driveway and Crawford noticed something on the yellow front door.

He and Ott got out of the Crown Vic. "Two shades of yellow," Ott said. "Not a good look."

He was right. The shutters were bright yellow and the door a more neon yellow. As they approached the front door, Crawford could see there was a note scotch-taped to it. It said in neat penmanship:

Dear Detective Crawford and sidekick (didn't catch your name),

Sorry, I missed you boys and sorry I had to sue you but you were turning into real pains in the ass, if you'll excuse my French. Anyway, I had to move since you and that genius from Melbourne were getting too close for comfort. Good luck trying to catch me as I think you'll find I'm slippery as an eel.

Sincerely,

John Reynolds Cotton the third

"What the fuck?" Ott said, as Crawford noticed a man cross the street walking toward them.

"Like he's playing a little cat and mouse game," Crawford said, as the man walked up the path of Cotton's house. Or former house, it would seem.

"You lookin' for him?" the man asked.

Crawford nodded. "Yeah, we are. We're Palm Beach Police."

"He just moved out this morning," the man said. "Good riddance, I say."

"Why?" Ott asked. "What did he do?"

"Shot squirrels with an automatic pistol for one thing," he said. "I called the Lake Worth cops but they never came. Had hookers over, for another."

Crawford put his hand over his eyes to shade them from the sun. "How do you know they were hookers?"

"Everybody knows what hookers look like," the man said. "I'm Wesley, by the way."

"Well, thank you for the information, Wesley," Crawford said. "You said he moved out, did a moving van come?"

"Nah, just a big pickup. He and another guy filled it up, took it away, and came back later and took another load."

Ott glanced over at Crawford. "So he can't have moved too far away."

Crawford nodded. "The pickup...can you describe it? Did it say anything on it?"

Wesley shook his head. "No, just a white Ford 150. Florida plates, I'm pretty sure. Nothing really stood out about it."

"Do you remember anything at all about it that caught your attention?" Crawford asked.

Wesley thought for a second. "Um, it had a gun rack but no gun. And a red Marines decal."

"Where was the decal?"

"Rear window."

"Anything else?"

"Couple dents on the passenger side."

"Where?"

"Down low on the door, I think."

"That it?"

"All I 'member."

"Thanks," Crawford said. "That helps."

"And after these two took off with the first load, how much later did they come back?" Ott asked.

"I'd say an hour and a half."

"How do you know this?"

"'Cause I just hang out on my porch all day long and watch shit." Wesley chuckled. "Pretty exciting life."

Crawford smiled. "And how long would you guess it would take them to unload the truck?"

"An hour, maybe a little more."

Crawford nodded.

"So, he wasn't the dream neighbor?" Ott said.

"Not unless your idea of a dream neighbor is a guy shooting guns, doin' hookers, and playing loud music."

Crawford and Ott nodded. "Well, thank you for the information," Crawford said, reaching for his wallet. "If he comes back or you see him anywhere, give me a call right away, will you?"

He handed Wesley a card.

"You got it," Wesley said. "What'd he do, anyway?"

"We don't know for sure," Crawford said. "It's important we find him, though."

"Okay, well, good luck." Wesley turned and walked away.

"Shooting squirrels with an automatic," Ott said. "Can you imagine if someone did that in Palm Beach?"

"There'd be a SWAT team there in five minutes."

Ott nodded. "What do we do now?"

Crawford shrugged. "Find the guy. Seems like he couldn't have moved more than fifteen, twenty minutes from here. Half hour max. We figure out a perimeter and start looking."

Ott groaned. "Fuuu-ck. That's a big area, man."

"You got a better idea?" Crawford said. "We get Rutledge to requisition a bunch of uniforms to find a person of interest who's driving a little black car and a guy driving a white Ford 150 with dents, a Marine decal and an empty gun rack?"

"Yeah, but there must be hundreds of little black shitboxes and white Ford 150's within a fifteen-minute radius of here."

"Yeah, but only one little black shitbox with the plate REM441." Crawford started walking toward the Crown Vic. "Come on, let's start cruising."

THEY DIDN'T HAVE ANY LUCK CRISSCROSSING THE SECTION OF Lake Worth that they covered but had better luck with Norm Rutledge.

Crawford spent ten minutes filling Rutledge in on John Reynolds Cotton III.

"It's like the guy's playing with you," Rutledge said.

Crawford didn't disagree.

"I'll let you have every uniform in the department." Which was thirty-one. "In case I haven't made it clear, this is about the highest priority case we've ever had."

"You made it clear. I just wasn't sure how many you could spare," Crawford said. "I'll get you a map that shows the area they need to cover, then you can deploy 'em. How's that?"

Crawford knew Rutledge was pretty decent at organization. Maybe his best skill. Maybe his only one.

"All right," Rutledge said. "Get that map to me as soon as you can. I'll do a grid."

"You'll have it in fifteen minutes."

"And I'll get the guys on the streets in an hour."

THE FIRST THING JOHNNY COTTON DID AFTER FOLLOWING Crawford around Palm Beach and watching him walk out of Green's Pharmacy with the hot blonde was swap the black Honda's license plate for one from another car in the Walmart parking lot. Took him about thirty seconds to exchange the two. He picked a car that looked very similar to his, a black Corolla with darkened windows and tires that were a few hundred miles from being completely bald. The second thing he did was buy 200 rounds of 115 grain FMJ 9mm ammo for his Glock. And it wasn't because his new neighborhood had a lot more squirrels than his old one.

THIRTY-SEVEN

THEY HAD PLENTY OF MANPOWER ON THE STREETS OF LAKE Worth and neighboring Lake Clarke Shores, Palm Springs, Lantana, Greenacres, and West Palm Beach. Crawford had even gotten the okay to use the PBPD helicopter to perform visual sweeps of the streets. Still, it was a lot of area to cover, and Crawford was sure that Johnny Cotton would be lying low and definitely not joyriding around town.

And the guy in the white pickup wouldn't be making himself easy to find.

In the meantime, Crawford and Ott had split up and gone back to Palm Beach. They were going around to the various real estate agencies with big blowups of the photo of Cotton, which they left behind, while urging agents to insist on meeting at their office if an unfamiliar man called and asked to see a house. In case they recognized Cotton from the photo, the agent should try to stall him and call the police right away.

So far, all the agents seemed to be taking their warning seriously, though none had apparently ever seen Cotton before.

One job that Crawford had pawned off on Ott was a call to Stark

Stabler. It was partly motivated by the fact that Stabler had also threatened to sue Crawford, Ott, and the Palm Beach Police Department for harassment and, in so many words, accusing him of murder. The last thing Crawford needed was another frivolous suit in addition to Johnny Cotton's, never mind the threatened leak to the newspaper by Dennis Shaw about the Holly Pine incident.

Crawford got a call from Ott between Realtor visits.

"Guy wasn't very gracious in accepting my apology," Ott said, referring to his recent call to Stabler.

"Why, what did he say?"

"'Bout time you jokers figured out I was innocent. You don't go around harassing a man who's on the Board of Governors of the Poinciana Club and past president of the Toastmasters Club.'"

"'Jokers'?"

"Yeah."

"So Troy Price calls us 'clowns' and Stark Stabler calls us 'jokers.' Which is it?"

Ott chuckled. "Personally, I prefer jokers. It's got a little more...I don't know, substance to it."

Crawford laughed. "Meantime, I got something more on Johnny Cotton. Got a psych profile from Malpaso Correctional. My friend the assistant warden emailed it to me."

"What's it say?"

"Buckle your seat belt," Crawford said. "So, according to some shrink somewhere along the way, Cotton apparently went to a Catholic school when he was a kid. Claimed that when he was eight years old he got molested by a nun."

"A nun? That's a first. I mean priests, yeah, okay, but I never heard of a nun before."

"Thing is, we have no idea any of this really happened," Crawford said. "All that matters is Cotton said it did. Guy told the prison people a lotta stuff, and some of the details are pretty scary."

"Like what else?"

"Married his high school sweetheart at age eighteen. Came home from work one day, about six months after they got married, and found his bride in bed with his brother."

"Shit, man, so far he's got to have a pretty high opinion of the opposite sex."

"Exactly the point," Crawford said. "So he got divorced, and after that it looks like he had himself a pretty steady diet of strippers and hookers. One of them charged him with throwing a frying pan full of scalding bacon grease on her ass when she was in bed."

"Jesus, wonder what she did to deserve that."

"No clue. Another thing, when he was a kid, he went around with a BB gun, shooting alley cats and stray dogs. Pulling the wings off of butterflies, fun shit like that."

"Normal kid stuff, huh?" Ott said, shaking his head. "What a sick fuck. Sounds like he basically just ratcheted up everything later on. Instead of a BB gun, a Glock; instead of throwing grease, strangling 'em."

"Exactly what I was thinking. We gotta get this guy, Mort."

"We will."

"I mean before he goes after someone else," Crawford said. "No telling how many women he's killed. Like that art teacher, Luna Jacobs. No proof it was him, but it was him."

Crawford's call waiting clicked in. "Got an incoming," he said. "Stay there." He clicked over. "Hello, this is Crawford."

"Hey, Charlie, it's Bob Shepley" —a Palm Beach uniform cop— "I just made that black Corolla you been looking for. Plate number REM441, right?"

"Yeah, that's it. Where are you?"

"Mid-block Dolphin Circle, Palm Springs."

"Hang on," Crawford said, programming the street name into his GPS. "You're driving an unmarked, right?"

"Yup."

"All right, stay close but not too close, and be careful," Crawford said, stepping on the accelerator. "The guy's armed and extremely dangerous. Put your phone on speaker and keep giving me locations. Me and Ott are on our way."

"Roger that," Shepley said.

Crawford clicked back to Ott. "All right, here we go," he said. "Cotton's car sighted at Dolphin Circle, Palm Springs. Bob Shepley's on him, he'll keep us apprised of where he goes next."

"Roger that," Ott said. "I just GPSed that location."

"We don't need to get anyone else on it. Between you, me and Shep, we oughta be enough to take him down."

"You don't want to call in that helicopter maybe?"

"Nah, what I'm afraid of is a chase. Anything could happen. Don't want any civilian casualties."

"I hear you. I'm about ten minutes away."

Crawford heard the sudden roar of Ott's Crown Vic Police Interceptor engine through his cell phone. Ott yearned for any opportunity to drive like a bat out of hell.

"Put your phone on speaker. I got Shep on it too. He'll tell us where he is. You hear me all right, Shep?"

"Loud and clear," Shepley said. "He just turned onto Luzon Avenue."

"Ideally, we want to triangulate him," Crawford said. "Come at him from three different directions, rather than all from the same one."

"All right, Charlie, you quarterback it and I'll just stay behind him," Shepley said. "I just worry about him making me."

"Yeah, me, too," Crawford said. "But we're gonna be there soon."

Shepley gave them a few more street names and reported that the black Corolla seemed to be driving randomly and without a destination.

"Where you now, Mort?" Crawford asked as his cell phone rang.

He looked down and saw it was Rose. He let it go to voice mail.

"Coming at him from the east," Ott said.

"Good. I'm a block away, coming from the west," Crawford said, reaching in the back seat for a bullhorn.

"Half a block behind him now," Shepley said.

"All right, let's take him," Crawford said just as the black car came into view up ahead.

"Roger that," Shepley said.

"I got him," Ott said, and he pulled out of a side street, steered in front of the Corolla and jammed on his brakes. He raised his gun and pointed it at the Corolla's windshield.

Crawford screeched to a stop twenty-feet from the driver's door and quickly raised the bullhorn. "All right, Cotton, out of the car, hands in the air, flat on the pavement."

Shepley had gotten out of his car, opened his door and was positioned behind it, his pistol pointed at the driver's side of the Corolla.

Ott had slid down in his seat, gun aimed at the Corolla, waiting.

There was no movement from the Corolla.

"Get the hell out of that car!" Crawford shouted into the bullhorn.

The Corolla's door opened a crack, then all the way.

"All right, down on the pavement," Crawford said.

A blonde woman slid out and went facedown on the pavement.

The three cops approached her, guns pointed.

"Who are you?" Crawford asked, ten feet away.

"Barbara," the woman said.

"Where's Cotton?"

"Who?"

"Johnny Cotton," Crawford said.

"I don't know who that is," Barbara said. "Why are you doing this to me?"

By now Crawford knew she was innocent.

"Okay, ma'am. You can get up," he said as he heard his cell phone ring again.

Ott went to the passenger side door, opened it, and slid inside. He found what he was looking for in the console. "Her plate number is actually AS7313," he said to Crawford, reading from her registration.

Crawford shook his head and frowned. He slipped his Sig Sauer into his shoulder holster. Then to Barbara, "You have no idea who Johnny Cotton is?"

"Never heard of him."

"Go 'round and look at the license plate number," Crawford pointed to the rear of the car, "and tell me if it's yours or not."

She looked at him uncertainly. "Okay to—"

"Yes, go ahead."

She walked back to the rear of the car, looked at her plate, then shook her head. "That's not mine. Like he said, mine starts with A-S. Don't know what's after that."

"Give us your full name, address and phone number, please," Crawford said.

She did.

"We're sorry this happened," Crawford said. "We're looking for a car like yours with that license plate, but obviously someone switched them."

The woman shrugged. "Who would do that?"

A man with a long list of homicides on his resume, Crawford chose not to say.

THIRTY-EIGHT

Crawford, Ott, and Bob Shepley were seated at the Dunkin' Donuts on South Congress Avenue in Lake Worth.

"Yet another person who can sue us," Ott said referring to the woman named Barbara.

"Not funny," Crawford said, taking a sip of his extra-dark, one-sugar coffee.

"So, you think Cotton's using her plates?" Shepley asked.

"Yup," Crawford said. "But by now he could have swapped 'em again or gotten another car."

"Or just garaged it, staying inside 'til we give up," Ott said.

"We need to take his picture around," Crawford said. "Door-to-door."

"Christ, you're talking thousands of houses," Ott said.

"You got a better way?"

Ott stuffed half a donut with pink sprinkles in his mouth and shrugged. "I don't. It's just...even if we knock on the door of the house he's in, he's not gonna answer."

"Yeah, I know," Crawford said. "Ideally what we're looking for is a neighbor who recognizes him. Says to us, 'Oh yeah, guy just moved in next door.'"

Ott nodded and took a sip of coffee.

"When you started out in Cleveland, wasn't it all about wearing out shoe leather? Getting leads talking to people?"

Ott nodded grudgingly. "Yeah, good ol' beat cop days. Don't remind me."

"But it got the job done, right?"

Ott shrugged. "Yeah, it did."

"And you got your guy?"

Ott shrugged again. "Once in a while."

"Well, there you go."

Shepley leaned back in his orange plastic chair. "Maybe you could borrow guys from West Palm. Seeing how this is their turf. You're tight with Red Noland, right?"

Crawford nodded. "That's a good idea."

He looked down and saw he had three voice mails. Two from Rose and one from Norm Rutledge. He wanted to talk to Rose more than Rutledge but figured he'd better see what the chief wanted. Plus, he could take the opportunity to suggest that Rutledge call the West Palm police chief to borrow some men. Red Noland was high up but wasn't the chief. It was better to go chief to chief.

"Okay, I'm gonna head back to the station," Crawford said, standing. Then to Ott, "Rutledge called. I don't know what he wanted."

"Probably to say he tracked down Cotton single-handedly."

"Yeah," Crawford said. "Hey, Shep, thanks for helping out; sorry it was a false alarm."

Shepley nodded. "Thanks for the coffee and good luck with this thing. I'll keep pounding the pavement."

"Appreciate it," Crawford said. Then to Ott, "Later."

ROSE HAD JUST GOTTEN A CALL FROM VERA, UNOFFICIALLY THE oldest cleaning lady in Palm Beach. Still going strong in her mid-seventies. Vera told her the water was running in an upstairs bedroom at Rose's listing on Angler. Rose started to tell her how to fix it but decided that was a job well above Vera's pay grade. She thanked her and started to call Leon the plumber. Then she thought, *Screw it, so he can charge me a hundred fifty bucks for ten minutes worth of work?* She'd do it herself.

And while she was at it, she decided to "make her rounds." That was what she called something she did religiously every week, go from the north end of the island to the south end giving her fifteen listings their weekly checkup. Making sure the windows didn't need to be cleaned, or a dead stinkbug hadn't breathed its last atop a bathroom vanity, or a palm frond hadn't fallen on the driveway. It was normally a pretty quick process. Just a fast walk-through of a house, guesthouse, and the property. Usually she didn't need to do a thing because her chosen landscapers and cleaning people had already performed their appointed tasks. Rose didn't know of any other agent who put as much house-care time into their routine as her, which was probably part of the reason she was the only agent who averaged more than $250 million in annual sales.

Part of her success was doing everything she possibly could to make a house look the best it possibly could. In ninety percent of the cases, she recommended a buyer make certain improvements to enhance the house's desirability and salability. Sometimes, if a job was too big for Vera, that meant bringing in her "Brazilian SWAT team"—five young cleaning women who bustled around a house, yakking away in Portuguese for a few hours, then left it spotless and gleaming. For other houses, Rose often had a long list of things she urged a seller to remedy. Sometimes it could get costly, too. Replacing tired, outdated kitchen cabinets or tearing up carpets stained by countless cats, dogs, and an exotic bird or two. Relandscaping the front of a house frequently made her list. She insisted that a potential buyer's initial impression was almost as important as the appearance of the kitchen and master bathroom. If a buyer frowned as they drove in the front driveway or even had a neutral response, it made selling the house much more difficult. It was like starting in a hole and having to climb out of it.

She had hastily calculated the risk that the killer might be cruising the streets of Palm Beach looking for his next victim and decided the odds were, worst case, so minimal as to be virtually nonexistent. One in a million, or thereabouts, especially given the fact that the cops were out in force, making Palm Beach look like it was a police state. Her guess was that the killer had fled and was no longer within a hundred miles of her beloved little island right now. She even had a theory, which she had called Charlie Crawford about and was eager to run by him. It was based on an article in the *Daily Mail*—okay, maybe not the most reliable paper around—about a serial killer who had hit Savannah a year ago, then Jacksonville six months back. She theorized that the same man, working his way south, had gone on to terrorize Palm Beach next but, because it was a small, island town, had since moved on. Her guess was he was now on his way down to Miami, maybe the Keys.

Plus, she had recently taken the COBRA self-defense course, could clean and jerk a hundred fifty pounds and could outrun most twenty-five-year-old men, so what guy in his right mind would ever mess with her? Not only that, she had a can of high-powered pepper spray that would drop a man to his knees and make him cry out for mercy.

Combine that with how restless she had become. And bored. She didn't play tennis or garden or belong to a book club...selling houses was all she knew. She'd had seven clients cancel showings, and it was driving her crazy. Because if she couldn't show, she couldn't sell. And selling was her lifeblood, the same way catching killers was Charlie's.

Speaking of Charlie...she wondered why hadn't he called her back. She really wanted to share her killer theory with him.

Oh, well, he'll check in when he can, she thought as she walked out of her office and got into her Jag, headed to her listing on Indian

Road. Her listings came in all shapes, sizes and conditions. Several looked as though they had been decorated by a team of top interior designers, several others were vacant, some looked as if no one had spent a dime on them in the last twenty years. But they all had one thing in common: they were in Palm Beach. And whether the house was a teardown or exquisitely maintained and furnished, it was sure to find a buyer sooner or later. Homeowners hired Rose Clarke because she had a reputation for hastening that process.

She drove up North Ocean Boulevard, almost to the end of the island, and took a left onto Indian. She got out, walked up to the porch and unlocked the door of the white-brick colonial.

She went through the house quickly and efficiently. No stinkbugs, no palm fronds in the driveway...this sucker was ready to be *sold*! She locked up and headed down to her listing on Arabian. It was a house she'd had under contract three weeks ago, but it had fallen through because the buyer didn't like the results of the home inspection. She just figured he had used that as an excuse because the house was so far north.

As she drove south, she didn't notice the black car parked a few houses down on Indian. It pulled away from where it was parked as Rose took a right on North Ocean Boulevard and went one block south to Arabian. She took another right and stopped in front of 215 Arabian Road, a two-story house with four square columns. It had been on the market longer than any of her other listings. Part of the reason was that many buyers had a reluctance to buy a house that far north. Having a twenty-five-minute round trip to get your daily bagel did not appeal to that many buyers.

Rose got out of her white Jag and walked inside.

The driver of the black car pulled over to the side of the road three houses past 215 Arabian and looked back in his rearview mirror. He opened the car door and started to get out but saw a tan Lexus pull into the 215 Arabian driveway. He slid back inside and shut the car door.

"Hello, anyone here?" a man said as he pushed open the door at 215 Arabian. He stepped into the foyer, his wife just behind him. "Hello," he said again.

Rose, who was in the house's kitchen, reached for the can of pepper spray in her purse but didn't take it out. "Who is it?" she asked, trying to sound unperturbed. "Who's there?"

The man and his wife walked into the kitchen. "Oh, hi, we're the Clearys," the man said with a smile. "We just got into town and were driving around. Are you the agent for this house?"

"Yes, yes, I am," Rose said, at ease again.

"Can we take a look at it?" the woman said. "My sister lives close to here. Down on Mediterranean." Two blocks to the south.

The man smiled. "They want to spend their sunset years together."

His wife gave him a look.

Rose stepped in seamlessly. "Well, then, this house will be perfect for you," she said, extending her hand. "I'm Rose Clarke. Nice to meet you."

"Dan Cleary and my wife, Dina," Cleary said, shaking hands. "Nice to meet you too. So, the big question is...how much?"

"The asking price is two million five, originally it was three million two." Rose said. "Off the record, the owners are quite motivated. They bought a condo at the south end and don't like carrying two places at the same time."

"Can't blame 'em," Cleary said. "So let's have a look. That seems like a pretty reasonable price for Palm Beach."

"Oh, it is, it is," Rose said. "The house is a shade over five thousand square feet, so it works out to about five hundred dollars a square foot, which is well below the average here."

"So what's wrong with it?" Cleary asked.

"Nothing," Rose said. "Some people think of it as a teardown, but I don't agree. I just think it needs the bathrooms to be renovated, put a new appliance package in here" —she gestured around the kitchen — "and probably new countertops, and you'll have yourself an incredible place."

Dina Cleary, who had an iPhone in hand, held it up. "Do you mind if I call my sister and get her to look at it with us?"

"No, not at all," Rose said. "The more the merrier." She was thinking that the sister, who apparently had no problem living this far north, might actually help her with the sale.

As Dina Cleary dialed, Rose's phone rang. She looked down at the caller. *Charlie.*

Too bad. Because when Rose Clarke was on the verge of making a deal, she took calls from no one, not even God.

Dina Cleary's sister walked in, and Rose recognized her immediately. She had sold her the house on Mediterranean five years before.

The sister recognized Rose right away. "Oh, wow," she told Dina. "You're in really good hands. Rose is the best agent in town. How are you, Rose?"

Rose shook her hand. "Couldn't be better," she said. "Long time, no see."

Rose took all three of them through the house. They liked it. Dan Cleary asked Rose how much it would cost to redo the bathrooms and put new appliances and countertops in the kitchen. Rose gave them ballpark numbers and said she had the perfect contractor for the job.

"We love it," Dan Cleary said. "The only problem is we have to sell our house in New York first."

That was a scenario Rose had encountered many times before. But, as always, she had a solution. "What if we did a contract that stipulated we have a long closing? So you can have plenty of time to sell your house?"

"What's long?" Cleary asked.

"Oh, I don't know, two and a half months, maybe?"

"No, we'd need more than that," Cleary said. "How about four months?"

The seller just might go for it, Rose thought. "Mm, that's pretty long. I can try it, but I'm guessing the most they would do is three months."

"But what if we offered the full asking price?" Cleary asked.

The seller would almost surely go for the asking price and a four-month closing. "I think that would be a strong offer. Let's give it a shot."

Cleary turned to his wife. "Are you good with that?"

Dina Cleary nodded eagerly. "The good thing is, we'll probably have plenty left over from the sale of our house to do the renovation."

Cleary looked at his sister-in-law. "What do you think?"

"I think I'd love to have you guys this close," Laura said, turning to her sister. "You could come borrow sugar anytime."

"The hell with that," Dina said. "Borrow wine."

All four laughed and Rose made arrangements for the Clearys to come down to her office later that day, when she'd have a contract ready for them to sign. She hadn't closed a deal this easily in a long time.

She hit speed dial for Charlie but it went to his voice mail. "Hi, Charlie, you'd be proud of me. I just made the fastest deal in the history of Palm Beach real estate. Anyway, get back to me when you can. I'm driving down the island, just left Arabian, doing my weekly house checks."

The man in the black car watched as the two cars pulled out of the driveway and drove past him. In the tan Lexus were a man and two women. In the white Jaguar, the hot blonde was smiling ear to ear. Johnny Cotton turned the key and his car started up. Both of the cars drove south on North Lake Way. Then the one with the man and two women turned left onto Mediterranean, but the blonde continued straight. Finally, she turned left onto Angler Avenue and pulled into number 208. Cotton liked the location for two reasons. It had a Chattahoochee pebble driveway, so you could hear if a car pulled in, and it had a long, tall hedge that made the house impossible to see from the street.

AFTER CRAWFORD'S MEETING WITH A CRIME SCENE TECH AT the station, he listened to Rose's message. He shook his head and groaned. His immediate reaction was that making house checks with a killer on the loose was about the worst idea Rose had ever had. But he knew Rose and how fearless, and sometimes pigheaded, she could be.

He tried her again, and again it went to voice mail. Suddenly he thought back to his lunch with Rose two days before and the mysterious black car that had followed him to Green's. And, as he later found out, the driver was John Reynolds Cotton III, who no doubt had seen him leave with Rose after lunch.

He dialed her again. Voice mail. "Dammit, Rose, stop what you're doing and go home. Then call me."

Without hesitating, he ran to the back of the police station and got in his car. He drove up to Rose's office building going twice the speed limit. He rushed into the building and went straight into the manager's office, almost plowing over an elderly female agent.

The manager, Brook Cavanaugh, started to say hello, but Crawford cut her off. "I need to know the addresses of all of Rose's listings."

Cavanaugh hesitated a split second. "Why—"

"Right now, Brook," Crawford said. "This is life or death."

Brook waved her hand for Crawford to follow and walked quickly toward Rose's office. Rose was just one of two agents who had an actual office. The rest of the agents were located in a big bull pen area similar to Sotheby's.

Brook pushed open the door, walked in, sat down in Rose's chair and opened a file cabinet. "Grab that pad," she said to Crawford pointing at a yellow, lined pad.

Crawford pulled a pen out of his jacket pocket and reached down for the pad.

"Ready?" Brook asked.

Crawford nodded.

"Here goes: 114 Indian, 215 Arabian, 208 Angler Avenue, 310 Palmo Way," Brook said, leafing through Rose's files and giving Crawford all fifteen addresses.

As soon as she was done, Crawford ran out of the office, jumped in his Vic and headed north.

COTTON WAITED A FEW MOMENTS TO SEE IF ANYBODY ELSE drove in. He didn't know whether the blonde was showing the house to a prospective buyer.

After a few minutes, no one had followed her in.

Time to make his move.

He reached into the center console, took out the nylon stocking, and stuffed it into the pocket of his jeans. He stepped out of the car and started walking toward the house.

As he walked, his anticipation peaked, causing a surge of adrenaline. The sensation triggered a memory... The nun who had taken his eight-year-old hand, placed it on one of her breasts, then started to disrobe... He flashed to playing strip poker with his friend Neil and two girls whose names he had long since forgotten—how they'd laughed at his naked fourteen-year-old body and his undersized symbol of manhood...

It got worse. Four years later, he'd married his child bride, Natalie.

Natalie wasn't particularly pretty or smart but certainly had a knack for spending money like no other girl in Wheeling, West Virginia. So it had fallen to Cotton to keep her in clothes and dresses, which she'd wear to nothing more fancy than dinner at the Olive Garden. That was another thing about Natalie, she didn't like to cook. As a consequence of her wanting to be first on her block with toe rings, anklets, Joe Boxer watch rings, puka-shell necklaces, and sunflower cord chokers, then go out for dinner almost every night, Cotton had been working two and sometimes three jobs. He drew the line, however, at working in a coal mine since black lung had killed his uncle, grandfather, and great-grandfather.

While he toiled, unbeknownst to him, his older brother and Natalie fornicated. Until the night he came home early from his job as a short-order cook. They admitted it had been going on for three months, so the next day Cotton left her and hit the road with only a handful of possessions. Realizing that an honest living had gotten him nowhere, he decided he was too smart to be a working schlub making minimum wage. So, soon thereafter, he launched into a career of crime.

At first, it was tough to tell what he was good at. He started out with burglary 101, shoplifting and breaking into empty houses. Lifting flat screens, jewelry and silverware. Then he graduated to cars. First, anything with four wheels, then exotic, foreign cars. He had moved down to Florida and bumped into a guy in a bar in Fort Lauderdale who peddled Porsches, Maseratis and Ferraris to a Colombian gang that shipped and sold them to South American drug dealers and businessmen. That was a profitable gig until he crashed a Testarossa into a Lauderdale canal with three cop cars on his ass.

That resulted in jail hitch number one. At Redfern Correctional. Much like Malpaso, Redfern had an art program, and Cotton wasted no time signing up for it. He gravitated toward Impressionism and found that he had an innate talent for copying famous paintings. The two artists who taught at Redfern urged him to become an artist when he got out, assuring him he had a great future ahead of him. But it soon became apparent to Cotton that while he had a tremendous knack for painting a Monet that was a dead ringer for a Monet, he was incapable of coming up with original subjects that would captivate serious buyers. But as far as copies went, he was a master, good enough, he was confident, to fool museum curators.

During his second year at Redfern, he approached one of the art teachers and proposed a plan. Something told Cotton that the teacher was not thrilled with being a starving artist and might be tempted by his proposition. Cotton laid it out in minute detail: He would paint copies of lesser known but still desirable Impressionist painters. The teacher, Richard Heyman, who was articulate, cultured, and looked the part, would then go to galleries in places like Atlanta, Jacksonville, Orlando, and New Orleans and peddle them as originals. "Art forger" had a much sweeter ring to it than "burglar" or "car thief," and Cotton was convinced he could be one of the best in the business. Richard Heyman embraced the project with enthusiasm, and as soon as Cotton finished his five-year hitch, he set up his easel in the garage of his $700-a-month rental apartment.

His first sale was a "Willard Metcalf" painting of haystacks in the foreground and cows in the distance. Heyman sold it to a gallery in Atlanta, after claiming that he found it in his recently deceased great-aunt's attic. Next to be sold was a "Valentin Serov" portrait of an unknown nobleman with a very impressive mustache and bulky muttonchop sideburns. Heyman sold this to a gallery in Tampa and, to keep things uncomplicated, again said he had discovered it in his great-aunt's attic. The next paintings of Johnny Cotton's were in the distinct styles of Impressionists Frédéric Bazille, Eugène Boudin, and Eliseu Visconti.

The money was starting to roll in, and Cotton was only in his mid-twenties. He believed that as an artist it was his birthright to play the role of reckless bohemian and live a life in which drugs, alcohol, and wanton women were part of his daily activities. So, in short order, he graduated from cocaine to crack and, in a nod to certain nineteenth-century Impressionist artists, started imbibing absinthe at the rate of a bottle a day. Lastly, he began picking up women at a nearby junior college, posing as Gianni, a young Italian artist from an aristocratic family. He was able to pull off an Italian accent quite credibly, but playing a suave, young aristocrat...not so much. Still, it turned out that eighteen- and nineteen-year-old girls were rarely short on gullibility.

A pretty freshman named Christie Hart, however, proved to be his downfall and the reason he ended up doing a ten-year stretch at Malpaso. His jail term could have been a lot longer, or even resulted in the death penalty, if Cotton hadn't banked enough money to hire a good lawyer instead of the public defender he had gotten stuck with in Fort Lauderdale. It turned out that the more absinthe and high-grade weed Cotton consumed on his first (and only) date with Christie Hart, the more she started to resemble his ex-wife. What finally sent him into a homicidal rage was something innocuous Christie said about him helping her pay for a new dress. He choked her and choked her for a full ten minutes, long after she had stopped breathing.

Cotton's teacher partner, Richard Heyman, was the one who hired the lawyer. Figuring that Cotton was his meal ticket and wanting to do everything he could to keep the income stream from Cotton's copies flowing, he hired the best trial lawyer he could find—cost be damned.

When Cotton first met the lawyer, they had a brief conversation.

"You're innocent, right?" the lawyer said. It was more a statement than a question.

"Ah..."

"Because the circumstances of the unfortunate victim's death are remarkably similar to a case I had a few years ago where a man and a woman were involved in what's called asphyxiophilia, which is sex where oxygen is depleted by—in that case—partial strangulation, thus heightening the sex act. Unfortunately, the strangulation went too far, and the woman lost consciousness and died."

It was apparent the lawyer was spoon-feeding Cotton an alibi.

Cotton started nodding. "Yes, that's exactly what happened. It just went too far. And we both had had a lot to drink."

What started out as unpremeditated murder and a life sentence ended up getting pled down to involuntary manslaughter. Cotton became an inmate at Malpaso and resumed his career as a forger under the eyes of Malpaso prison officials.

Then under the patient, expert tutelage of Marty Sanchez, Cotton read and studied everything he could get his hands on about artists and their creations. Shortly thereafter, he got to know Luna Jacobs. She was overweight and not much to look at, but he *was* in prison after all. They began having a broom closet affair and, as others observed, she spent more time teaching him than any of her other students.

The other thing Luna Jacobs did was speak on his behalf at his parole hearing. She stood up and rhapsodized about Cotton's good behavior, exceptional talent as an artist, and her certainty that he would be a positive addition to the community upon his release.

Her recommendation was instrumental in getting Cotton sprung from Malpaso fifteen months before his scheduled release date. One of the painters he had been drawn to was Amedeo Modigliani, who had been born a Sephardic Jew in Italy but spent the bulk of his short career painting, experimenting with drugs, and drinking to excess in Paris. It was his hedonistic, bohemian lifestyle—which Marty Sanchez described in vivid detail—that initially drew Cotton to the famed artist. One of his favorite Modigliani paintings was entitled *Portrait of Woman in a Hat*. On the day of his release, he went to a women's clothing store in Melbourne and bought a wide-brimmed brown felt hat, the closest thing he could find to the hat worn by the woman in Modigliani's painting.

He gave it to Luna, telling her it was for all that she had taught him and for everything she had done for him. She thanked him but was somewhat befuddled why he had chosen the hat. Then Cotton sat down and watched a football game on Luna's living room TV while he knocked back a six-pack of beer. After that he went into

Luna's makeshift studio in her second bedroom, calmly jammed a sock in her mouth, and choked her to death. Then he took her clothes off, sat her in a chair, and put the brown floppy hat on her head.

He had a similarly special yet dramatically different pose planned for the blonde, whose name he found out was Rose Clarke. When he first laid eyes on her, she reminded him of a sexy version of Edward Hopper's wife, Josephine, whom Hopper featured in many of his paintings. And, as it turned out, Rose had been wearing a pink dress the day he first saw her at Green's Pharmacy having lunch with Crawford. The moment Cotton first saw Rose, he'd flashed to a painting of Hopper's that haunted him. It was called *Morning Sun*, and it pictured Josephine sitting on a bed with no top sheet, looking pensively out a window. Her blonde hair is pulled back in a bun, and her pink nightgown rises up over her thigh. It was that detail that aroused Cotton, but what captured his interest was Hopper's deft use of light and shade to convey that it was, in fact, morning sun.

In case Rose was not wearing her pink dress again, Cotton had bought a pink negligee from a woman's store on South Olive. He planned to position Rose in a position similar to Josephine's in *Morning Sun*—on a bed with only a bottom sheet, looking out a window.

The only difference was that Rose Clarke would be dead.

Cotton walked up Angler, looking both ways down the street, and slipped in between two hedges separating the house Rose Clarke had entered from the adjoining one. He walked between the two hedges and saw it was the right house. He walked past it until he spotted a space in the hedge then squeezed through it.

The running toilet that Vera had told her about was off of the fourth bedroom on the second floor. Being handy by necessity, Rose had taken off the top of the tank and rested it on the floor. Next, she flushed the toilet as she looked for a fill-valve leak.

Her cell phone rang. It was across the master bathroom from her, on the white Carrera vanity top. Charlie probably. Could the man's timing possibly be any worse? She continued performing her function as plumber and let the call go to voice mail.

She lifted up the float arm while the tank filled to see if the water had stopped. She bent the float arm slightly so the tank stopped filling an inch below the overflow pipe.

Problem solved. Whoever thought the real estate business was even remotely glamorous, Rose chuckled to herself, failed to take into account toilet-fixing and dead-insect-removing duties. She turned to exit the bathroom, planning to leave for her next house, on Palmo Way.

As she walked into the bedroom from the bathroom, she heard a sharp noise behind her, then as she turned, felt an arm around her neck. Suddenly she felt something swipe across her mouth. Whatever it was, it prevented her from screaming or emitting anything other than a muffled cry, which she knew couldn't be heard outside of the room. But Rose was a gym rat and could do barbell back squats for ten long minutes. Feeling two hands around her neck, she raised her right arm, then thrust it back and into the ribs of the person behind her. He groaned, his hands loosened around her neck, and she ran for the stairway. She heard him right behind her as she started running down the steps. She took them two at a time, but her attacker was only a step or two behind. She got to the bottom and sprinted for the front door. But then she felt his hands around her thighs and knew he had dived to tackle her. She went down, knees first, with a painful thud on the hardwood floor.

Facedown and unable to scream, she felt his hands around her neck again. She heard him panting for breath as the hands tightened, cutting off the flow of oxygen.

"Now we're going to have some fun," the man said, loosening his grip from around her neck. Then she heard the unmistakable sound of duct tape being ripped from a roll and felt it being tightly wrapped around her wrists.

"Stand up," the voice said.

She struggled to get to her feet.

"Okay, now go back up the stairs."

"Please," Rose said, "I have six hundred dollars in cash in my purse."

He slapped her on the back of the head and laughed. "Think I'm a cheap date or something? Come on, up the stairs, bitch."

She smelled his dank, foul breath as he pushed her toward the stairs. "I can get you as much as you want," Rose said as she climbed the stairs.

He pushed her. "It ain't about the money, girlfriend."

Rose's mind amped up to hyper speed. "What do you want?"

"I want to see you in a pink negligee...Josephine."

She reached the landing. "You got the wrong woman, my name's not—"

He whacked her on the back of the head again. "It is now."

He pushed her hard toward a bedroom. She stumbled but kept her balance.

"In there," he said and pushed her again.

She went through the door.

"Okay, on the bed. Facedown."

She hesitated. He kicked her hard in the butt. "Do it," he shouted.

She tried to scream but it was just a muffled nothing.

"Don't make me hit you again, bitch."

He shoved her hard, and she flopped onto the bed, her hands taped behind her back. Then he put his knee on her upper back so she couldn't get up. "Okay, I'm gonna take off the tape, make your hair into a bun. Get all pretty for me. Then you're gonna take your clothes off and get into this nice little negligee I brought you."

She didn't move but felt his hands peeling off the tape. Then her hands were free, but he still had his knee pressed into her back. Now was her only chance, even though she was at a huge disadvantage, to quickly roll over so his knee didn't have her pinned, and either fight him with all she had left or run again and, this time, get away.

Just as she was about to make her move she heard a sound. A footstep maybe. Then another one. Out of the corner of her eye she saw the man above her turn his head toward the door.

A voice rang out, "Get your goddamn hands off her!"

It was a voice she knew well.

She looked to her right. Charlie Crawford was pointing his pistol at the man above her. Never had a gun looked so beautiful. "You okay, honey?"

She nodded, thinking, inanely, *He never called me honey before.*

He reached down with his left hand, still covering the man behind her with the gun in his right, and slowly peeled the duct tape off of her mouth.

"Thank you, Charlie," she said, trying to muster a smile. "'Bout time you showed up."

He helped her to her feet. "Sure you're okay?"

"Knee's a little sore, so's my head," Rose said, turning to glare at Johnny Cotton. "I hope you get a chance to sit in Old Sparky's lap, you son of a bitch," Rose said, referring to the electric chair.

"Get up," Crawford told Cotton.

Cotton put a hand on the floor and, one knee cracking, got to his feet. "Hands up," Crawford said. "Take that thing off."

Cotton pulled the nylon stocking up over his face and off his head.

"So, this is the guy?" Rose said to Crawford. "He looked a whole lot better with that thing covering his face."

THIRTY-NINE

Rose decided not to share her theory about the killer on his way down to Miami with Crawford.

Dennis Shaw, head of the Board of Realtors, had called and requested a meeting with Norm Rutledge. He hadn't told Rutledge what the meeting was going to be about but Rutledge accepted anyway, thinking how could it possibly be bad? They'd scheduled it for four thirty in the afternoon.

This time Crawford and Ott were on time as Shaw, David Crane, and Rose Clarke filed into Rutledge's office. Rose snuck a wink at Crawford, who smiled back at her. Dennis Shaw was carrying an old-fashioned leather briefcase with the handle on top. Exactly like the one Crawford remembered his father carrying as he humped into New York every day on his way down to Wall Street.

"So, welcome back, gentlemen," Rutledge said with a jaunty smile. "What can we do for you today?"

"As head of the board" —Shaw broke into a wide smile— "this time it's all about what we can do for you. So, on behalf of David and Rose" —he glanced at his colleagues— "and all of the other Realtors in Palm Beach, I would like to express my gratitude for a job well done. You have made it safe again for agents to go about their business without fear for their lives. And, for that, we're all eternally grateful."

"Well, thank you," Rutledge said, never one to shy away from an opportunity to take credit for something he had absolutely nothing to do with. "I'd just like to say that it's been a pleasure meeting you three, and if we can ever do anything for you again, please don't hesitate to ask."

"Thank you, Chief," Dennis Shaw reached into his leather briefcase. "As a demonstration of our appreciation for solving the tragic murders of our two beloved agents, I would like to present you with these." The objects were two-foot-high gold keys mounted on mahogany stands. "They're what we call Golden Keys, which symbolically represent the real estate industry and are awarded to those individuals who contribute positively to our community and make it a better place to live and work. In the past, recipients of Golden Keys have included the governor of the state of Florida, astronaut Nancy Steadman, and Miami Dolphins star linebacker Rich Pawlichuk, among other prominent individuals."

Crawford could see Rose trying to suppress a chuckle.

"So, to you, Detective Crawford and Detective Ott" — Shaw stood up and held golden keys in both hands— "I would like to present you with the highest honor we have in our industry."

Crawford stood and took the golden key from Shaw's outstretched hand, and Ott did the same with the other.

"Well, thank you, Mr. Shaw, I am honored," Crawford said simply.

"Yes," Ott said. "I appreciate it."

Rutledge's expression was somewhere between bewilderment and a frown, clearly wondering where his golden key was.

"I'd just like to add my own personal thanks," David Crane said. "As a close personal friend and coworker of Mimi Taylor, I'm sure I speak for her family and friends along with those of Mattie Priest in thanking you fellas for your diligence, skill, and resourcefulness in bringing this cold-blooded killer to justice."

"Yes, great job, guys," Rose said, knowing that at least a few words were expected of her.

Rutledge leaned back in his chair. "Well, again, we thank all of you." He had apparently gotten past the snub. "And we certainly appreciate your recognition."

Crawford felt as though they had been thanked, thanked again, and re-thanked. It was time for this meeting to end.

Rutledge stood up and put his hand out to Shaw. Seemed like he agreed. Everyone shook hands, and Shaw and Crane left.

Rose, Crawford, Ott, and their Golden Keys went back to Crawford's office.

Rose and Ott sat across from Crawford. Ott hefted his Golden Key. "Got a spot between my bowling trophies for this little beauty."

Rose and Crawford laughed.

She looked at her watch. "You boys done for the day?"

"Oh, yeah," Crawford said. "We're done."

"Feel like a drink?"

"Several," Ott said.

"How 'bout this?" Crawford said. "A couple pops at Mookie's. Then the Palm Beach Police Department buys us dinner at the restaurant of our choice."

"Sounds like a plan," Ott said. "You available, Rose?"

"Of course. Dinner with you two studs? What girl would ever say no?"

Crawford asked Red Noland to join them at Mookie's.

The four of them were sitting at a table in the back, Rose being one of only three women in the less-than-elegant cop bar. A few cops had bought them drinks for having busted the killer, so they were on round three.

"I got a feeling Cotton's got Ted Bundy, Aileen Wuornos, and Gerard Schaefer kind of numbers," Noland told the group.

"What do you mean?" Rose asked.

"Florida serial killers," Noland said. "They killed a lot of people between them."

"Who's Gerard Schaefer?" Ott asked. "Never heard of him."

"Oh, Christ, he mighta had the most of all," Noland said. "He was a sheriff's deputy up in Martin County who moonlighted as a mutt who got his jollies dismembering young girls. They think he may have done thirty or more. A relative of one of 'em took him out in prison."

Rose shook her head. "What's with this state, anyway? So many murderers."

"Simple," Ott said. "Killers like nice weather."

"I guess," Rose said.

"So, Rose," Ott said, "when that guy came after you, what did you think?"

"Come on, Mort," Crawford said. "She doesn't want to talk about that."

Ott put his hands up. "I was just—"

"I don't mind at all," Rose cut in. "Tell you the truth, I was just trying to figure out how I could twist around and knee him in the balls."

THE DECIDED ON A RESTAURANT IN CITYPLACE IN WEST PALM called Shell. It was a place that some friends of Rose's had said had fabulous seafood. They asked Red Noland along, told him it was on Palm Beach PD's tab, but he said he had to get home. The restaurant was on the second level at CityPlace, two doors down from the AMC movie theater.

Since they didn't have a reservation, the only table they could get was all the way back next to the entrance to the kitchen. But after having had three drinks apiece, they didn't much care.

They sat and ordered a bottle of wine.

"Turn slowly to your right," Rose whispered to Crawford.

Crawford did. Sitting at a nearby table, wearing sunglasses and a stereo headset complete with mike, was Stark Stabler. And a woman, who Crawford knew was way too good-looking to be bitchy Sally Stabler.

"Did you ever hear of a model named Lola Sandwood?" Rose asked in a hushed tone.

Crawford and Ott shook their heads.

"Well, she was very big at one time," Rose said. "Did ads for Gucci, Bulgari, Jimmy Choo, you name it."

"Well, I've heard of Gucci anyway," Ott said.

Rose laughed. "Sorry, I know fashion isn't exactly your wheelhouse, Mort," she said. "Anyway, that's who she is."

"What's she doing with that slimeball?" Ott asked.

"I heard she's had a hard time of it," Rose said. "Most models have the shelf life of professional athletes. I think she went from making a fortune to nada. As I remember, she had a drug problem too. Declared bankruptcy. Ended up down here, trying to marry a rich man."

"Well, then, what's she doing with him?" Crawford asked. "He's only rich because his wife is. And something tells me his wife's got an airtight prenup."

"Something tells me you're right," Rose said.

"Wonder if they're headed over to the L.N. after?" Ott asked Crawford, raising his eyebrows.

Crawford laughed.

"You never told me what that stands for," Rose said to Crawford.

"A place you'll never go," Crawford said.

Ott flicked his head in the direction of Stabler. "Look at that guy," he said. "Dude looks like an airplane pilot." Ott rolled his eyes. "Like he's about to bounce a 747 off a runway or something."

Crawford shot a quick look over at Stabler. "Guys who wear those things always strike me as wanting people to look at them."

"Yeah," Rose said. "And they always talk really loud on them. Like they want you to think they're making a business deal you're going to read about in *Forbes* next month."

Crawford turned away from Stabler and his date and sighed. "Mimi Taylor's body's not even cold, and this guy's already on to the next. I can't believe it." He shook his head. "So, back to the subject of models," he said to Rose. "I have a question."

"Okay, fire away," she said. "I didn't realize that was something that interested you much."

"Well, I mean, what guy doesn't like to look. Fantasize a little," Crawford said. "But I was in my doctor's office and there was this *Vanity Fair* magazine there. So, never having been lucky enough to read a *Vanity Fair* magazine before, I started turning the pages. And I gotta tell you, the models in that thing were complete turnoffs. I mean, the clothes they were wearing were bad enough, but the women themselves...you ever hear that expression *from hunger*? Like there was this Gucci ad with three models who had hairdos out of a really bad prom night back in the fifties. And the clothes...made Norm Rutledge look stylish. Whatever happened to the Lauren Huttons and the Cheryl Tiegs, the women who rocked my world when my hormones were just starting to rage?"

Ott was eyeing Crawford with complete disbelief. "Will you listen to yourself, Crawford? You're talking about hairdos and models. I can't believe my friggin' ears."

Crawford raised his hands in protest. "All I'm saying is I got three-quarters through the magazine before there was something to actually read...instead of ads for things you'd expect to see at Salvation Army."

"Charlie, Charlie, Charlie." Ott spoke as if scolding a child. "Fortunately, when I remind you of this conversation tomorrow morning, you can blame it on the fact that you'd been drinking heavily and had no idea what was coming out of your mouth."

FORTY

THEY FINISHED THEIR BOTTLE OF WINE AND HAD ANOTHER ONE while they ate. Crawford had swordfish, Ott had yellowfin tuna, Rose had salmon, and everyone was happy. All of them ignoring Stabler at the next table. But it became particularly hard not to stare when he moved his chair closer to the model, put his arm around her, and started kissing her—more like slobbering on her—without restraint. He didn't even take off his sunglasses or the headset.

At a little past ten thirty, Crawford, Rose, and Ott got up and left. They had jointly decided that it would be an Uber night, that they'd leave their cars in the parking garage. They peeled off in separate directions, Ott by himself, Crawford saying he was going to take Rose to meet her Uber then find his.

But Ott was no fool. He knew the drill. Crawford was actually going to slip his Uber driver a ten, then hop in with Rose and head over to Palm Beach. The giveaway would be when Crawford rolled into the station the next morning smelling like Jean Patou Joy. Even after a shower, the scent lingered.

"You think Mort knew?" Rose asked.

"He is a detective," Crawford said. "So, my guess is...he suspected."

"I'm just glad we don't have to look at Stabler anymore," Rose said. "Poor Lola. How the mighty have fallen."

"What would she possibly see in him? I mean, she's still attractive. He's like this worthless, has-been tennis player. Actually, more like a *never-was*."

THEY DECIDED JUST BEFORE THEY GOT TO ROSE'S HOUSE THAT IT was a perfect night for a skinny-dip. A full moon shone above, and it was about seventy-five degrees. The thought crossed Crawford's mind because that's the way his mind worked, that they could make love in the pool. Or maybe in the two-person chaise longue next to the pool—which Rose referred to as her "double-wide." Or in her king-size bed with the crisp, 1,000-count Egyptian sheets. Or, if they couldn't make it to her bedroom because they were so overwhelmed with passion and lust, the sofa in the living room with the little buttons that had once left a mark on Rose's perfect, round ass.

Speaking of models, which they no longer were, Rose made her entrance into the pool as if she were just coming off the runway. She had a perfect strut, erect posture, and did it all nice and slow, with great deliberation. Crawford watched from the shallow end as she got to the bottom step, then stretched out her arms, dived in, and swam to the deep end.

She turned and put one hand on the diving board. "Ah, perfect temperature," she said.

Rose let go of the diving board and starting swimming underwater toward Crawford. Just before she got to him, she came up out of the water until their bodies were barely touching. Crawford put his arms around her, drew her closer, and kissed her. And kissed her. And kissed her some more.

Finally, she drew back. "You get me in the mood in about five seconds."

He smiled. "So, what do you think...right here?"

She put her hand on his cheek and gave it a soft caress. "I think it would be amazing. I think it would be incredible—" she gave him a quick kiss on the cheek "—but it's not happening tonight."

"What?" This was a first.

"You know, Charlie, it's time you decided."

"Decided what?" He played dumb.

"You've got the best of both worlds. The world of me and the world of Dominica. And now the time has finally come when you need to choose between us."

Oh, God, why? Crawford wasn't prepared for a heavy conversation. He had figured a few drinks, a nice dinner, good conversation, then fantastic sex. The usual.

This was a curveball he was totally unprepared for.

"But, Rose, here we are...naked, and, and it's this beautiful moonlit night, and—"

"You're a tough man to say no to. In fact, come to think of it, I never have. *Ever*. But this time I am."

He was near panic. The thought flashed through his mind to say, *Rose, I'm ready to immediately commit to you and dump Dominica.* Then, during breakfast in bed tomorrow morning, he could say, *I was really drunk last night. Whatever I said, don't hold me to it.* But that would just be so incredibly low rent, no way he could ever go there.

Instead, he thought about kissing her again. Giving her his very best work. Maybe she'd change her mind. It had worked before.

But instead, he simply put his hands on her shoulders and stared into her eyes. "You know what?" He couldn't believe what he was about to say. "You're right."

Rose cocked her head. "Why, Charlie, that's so understanding of you. I was sure you were going to try to talk me into the double-wide or my bed."

"Not this time, Rose. 'Cause, like I said, you're right. And, by the way, I know Dominica thinks you're right too."

"Maybe it's just not in you to commit."

Crawford sighed. "Maybe."

He gave Rose a kiss on the cheek, walked up the pool steps, toweled off, got into his clothes, and dialed Uber.

THE END

AFTERWORD

I hope you liked *Palm Beach Predator*. If you did, please **tap here to leave a quick review on Amazon**. Thank you!

Charlie Crawford and Mort Ott return to investigate the death of a Silicon Valley wonderboy whose company just tanked in *Palm Beach Broke*—**now available on Amazon**.

And to receive an email when the next Charlie Crawford Palm Beach Mystery comes out, sign up for my free author newsletter at **tomturnerbooks.com/news**.

Best,
Tom

PALM BEACH BROKE (EXCERPT)

When a Silicon Valley wonderboy whose company just tanked is found dead in a gruesome pose, Detective Charlie Crawford and his partner Mort Ott swing into action. Only problem is the crime scene is scrubbed clean, and leads...not a one.

This comes the day after the cold-blooded murder of an owner of Palm Beach's most exclusive health club. Who said the high walls and privacy hedges of Palm Beach make it one of the safest places in the world?

PROLOGUE

It reminded Thorsen Paul of when he used to smuggle girls up to his bedroom in his parents' house in Greenwich. Except now he and his lady friend were in the guesthouse of his parents' house in Palm Beach and it was twelve years later. His parents had stopped trying to catch him in the act a long time ago.

The only real danger was the boyfriend of the woman he was in bed with. The guy's name was David Balfour and he had a nasty temper. Thorsen and Bree had just made love and were lying next to each other naked and sweaty, the top sheet up to their waists. It was one o'clock in the afternoon and Bree had to get back to the gallery on Worth Avenue where she worked.

"I love our little nooners," Bree said, getting up out of bed.

Paul grabbed her arm gently. "Do you have to go?"

She pulled her arm away. "Sorry, gotta get back. You know, another day, another Picasso to sell."

"Really?"

"I wish," Bree said, sliding into her panties. "Don't you have to go see your bankers and lawyers?"

Thorsen groaned. "Just my lawyer. And it's not going to be fun."

Bree pulled up her short white silk skirt over her hips and buttoned it. Then she lifted her black spaghetti strap shirt over her head and pulled it down.

"I love women who don't wear bras," Paul said, a lustful look in his eye.

Bree walked over to the bed and leaned down and kissed him. "You love *all* women." She put a finger up to his lips. "Bye, my love."

"Hurry back."

She walked toward the back door, opened it and left.

Thorsen Paul looked at his watch. He had two hours until he had to see his lawyer.

Five minutes later he was sound asleep.

The second-floor door suddenly flew open and two people burst in. One had a Glock and the other, a short, heavily tattooed man, brandished a long knife.

"Don't say a word," said the one with the Glock. "Get out of bed."

"But—"

"*Now.*"

Two days later.

Charlie Crawford and Mort Ott, the full complement of Palm Beach's homicide department, were on their way back from lunch in West Palm Beach. The radio was tuned to a local news station.

Former billionaire and twenty-eight-year-old founder of NextRed Corporation, Thorsen Paul, has been reported missing by his attorney. The San Francisco resident and son of Palm Beach philanthropist, Roderick Paul, was last seen at his parent's home yesterday afternoon by a source who asked to remain anonymous. The family has requested that if anyone has any knowledge of Mr. Paul's whereabouts, to please contact...

The news anchor provided a phone number identified as that of Mr. Paul's attorney.

Ott nodded. "NextRed was that company that went from being worth billions to worthless in about five minutes, right?" he asked as he drove their Crown Vic over the middle bridge from West Palm to Palm Beach.

"It was a little more than five minutes, but yeah, it got totally crushed," Crawford said. "I read somewhere that Paul declared personal bankruptcy and was like...close to homeless."

Ott shook his head. "Poor bastard," he said. "Not to be a downer, but you think maybe the guy offed himself?"

Crawford shook his head. "Jesus, Mort, you just heard this and already you got the guy dead and buried."

ONE

Charlie Crawford got the call from dispatch the same day, a few minutes after 8 p.m. Dead woman ID'd as Adriana Palmer, had been shot four times, at 897 North Ocean Boulevard. He drove quickly from his West Palm Beach condo, and reached the Palm Beach residence a few moments before Mort Ott arrived.

Ott rumbled in behind the wheel of his tricked out 1969 Pontiac GTO Judge Ram Air IV, a car their boss, Chief Norm Rutledge, thought inappropriate for a homicide cop. Ott slid his two-hundred-fifty-pound frame past the steering wheel, got out, and looked over at Crawford.

"Just when I was all hunkered down, ready to binge out on *Bosch*," he said, referring to the TV show.

"Maybe we can solve it quick," Crawford said. "Get you right back there."

"When does that ever happen?"

"Yeah, true."

Three uniforms were there already. One of them, Bob Shepley, introduced Crawford and Ott to the victim's twin sister, Amanda Palmer, who was sitting in her sister's living room. Shepley explained that a next-door neighbor said she'd heard several loud pops and called the police.

Amanda, who lived in a house on the other side of her sister, had told Shepley that she had just arrived home, heard sirens and seen the flashing lights of arriving police cars. She was a medium-height, fit-looking blonde who had mascara pooling below her eyes, and a splotchy red nose. She wore tight jeans and a blue T-shirt with *St. Barth's* on it.

"We're sorry about your loss, Ms. Palmer," Crawford said, showing her ID. "I'm Detective Crawford and this is my partner Detective Ott. Can we ask you a few questions? We want to find who did this as soon as possible."

"Yes, sure," she said, wiping her eyes on the short sleeve of her blouse. "What do you want to know?"

It turned out Amanda and her sister owned The Max, an exclusive fitness club that Crawford had heard of a few times. She said Adriana had left work at a little before six and that she had left around seven-thirty. Amanda said her sister had told her she needed to run a few errands before she headed home.

Amanda shrugged. "Sorry, I wish I could tell you something really helpful."

"Are you aware of any recent burglaries in the neighborhood, Ms. Palmer?" Crawford asked. Theft wasn't Mort's or his beat.

Amanda shrugged. "No, not that I'm aware of."

"Did your sister ever mention anyone she was afraid of?" Ott asked. "Anyone who may have threatened her, possibly?"

Amanda shook her head. "No, and I would certainly know about that."

"Nobody at all?" Ott pressed.

Amanda shook her head

Crawford nodded. "Okay, well, thank you. We're going to look around your sister's house, if that's okay. Then I'm sure we'll have more questions. You'll be here for a while, right?"

Amanda nodded and sniffled.

As they walked out of the living room, Crawford and Ott each donned a pair of vinyl gloves.

They walked through the living room and out to an enclosed sun porch.

Ott pointed at a window, opened a crack. He and Crawford walked over to it.

"Remember when there was that string of burglaries? Houses on the beach?" Ott said.

"Yeah, just before I came down," Crawford said. "A gang from Miami, right?"

"Yeah, Cuban guys, in a Donzi." A so-called *go-fast* boat. "Took a while to get 'em, but eventually they did."

"So that's what you're thinkin'?"

"Just that it's a possibility," Ott said. "Not necessarily by boat, but houses on the ocean are easier to hit. Just walk down the beach."

Crawford nodded as he looked around for anything else out of place.

"Plus, most people who live on the ocean have expensive shit," Ott said.

"You've made a study of that?"

"Yeah, you name it: jewelry, flat screens, furs, silverware, hell of a lot nicer here than in my neighborhood."

Crawford nodded.

"Not that someone's gonna drag a flat screen out of here. But all that other stuff's pretty portable."

"Yeah," Crawford said. "I'm gonna go out to the car. Get my Maglite and look around out back."

Ott nodded and they both went and retrieved Maglites from their cars, then walked through the house and out the French doors, which led to a big stone terrace and a pool beyond.

Outside, they shined their Maglites on the ground below the open window. The beams illuminated a large shoe print in the dirt, pointed away from the house, toward the ocean.

"Bingo," Ott said.

Crawford crouched and studied it. "Should be able to get a good impression." He pointed at the print. "Tread looks like a sneaker."

Ott nodded. "About a nine or ten," he said, looking around for more prints but seeing only the one.

Walking in a straight line, four feet apart, they walked toward the ocean, then back to the house, covering a small grid pattern.

"Hey, check this out," Ott said, his Maglite pointing at something in the grass. It was a string of pearls.

Crawford reached down to pick up the pearls with a vinyl-clad hand.

They spent the next half hour scouring the beach but found nothing more. At the water's edge, they walked along the sand, looking for any sign of a boat having landed on the beach or been pushed off from it. But the tide had recently come in, so if there had been any footprints or signs of a boat, they'd been washed away.

They walked back up to the house. "Let's check the security system," Crawford said, and they went into the foyer and found the keypad. It looked expensive and state-of-the-art. Not surprising. But what *did* surprise them was...it was off.

"Why would you ever turn it off?" Ott asked.

Crawford shrugged. "Damn good question. Let's go talk to the sister."

Ott nodded and they turned and walked toward the living room.

"You know anything about The Max?"

"Just that it's a little out of my budget."

Ott chuckled. "I heard they get like a grand a month."

"Make that way out of my budget."

Amanda Palmer was sitting in the living room, having a glass of wine. Bob Hawes, the medical examiner, had arrived, along with two crime-scene techs. Crawford was disappointed that neither of them was Dominica McCarthy, with whom he shared a special relationship. He also believed she was the best tech in the department—but, then, he might have been a little biased.

Crawford and Ott approached Amanda Palmer. "Mind if we ask you a few more questions, Ms. Palmer?"

"Sure, whatever I can do to help," she said, gesturing toward the couch opposite her. "Have a seat."

Crawford and Ott sat as Crawford pulled out the pearl necklace from his jacket pocket. "Is this your sister's?"

Amanda nodded, wide-eyed. "It sure is. Where'd you find it?"

"On the lawn out back," Crawford said. "Our theory is your sister may have walked in on a burglary. Could have tried to resist the burglar, or burglars, with the pepper spray found in her possession, and was shot."

"Oh, my God," Amanda said. "Did you find anything else?"

"We found a well-preserved footprint just below where we believe the suspect entered and exited the house," Crawford said.

"Can you track someone down with a footprint like that?"

"It's not easy," Crawford said. "But it's a start." He remembered the keypad. "Do you know why your sister's security system was turned off?"

Amanda shrugged. "No, sorry. That seems odd."

"That's what we thought."

"On another note," Ott said, "was Adriana going out with anyone, seeing someone?"

"Yes," Amanda said, "a man named Ed Bertoli."

Crawford heard footsteps from the foyer. A tall man in blue jeans and a polo shirt burst into the living room. "Oh, my God," he said, running up to Amanda. "I just heard. Are you all right, honey?"

Amanda stood, threw her arms around the man, and started to sob. "I—I just can't," she started. "I can't even comprehend it."

The man kissed her. "I am so damned sorry."

"These nice men are Detective Crawford and...sorry I forgot—"

"Detective Ott," Ott said with a smile.

"I'm Ted Bartow," he said. "Amanda's boyfriend. Do you have any idea how it happened?"

"It's too early to know for sure," Crawford said. "We think Adriana may have walked in in the middle of a burglary."

Bartow looked back at Amanda. "I'm so sorry, honey," he said again, putting an arm around her shoulder.

"Thank you." Amanda wiped her eyes, spreading mascara. "I think I want to go home unless you have some more questions," she said to Crawford.

"We'll make it brief," he assured her. "I'm assuming your sister had people who worked at the house on a regular basis. Like a cleaning lady? Pool cleaners? Landscapers, probably?"

"All the above," Amanda said. "Plus, she had a man come and detail her car every two weeks."

"Do you use the same people your sister used?" Crawford asked.

"Yes," Amanda said. "We vetted them all pretty thoroughly. They've all been working for us"—she thought for a second— "for over five years."

"Why?" Bartow asked Crawford. "Were you thinking it might be an inside job? One of them decided to rob the place?"

Crawford nodded. "We've seen it before," he said, then to Amanda. "But you never had any kind of problem with anything disappearing before?"

Amanda shook her head. "No. Nothing like that."

Crawford glanced over at Ott, who was taking notes in his old leather-bound notepad. His partner looked up and shrugged.

"Well, I guess that'll do it for now," Crawford said, reaching for a card in his wallet. "If you think of anything else, please call me." He handed cards to Amanda and Bartow. "In the meantime, we'll be in touch and keep you up to speed on our investigation."

"Thank you very much," Amanda said.

Crawford nodded.

"Again, sorry for your loss," Ott said.

Amanda gave the detectives a pained smile, still clinging tightly to Bartow.

Crawford and Ott walked to the foyer, where the ME and the two crime-scene techs were still studying the body and the area surrounding it.

"Perp came in through a window in the sun porch," Crawford said. "It's on the other side of the living room."

"And there's a good footprint outside below the window," Ott added. "Perp exiting the house."

Crawford asked Hawes, "Can you measure it, and let me know what its size is?"

Hawes nodded. "For you, Charlie, anything."

"We also found this string of pearls owned by the vic out in the lawn behind," Crawford said, handing it to Hawes, who promptly bagged and tagged the necklace.

"So, burglary gone wrong, huh, Charlie?" the ME said.

"Maybe."

"What do you mean, maybe?"

Crawford looked at Ott, then back to Hawes. "'Cause, having done this for a while, I've seen my share of curve balls."

Ott nodded. "Yeah, especially in this town."

END OF EXCERPT

Tap here to get your copy of Palm Beach Broke on Amazon now

ALSO BY TOM TURNER

CHARLIE CRAWFORD PALM BEACH MYSTERIES

Palm Beach Nasty

Palm Beach Poison

Palm Beach Deadly

Palm Beach Bones

Palm Beach Pretenders

Palm Beach Predator

Palm Beach Broke

Palm Beach Bedlam

Palm Beach Blues

The Charlie Crawford Palm Beach Mystery Series: Books 1, 2 & 3

The Charlie Crawford Palm Beach Mystery Series: Books 4, 5 & 6: Box Set #2

THE SAVANNAH SERIES

The Savannah Madam

NICK JANZEK CHARLESTON MYSTERIES

Killing Time in Charleston

Charleston Buzz Kill

STANDALONES

Broken House

Dead in the Water

ABOUT THE AUTHOR

A native New Englander, Tom dropped out of college and ran a bar in Vermont...into the ground. Limping back to get his sheepskin, he then landed in New York where he spent time as an award-winning copywriter at several Manhattan advertising agencies. After years of post-Mad Men life, he made a radical change and got a job in commercial real estate. A few years later he ended up in Palm Beach, buying, renovating and selling houses while getting material for his novels. On the side, he wrote *Palm Beach Nasty*, its sequel, *Palm Beach Poison*, and a screenplay, *Underwater*.

While at a wedding, he fell for the charm of Charleston, South Carolina. He spent six years there and completed a yet-to-be-published series set in Charleston. A year ago, Tom headed down the road to Savannah, where he just finished a novel about lust and murder among his neighbors.

Learn more about Tom's books at:
www.tomturnerbooks.com

Made in the USA
Middletown, DE
01 December 2022